Rayna touched his arm.

"I suggest you wait until the DNA results are back. We don't know for sure it's her."

Gazing down at her, he appeared to be struggling to speak. And then he covered her mouth with his and kissed her.

Shocked, stunned and, yes, aroused, she kissed him back, helpless to resist. Her arms somehow found their way around his neck, her body full up against his with her back against her car.

Somehow, they made it inside the car. Apart, no longer locked together like a couple of horny teenagers. A good thing, she thought, trying to catch her breath. Because if someone had seen them, she'd have been the topic of gossip for the next several days.

"That was..." She struggled to express herself.

Parker simply gazed at her, his expression hidden in shadows. "I want you," he rumbled.

* * *

If you're on Twitter, tell us what you think of Harlequin Romantic Suspense! #harlequinromsuspense

D0043490

Dear Reader,

I love west Texas. I don't know what it is about the landscape that I find so enchanting. Maybe it's the wide-open vistas and the hardscrabble trees clinging tenaciously to life in the dry dirt. Or the amazing sunrises and sunsets. And definitely it's the people.

When I created the imaginary west Texas town of Getaway, I knew that I wanted to set several books there. *Texas Sheriff's Deadly Mission* is the first. The heroine, Sheriff Rayna Coombs, introduced herself to me and I knew exactly who she needed. Sexy biker Parker Norton rolls into town on his Harley, looking for his best friend's missing niece. The attraction is instant.

Throw in more missing young women and the possibility of a serial killer in a small town, and this was a fun story to write. I hope you enjoy reading it!

Karen Whiddon

TEXAS SHERIFF'S DEADLY MISSION

Karen Whiddon

HARLEQUIN®
ROMANTIC SUSPENSE™

Recycling programs
for this product may
not exist in your area.

ISBN-13: 978-1-335-75935-1

Texas Sheriff's Deadly Mission

Copyright © 2021 by Karen Whiddon

This edition published by arrangement with Harlequin Books S.A.

For questions and comments about the quality of this book,
please contact us at CustomerService@Harlequin.com.

Harlequin Enterprises ULC
22 Adelaide St. West, 40th Floor
Toronto, Ontario M5H 4E3, Canada
www.Harlequin.com

Printed in U.S.A.

Karen Whiddon started weaving fanciful tales for her younger brothers at the age of eleven. Amid the gorgeous Catskill Mountains, then the majestic Rocky Mountains, she fueled her imagination with the natural beauty surrounding her. Karen now lives in north Texas, writes full-time and volunteers for a boxer dog rescue. She shares her life with her hero of a husband and four to five dogs, depending on if she is fostering. You can email Karen at kwhiddon1@aol.com. Fans can also check out her website, karenwhiddon.com.

Books by Karen Whiddon

Harlequin Romantic Suspense

Colton 911: Chicago

Colton 911: Soldier's Return

The CEO's Secret Baby
The Cop's Missing Child
The Millionaire Cowboy's Secret
Texas Secrets, Lovers' Lies
The Rancher's Return
The Texan's Return
Wyoming Undercover
The Texas Soldier's Son
Texas Ranch Justice
Snowbound Targets
The Widow's Bodyguard
Texas Sheriff's Deadly Mission

Visit the Author Profile page at Harlequin.com for more titles.

To all my dog rescue friends—Laura Everitt, Audra Bishop, Reg Morgan, Kathleen DeAngelo. You work tirelessly to help save dogs, rejoicing when one is saved and finds their forever home, and grieving when one is lost. I see you, I appreciate you and I'm honored to work beside you.

Chapter 1

Looking up at the tall, muscular and very tattooed man who strode into her sheriff's department, Rayna Coombs flushed, all over her body. Mary Leeds, who usually worked the front desk, had just stepped out to grab them both lunch. Though Rayna wished she could let someone else assist this citizen, right now she was the only one there. Holding down the fort, as they liked to say.

"Can I help you?" she asked, her tone cool and professional, despite the way her every sense had sprung to life at the sight of him. From his massive chest and arms, cleft jaw and enigmatic brown eyes, he was everything that made her entire body sing. In other words, trouble. She'd learned the hard way to stay far, far away from men like him. Outside, she saw a black-and-chrome Harley. A custom job from the looks of it. Which only made him even more attractive, dang it.

"I'm looking for the sheriff," the sexy stranger drawled, his Texas accent letting her know that yes, he was from around these parts.

Though inwardly, she sighed and tried like hell not to melt, she kept her demeanor remotely law enforcement officer polite. "You've found her," she responded, bracing herself for his response. She'd more than earned the respect of the locals, but sometimes strangers, particularly men, had trouble accepting a woman in a position of power. Even in this day and age.

At first, he didn't reply. Instead, he looked her up and down, as if waiting for her to laugh and say she was joking. Instead, she let her gaze travel over him in the same sort of slow assessment. "Now, once again, how may I assist you?"

Finally, he jerked his rugged chin in a quick nod. "Parker Norton," he said, holding out his hand. "Sam Norton is my uncle."

Briskly, she shook it. Sam had been sheriff before her and the one who'd originally hired her as a patrol officer. "Then you know Sam's living the retired life down in Corpus," she said.

"I do." He glanced around before reaching into his pocket and pulling out a photograph, sliding it across the counter toward her. "My friend's little sister disappeared somewhere around here. Her name is Nicole Wilson. She was driving to Dallas from Texas Tech, where she was going to school. I'm here to get your help in locating her."

She instantly knew who he was referring to, but went ahead and studied the photo anyway. "We've already looked into this," she said. "Sam called and asked us to prioritize it as a favor to him. We did and we found nothing to indicate she'd even been in Getaway. She didn't stay at either of the motels, or get gas at any of the filling stations. We even reviewed video from some of the shops on Main Street, looking for a 1995 yellow Camaro. Nothing."

"She was here," he replied, his stubborn certainty at complete odds with what she'd just explained. "My friend John got a text from here at the city line. She took a picture with the sign. Here." This time he slid his phone over to her, revealing a photo of a smiling, carefree young blonde woman, posing in front of the Getaway sign. This was a popular spot with both tourists and those on their way to other places. Their little town northwest of Abilene was best known for its name.

"I'm sorry," she began, her voice gentle. "I don't know what else to tell you."

He looked down at that, gathering himself. She braced herself for insults or cuss words, not enough to get him arrested, but probably enough for her to be able to ask him to leave.

Instead, he swallowed hard and met her gaze. The pain in his dark eyes stunned and moved her. "You don't understand," he rasped. "John is my best friend and he's dying. Colon cancer. Nicole was on her way to Dallas from Lubbock to see him when she disappeared. All John wants in this world before he dies is to see her again and know she's safe. I'll do whatever it takes to give this to him."

"Again, while I sympathize, I'm not sure what you want me to say. We've already done an exhaustive search. We found nothing to indicate Nicole came in contact with foul play here in Getaway."

Though he winced at the words *foul play*, he didn't

look away. "What I want, Sheriff Coombs," he said through clenched teeth, "is for you to help me find her."

With sudden clarity, she realized he wasn't going to go away. No matter what she said or did. "You want me to reopen a closed case, is that correct?" Her crisp tone put her right back in professional mode. Sam's nephew would get what he wanted. She owed Sam that.

"I do."

She nodded. "All right. Will you text me that photo, the one of her with our city-limits sign? I'd like to print it out."

If her rapid capitulation surprised him, he gave no sign. He asked for her number, entered it, and a moment later her phone chimed. "Got it," she exclaimed, pushing the icon to send it to the printer. "Now, how can I reach you? I assume you'd like to be notified if there's any news on this case."

"You've got my number," he pointed out. "Just save it in your phone. I'm staying at the Landshark Motel, room 233. I'll be there for the next several days."

Damn. She managed to keep her face expressionless, despite her dismay. She should have known someone as determined as him wouldn't leave town until he had what he wanted. Which might just be pretty damn impossible.

She thought about explaining how thorough they'd been. Sam Norton never asked for personal favors and when he did, well, she sure as hell would work her fingers to the bone to try and get answers. Except nothing had turned up. Zero, zilch, nada. If Nicole had been here, she'd simply passed through. Whatever had happened to her must have occurred somewhere between Getaway and Dallas. Though Rayna had even called a state trooper friend of hers and had him check. Even then, nothing had turned up. No sign of Nicole Wilson's Camaro had been found.

Glancing at the hard line of the masculine jaw in front of her, she understood Parker Norton didn't care what might have been done before. He wanted them to try again. And again, until they somehow got the results he wanted. She couldn't blame him. She'd be the same way if someone she loved had simply disappeared.

"I'm sorry about your friend," she said softly. "And we'll be in touch with you if anything turns up."

"Thank you."

Again, she felt a sizzle low in her belly as his gaze met hers. Pushing it down, she gave a curt nod and turned away. Only when she heard the door close behind him and his motorcycle start up did she release the breath she hadn't even been aware of holding. Her entire body tingled, even though she'd barely touched him. Ridiculous.

Needing a distraction, she sat down in front of her computer and reviewed the case files regarding the search for the missing Nicole Wilson.

Mary returned a few minutes later, toting two Whataburger bags. "Here you go," she said, dropping one on the counter in front of Rayna. "Eat it while it's hot."

About to walk past, the older woman caught sight of the photo Rayna had printed. "Isn't that the girl Sam asked us to check on?"

"It is." Rayna sighed. "Sam's nephew came by a few minutes ago and asked us to reopen the case. I'll have Larry take another shot at investigating her disappearance when he comes in this afternoon."

Shrugging, Mary took her lunch to her desk. After

a moment, Rayna did the same. She only wished she could put the thought of Parker Norton out of her mind. Because the images running through her mind were not the slightest bit respectable or sheriff-like. She'd only had this kind of reaction to one other man, and that had nearly cost her not only her job, but her life. Acting on something like that was not a mistake she would ever make again.

Biting down into her burger, Rayna savored every morsel. Usually, her lunch consisted of salads or wraps—healthy food. The rare occasion she allowed herself a burger, she always, without exception, had a bacon-mushroom burger with pepper-jack cheese and a side order of fries. She wouldn't allow herself to taint her enjoyment of this rare meal with all these sensual images of the first man who'd piqued her interest in years.

By the time Larry Newsome arrived for his shift, Rayna had refreshed her memory with every aspect of the previous investigation into Nicole Wilson's possible disappearance. The family had filed a missing-person report, not only with Getaway PD but with the county.

Larry blinked when Rayna filled him in on what she needed him to do. "But didn't we already look into this?"

"Yes. But we're going to take another look. Sam's nephew came by and requested it."

Immediately, Larry's frown cleared. Anyone who'd ever worked for Sam would do just about anything for him. Larry was no exception.

"I'm on it," Larry said. "Where would you like me to start?"

"We're going to begin an entirely new investigation,"

Rayna answered. "All new interviews, reviewing camera footage, the works. As far as you're concerned, none of this was done before. Start from scratch."

"Sounds good." Larry ambled back to his desk, booted up his computer and started his own preliminary work. Rayna relaxed, knowing the investigation was in good hands.

"It's nearly five," Mary said, bringing a short stack of forms over for Rayna to sign. "I'm heading home right after this. How about you?"

Slightly surprised to find out the time, Rayna couldn't resist glancing at the clock to double-check. Yep, 4:58 p.m. Time to head home to her small family. Just the thought of seeing her baby girl made her smile. Her mother, Wanda, watched over Lauren during the day while Rayna worked, an arrangement that suited all of them just fine.

"I'm right behind you," Rayna said, rolling her shoulders a bit to help relax some of the kinks.

"I'll start making a few calls tonight," Larry promised. "I won't call anyone too late, but maybe I can question a few people over the phone in between the time they get home from work and eat supper."

"Sounds good," Rayna responded. "Let me know if you learn anything new."

Driving home with the summer sun still high in the sky, Rayna managed to keep her thoughts from returning to the handsome biker. She knew better, honestly she did, and she couldn't fathom why she'd even consider allowing herself to get all worked up over a guy who could only bring drama to her life. Everything about him screamed *bad boy*, from his black leather vest, tattooed muscular arms, right down to the custom black Harley he rode.

She knew the type well, she thought grimly. She continued to remind herself that her involvement with one had nearly cost her everything. She couldn't take that kind of risk again. Never ever.

Pulling up in front of the tidy ranch-style house, she parked and went in through the front door. The instant she stepped inside, five-year-old Lauren launched herself at her.

"Mommy!" she squealed. "You're home!"

"I am." Rayna bent down and scooped Lauren up in her arms. "Let me look at you. Yep, your hair is still red."

Lauren laughed and laughed, green eyes sparkling, her amusement real, even though Rayna said this every single time she came home. Heart full, Rayna hugged her daughter tightly before putting her back down. "Let me go change and I'll meet you and Grandma in the kitchen."

Nodding, Lauren went skipping off, her routine every evening.

In her bedroom, Rayna approached her closet and punched in the code to unlock her gun safe. Once she'd stored her weapon, she quickly shed her uniform, changing into a pair of running shorts, a tank top and flip-flops. In her small bathroom, she quickly washed off her makeup, scrubbed her face clean and tied her hair back into a ponytail.

Her mother sat at the kitchen table, cutting up a cantaloupe. "How was your day?" Wanda asked softly.

Rayna shrugged. She knew better than to discuss any aspects of her job with her mom. Wanda would worry herself sick if she had even the slightest knowledge of Rayna putting herself at risk. Today had been one of those days where she hadn't even left the office, but others she wasn't so lucky.

"I made a tuna casserole for dinner," Wanda continued. "Lauren asked me to, even though it's kind of too hot to use the oven, I did. It'll be done in about fifteen minutes."

"Sounds great." On cue, Rayna's stomach growled. "Thanks, Mom. I really appreciate all that you do around here."

A bright smile lit up Wanda's still-pretty face. "Honey, I really appreciate you putting a roof over my head and food in my belly. It's so nice not to be waiting tables and worrying about if I'll have enough money to make rent. Moving here was the best thing we ever did."

"I know." Looking over at her daughter, playing happily with stuffed animals in the small living room, Rayna smiled back. "I'm going to do whatever it takes to make sure we're always safe here."

Expression clouding, Wanda nodded. They hadn't been safe in Conroe, even though Jimmy Wayne had gone away to prison. He'd had too many contacts on the outside who might be willing to carry out the vengeance he'd sworn against Rayna. Even though he'd been incarcerated before Rayna had learned she carried his child, she'd never stopped looking over her shoulder.

Parker Norton rode away from the sheriff's office, his powerful Harley rumbling underneath him. He'd been surprised as hell by his physical reaction to the tiny redheaded sheriff. When she'd looked up at him, eating him up with her hot emerald-eyed gaze, his body had responded powerfully. Despite cruising aimlessly around town, he still hadn't settled down, which meant he'd need to head back to the motel for a cold shower, or find an isolated pond and go skinny-dipping. With the brutal afternoon heat of the west Texas sun burning down on him, he was inclined to search out the latter.

In fact, he still remembered a few of those refreshing ponds from his teenage years, if they were still there. He'd bet it was ninety-eight or ninety-nine in the shade.

He'd always loved Getaway, Texas. When he'd been a kid and his uncle Sam had been sheriff here, Parker spent almost every summer here. His mother drove northwest from Houston the first weekend after school let out, delivering Parker on her brother's doorstep with an indulgent and exhausted admonition that he stay out of trouble. Until his teens, Parker didn't have a problem promising his mother he would. Of course, once he noticed girls and cars, in that order, trouble practically became his middle name.

Only Sam, with his calm, confident manner, had been able to settle Parker down. Since Parker never had a father figure in his life, he looked up to the sheriff and respected him. What Sam said, went.

And Sam had known Rayna Coombs, too. In all the summers he'd visited Getaway, Parker knew he'd never met her. He sure as hell wouldn't have forgotten a woman like her. Ever.

Sam claimed she was good people, bestowing on her his highest compliment. He'd told Parker he hired her away from the Conroe Police Department, where she'd run into some kind of trouble, though Sam didn't elaborate on what that might have been. She'd worked as a patrol officer in Getaway for a few years, which must have been during the time Parker had been in the Marines. And when the time had come for Sam to retire, she'd run and won the job of sheriff hands down. If anyone could find Nicole, Sam said, Rayna Coombs could. Even though she'd already tried once and failed, Sam urged Parker to enlist her help again and give her another shot. Sometimes clues turned up that were overlooked or not present the first time, Sam had said.

Desperate to find Nicole before John died, Parker had agreed. And that was how Parker found himself back in the dusty west Texas town of Getaway after far too long an absence. After getting out of the Marines, he'd kicked around the country for a while. He'd hang glided in Tennessee, rode the waves off the coast of California and mountain climbed in Colorado. He'd somehow managed to forget the arid beauty of the flat, rugged land in west Texas. He'd always loved the expansive sunsets, tinting the sky with vivid oranges and pinks and reds. And downtown Getaway held fond memories, with its lovingly restored old-timey buildings and cafes, bars and shops where even now, folks still remembered his name.

If he'd been a settling kind of man, Getaway would be the kind of place he'd choose. Instead, he'd come to find Nicole, so John would know his sister was okay. All John wanted was to see her before he died. That hope was the only thing that kept John hanging on. Parker's gut clenched even thinking about it.

Both Texans, Parker and John had served together in Afghanistan. Though they hadn't even known each other before being assigned to the same unit, by the time they'd done their time and managed to get out alive, they'd become best friends. The kind of bond they'd forged wasn't easily broken. In fact, the instant Parker had learned of John's diagnosis of late-stage colon cancer, he'd abandoned his rental on Maui, where he'd been teaching scuba diving, and flown on a red-eye to Dallas.

Even though he'd come immediately, he'd been shocked by John's condition. A human skeleton, skin stretched over brittle bones. He knew right then John wasn't long for this world. What really sucked was that colon cancer was easily taken care of with early detection. John had simply not bothered to get himself checked out until it was too late. "I thought I was invincible, man," John had said, smiling a weak yet sardonic smile. "After surviving Afghanistan, I didn't think anything else would have the balls to go after me."

He had a point. This was why Parker had taken so avidly to extreme sports. He'd survived hell on earth. Nothing else would dare to touch him.

Clearly both he and John had been wrong.

Shaking off the melancholy, Parker eyed the road ahead of him. Pavement shimmered in the heat. Heading west, always west, he left downtown, drove through the stately restored Victorian houses, and then left the city limits behind. Past sunbaked fields of brown grass, the old grain silos near the train tracks, and the fruit-and-vegetable stand on Farm to Market Road 1560. He passed the cattle pasture where he, along with several other bored teens, had hauled a keg of Bud Light and built a huge bonfire. Kids started showing up before sunset, many even driving in from nearby towns. The party had been the talk of Getaway for months, especially after the bonfire had gotten out of control and nearly burned down the nearby cornfield.

If he remembered right, a huge stock pond sat around the curve in the road.

There. Smaller than he remembered, but easily accessible just the same. Pulling his bike over onto the dirt shoulder, he cut the engine. And sat for a moment, allowing the heaviness of his task to weigh him down. Due to the length of time Nicole had been missing, Parker figured she was most likely dead. If proof of this were found and delivered to John, the horrible news would most likely kill him.

Parker thought of his friend, dying and worried about his sister, and his stomach clenched.

As he pulled off his leather vest and T-shirt, his cell phone rang. His uncle's name appeared on the screen.

"Uncle Sam," Parker greeted him. "How are you?"

"Good. Any news on Nicole?"

Parker explained he'd met with Rayna earlier.

"Ah, Rayna." Sam chuckled. "What'd you think of her? She's single, you know."

Amused, Parker grimaced. "Tell me you're not matchmaking."

"I'm not. At least not much. She's a pretty little thing, though, isn't she?"

Parker conceded she was. "But she's the sheriff," he pointed out. "The one who's going to find Nicole." Might as well be positive.

"Hopefully," Sam replied. "But I don't see what her being sheriff has to do with you dating her."

"Aha! You *are* matchmaking."

"Of course I am," Sam groused. "She's alone and stubborn—so are you. You're both around the same age, and I think you might like each other, if you'd take a chance and get to know her." He paused, then chuckled. "Plus, she's easy on the eyes."

Parker didn't reply. No way in hell did he intend to agree with Sam, even though he found Rayna more than easy on the eyes. As far as he was concerned, she was downright beautiful.

"Maybe, but I'm not going to be here long enough to start dating anyone," Parker pointed out. "All I care about is locating Nicole. Once that happens, I'll be taking her back to Dallas to see John."

Sam understood what John meant to his nephew. After all, Sam had been the one Parker had talked to when those late-night demons had come calling, urging him to either do something really stupid or drown his sorrows in a bottle of Crown. He often joked that while he might have left Afghanistan, the things he'd experienced there had never left him. He'd often despaired if they ever would.

John had been the same way. It was one of the things he and Parker had in common.

But then cancer had come calling, and John had discovered he had worse demons to fight. Helpless, Parker could only stand by and offer support.

"Keep me posted if you get any new leads," Sam said. "And if there's anything I can do for you from a distance, give me a holler."

Promising he would, Parker ended the call.

That night, he grabbed a to-go burger and fries from Hardees, a pint of beer from Quick Trip and stayed holed up in his room watching television.

Once asleep, he dreamed of the beautiful sheriff, intermingled with John begging to see his sister, and IEDs going off in the desert. He woke sweating, his heart racing, and struggling a moment to remember where he was.

After showering, he went in search of breakfast and a cup of coffee, finding both at the Tumbleweed Café. Though barely seven o'clock, the café was crowded with ranchers wearing Stetsons and boots, farmers in overalls, truck drivers with big rigs parked in a gravel lot across the street and several shop owners needing a warm meal before their day started. Most of the customers appeared to be locals, except for maybe the truckers. Parker's motorcycle was the only one in the parking lot.

He took a seat at the breakfast bar and ordered coffee while checking out the menu. The waitress poured him a cup, piping hot, and promised to be back to take his order.

He decided on a basic breakfast—eggs, bacon, toast and hash browns. Order placed, he drank his coffee and listened to the ebb and flow of conversation around him.

Most of the talk from the table behind him seemed to be about the drought and what that might mean for the crops. From two tables over, he could hear two men discussing the best route to take a load to Kansas without hitting too many weight stations. And he'd be willing to guess that group of men occupying three tables pushed together were talking about cattle prices or some such thing.

No one discussed a missing woman. Of course, that would be old news. Two weeks had passed since Nicole had disappeared. The local sheriff's department had investigated, found nothing, and only then had John's parents called Parker. If they'd told him sooner, he'd have been here much earlier. As it was, he'd come quick. Like, immediately. He'd packed and hopped on his bike the instant he hung up the phone. All he told John was that he was going to get Nicole. John's parents had been emphatic that John not be told his sister was missing.

Talk about stress. Not only did they have to worry about losing their son to cancer, but now they had to worry because their daughter had disappeared. Parker couldn't imagine how it would feel to lose both your children at the same time.

His food arrived and he abandoned his efforts to eavesdrop and instead focused on his breakfast. While he ate, he figured out what he was going to do with his day.

The small town of Getaway was known for two things. First, its name. Legend had it that the first settlers wanted to keep strangers out of the area, so they named it Getaway. Despite some people taking the name the opposite way, claiming they'd found their own getaway in Getaway, the name had stuck.

The other thing was that syndicated advice columnist Myrna Maple lived on a farm about ten miles outside the city limits. Though eccentric, the older woman had been known to dispense random gems of wisdom to people she met on the street.

One of the reasons Nicole had detoured to Getaway had been a hope of meeting Myrna. Therefore, Parker felt talking to the advice columnist would be a good place to start.

Except he didn't know how to find her. He'd done an internet search of the county property tax records and nothing had come up under her name. Which only meant that Myrna Maples wasn't her real name or she'd purchased property under a corporation. Hell, she might even be a renter, for all he knew.

He'd bet the sheriff had her location. They'd probably even talked with her. Though Parker knew he could simply call her, the thought of seeing the gorgeous redhead again felt infinitely preferable.

Plus, he needed to keep an eye on things in person, right?

Signaling for the check, he slugged down the rest of his coffee. When the check came, he handed the waitress a twenty and told her to keep the change. He'd managed to kill an hour, which put it a little after eight.

Outside, the early-morning temperature only hinted at the heat to come. He stood on the sidewalk for a moment, inhaling the unpolluted air, and then climbed onto his motorcycle. Even with the single stoplight turning red, he made it from the motel to the sheriff's office in just under three minutes. It wasn't until he pulled into the parking lot that he wondered if the sheriff would even be on duty this early.

If not, he'd wait until she came in.

Parking his bike, he removed his helmet and strode in through the front door.

"May I help you?" An older woman with steel-gray, close-cropped hair, small silver glasses and a no-nonsense expression greeted him. Her name tag proclaimed her name to be Mary Leeds, dispatcher. She held a disposable up of coffee and took gulps from it as she eyed him. She appeared to be the only person in.

"I'm looking for the sheriff," he said, taking a second look around the place just in case he might have missed her the first time.

"She's not here right now," Mary said. "I can take a message or perhaps Officer Newsome can help you?"

A uniformed man pushed up from his desk behind

a cubicle and joined them. Judging from his bloodshot eyes, he hadn't gotten much sleep the night before. His name tag read Larry Newsome. Eyeing Parker, Officer Newsome patted his paunch. "What can I do you for?" he asked.

Parker repeated himself. "I'm looking for the sheriff. She and I spoke yesterday and she's checking into something for me."

Appearing unconvinced, the deputy scratched the back of his neck and yawned. "Why don't you let me check on that for you? Rayna—the sheriff—always logs everything into the system. That's how we work. That way, if something happens to one of us, the others can still work the case."

Which made sense. "Okay," Parker conceded. "She's looking into a missing-person case."

"Oh, you must mean Nicole Wilson." Straightening, Officer Newsome nodded. "Actually, she assigned that one to me. I refamiliarized myself with the files all last night. I got about four hours' sleep because I got so caught up in poring over them. I'm not even supposed to be here yet, but I've got so many people to talk to that I figured I'd give it a head start."

While Parker appreciated the other man's work ethic, one thing stood out to him. Sheriff Rayna Coombs, the woman his uncle Sam said could be relied on, didn't even care enough to work Nicole's case personally. She'd assigned it to this guy, Larry Newsome.

Infuriated and disappointed, he bit back a sharp response. "Any idea when the sheriff will be in?"

The other two exchanged glances. "Her daughter is sick," Mary finally said. "She's taking the day off to stay home with her."

"But in the meantime—" the deputy leaned forward, elbows on the counter "—I'll be more than happy to keep you in the loop on the case."

Jaw clenched so hard it hurt, Parker forced himself to nod. "That would be awesome," he managed to say. "When do you plan to start talking to people?"

"Unfortunately, it won't be today," Mary chimed in, her tone brusque. "With the sheriff out, we like to have an officer here at all times, just in case. We've got a couple others who are out patrolling."

The phone rang just then and Mary went off to answer it. Both Parker and Officer Newsome watched her go.

A moment later, Mary came back. "Well, you're in luck," she told Parker. "That was Rayna. Her little girl's fever broke. Wanda's going to keep an eye on her, so Rayna is on her way in."

"Wanda?" Parker asked before thinking better of it.

"Rayna's mother," Mary answered. "She lives with Rayna and Lauren."

Interesting. Though he knew he shouldn't have cared, Parker filed this information away.

"I see." Parker walked over to one of the hard metal chairs in the waiting area. "I'll just sit here and wait until she arrives."

Chapter 2

Nothing hurt worse than worrying over a sick child. Lauren had crawled into Rayna's bed around one in the morning, complaining of a headache and chills. When Rayna touched her little forehead, she'd realized her child was burning up with fever. A thermometer under the tongue confirmed it.

She'd dosed her with children's ibuprofen, gotten her to drink some water, and they'd both finally drifted to sleep shortly before three.

The alarm clock went off at six. Lauren opened her eyes, bright with fever, and then let them drift closed. She'd been lethargic, refusing water or food. Rayna checked her temperature. Finding it still high, she placed a cool washcloth on Lauren's forehead and went and woke her mother.

As soon as Wanda heard, she called Dr. Delpeccio's

home number, having confided to Rayna that he'd given her both that and his cell.

"He'll meet you at his office at eight," Wanda said once she'd ended the call. "His first appointment is at eight thirty, so he's going to squeeze you and Lauren in. He'll get her fixed up and good as new."

One thing Rayna envied about her mother was Wanda's absolute certainty that everyone loved her. With those kind of high expectations, everyone did. And with good reason. Wanda was the kind of mother who was always there for her, without judgment or comment. Just love.

When Rayna made the foolish mistake that almost cost her the career she'd worked so hard for, Wanda was the one who'd offered comfort. And then when Rayna learned she was pregnant, Wanda promised to help her with the baby, no matter what. That was what families did. Stick together.

Rayna hadn't even told Jimmy Wayne he had a daughter. The one time she tried to contact him in prison, he told her he'd kill her if he ever saw her again. In fact, he said, his tone dripping with venom, he'd have one of his friends on the outside do the job for him. Even though she had nothing to do with the huge drug bust that brought him down—hell, she hadn't even known he was involved with drugs or the cartel—he believed she was behind everything. Despite her denials, both to him and to the police department she worked for, everyone seemed to view her as the bad guy. A compromised cop.

Everyone, that is, except Wanda. Wanda knew Rayna had simply made a mistake, fallen in love with the wrong man. Lauren was the awesome result of that mistake, like a bonus rainbow after a particularly bad storm.

When the death threats had started coming in from cronies of the man Rayna had thought she loved, she'd worried about her mother first, before herself. So open and trusting, Wanda would never know what hit her in the event of an attack. That was why when Sam called with a job offer in a middle-of-nowhere town in dusty west Texas, Rayna had jumped at the opportunity. Sam hadn't even minded that Rayna was pregnant.

Another bit of serendipity. She and Sam had kept in touch since her days at the police academy, where he'd done a brief stint as one of the instructors. He'd been a father figure to her and he'd even told her he considered her an honorary daughter.

He'd told her later that he'd heard the news of her mistake through the grapevine. When she'd been suspended without pay—which she couldn't afford—his job offer had been a lifesaver.

She'd accepted, only telling Wanda after the fact. Unsurprisingly, Wanda had been totally on board with uprooting her entire life and moving. She'd gotten tired of waitressing anyway and was looking forward to spending her days looking after her grandchild.

Sam had kindly let them move into one of his rental houses, so they'd packed up their meager belongings into Rayna's SUV and made the six-hour drive to Getaway.

They never looked back. Lauren was born at Abilene Regional Medical Center, the closest hospital. Wanda made a new circle of friends, starting with the knitting club. And Rayna bloomed where she'd been planted, loving her job in the small-town sheriff's department.

So different from working in Conroe, a bustling suburb of Houston.

Even Lauren seemed to thrive in the fresh air and uncluttered lifestyle. In short, her life had become happy. Even Jimmy Wayne and his dire threats seemed far away.

Six months ago, she'd received word that he'd been killed in a prison fight. She'd been stunned, but not surprised. Most of all, she'd been relieved.

Bundling up her sick daughter into her cruiser, she drove the few miles to the doctor's office. True to his word, Dr. Delpeccio's pickup was already in the parking lot, along with a few other vehicles that must have belonged to his staff.

She got Lauren inside, letting her sick child lean on her for support. The instant she walked through the front door, one of the nurses shepherded her back into an exam room, where she took Lauren's temperature, did a throat and flu culture, asked a few questions and went to get Dr. Delpeccio.

The doctor came in shortly after, greeted Rayna with his gaze on Lauren. "Negative for strep or the flu. Seems to be a sinus infection with upper respiratory involvement." He wrote out a prescription and handed it to Rayna. "The nurse will be back in to give her a shot. She'll be good as new in no time."

Lauren started crying as soon as she heard the word *shot*. Rayna got her calmed down, fixed up, and they headed toward the front desk. "No charge," the receptionist said, waving her away. "Your mama has already promised to bring us a couple of peach pies."

Of course Wanda had. Thanking them again, Rayna got Lauren, who still sniffled but already seemed a slight bit better, into the car. A quick stop at the pharmacy to fill the prescription, and then Rayna got Lauren home and back into her bed. After turning on the television, Lauren snuggled under the blanket and drifted off to sleep.

"Sinus infection," Rayna told her mother. "And thanks for offering to bake them pies."

"They love my pies," Wanda said smugly. "Though honestly, I was going to bake them some even before Lauren got sick."

"Life in a small town," Rayna and Wanda said together, smiling.

Now that Lauren was on the mend, Rayna felt like a weight had been lifted from her shoulders. With Wanda shooing her away, promising to look after Lauren, Rayna decided to go into work. Any absence in a department this small could cause a problem, never mind when the sheriff didn't make it in.

She saw the shiny black motorcycle the instant she pulled into the parking lot, and her heart skipped a beat. Clearly, Parker Norton had returned. Surely he didn't expect results on the case in such a short time span. She figured he'd be persistent, but not have unrealistic expectations.

Steeling herself, she straightened her shoulders and strode up the sidewalk, entering through the front door like she did every day.

The instant she saw him, her insides went still. He stood as she approached, his expression serious. "Sheriff Coombs. Do you happen to have a moment?"

Brusquely, she nodded. "Certainly. Mary, will you please show Mr. Norton to my office? I'll be along in just a moment."

Mary nodded. "Please follow me."

Back ramrod straight, Parker followed the older woman. Watching him go, Rayna wondered. His military bearing seemed at odds with his biker appearance. Deliberate? She filed away the question for future reference.

Right now, she figured she'd be explaining how investigations worked.

After grabbing a cup of coffee, she stopped by to talk to Larry Newsome, who was on the phone. She waited him out, unabashedly listening in on his side of the conversation. He appeared to be talking to Getaway's self-proclaimed psychic, Serenity Rune, whose real name was something like Gertrude Reddoch. Serenity frequently called the sheriff's office with tips. More often than not, she was actually right. Because of this, Rayna had instructed her staff to always take her seriously.

Larry finally hung up, slightly pale. "Hey, boss," he greeted Rayna. "That was—"

"Serenity," she interrupted. "I got that. What did she have to say this time?"

Larry swallowed. "She claims Nicole Wilson is still alive."

"Interesting." This was news, no two ways around it. When they'd conducted the first investigation, Rayna sent one of her men to Serenity's downtown metaphysical bookstore, florist and rock shop, all combined into one. At the time, Serenity had said she couldn't see anything related to the missing girl.

Evidently, that had now changed.

Mary walked up. "He's all yours, Rayna," she said, and winked. "If I was twenty years younger…"

Rayna's entire body flushed, which meant her face had gone red, too. Being a fair-skinned, freckled redhead made it difficult to hide her emotions sometimes. "He's Sam's nephew," she reminded Mary. "We owe him respect."

Abashed, Mary nodded. "You're right. I'm sorry."

Larry snorted. "I should warn you, he wasn't too happy that you assigned me to work the investigation. I'm guessing he thinks you should handle it personally."

"Thank you." Turning to head back to her office, she smiled at them. "I'll get it handled."

Walking toward her office, she caught sight of Parker, sitting in the chair across from her desk, his back to her. For a moment, she allowed herself to admire his broad shoulders, his thick, dark hair, the masculine energy he exuded.

Then she squared her shoulders, reminded herself she was the sheriff and walked into her office.

"Sheriff Coombs." Standing when she entered, Parker dipped his chin in greeting. "How's your daughter?"

A bit surprised, she waited to answer him until she'd gone around behind her desk and taken her chair. "She's getting better," she replied. "I'm guessing Mary told you why I wasn't here?"

"She did." His easy smile faded. "As I'm sure you guessed, I'm here to talk to you about the investigation."

"I figured. We've already gotten started." She let her pleasant expression change into a frown. "Larry said you seemed upset that he'd been assigned to handle it." Might as well head him off at the pass. "I can assure you, Larry is a very capable law enforcement officer. He's good at what he does."

"Maybe so. But Sam said you're the best."

"I'm the sheriff." She dipped her chin. "I have other responsibilities."

He held her gaze. "Maybe so. But I'd appreciate you making this a priority."

The raw pain lurking under his mild tone touched her. "I'll oversee it very closely."

Instead of replying, he simply looked at her. She looked back, resisting the urge to squirm under his regard. Damn, he had beautiful eyes. Again, she felt that tug of attraction. She couldn't help but wonder if he felt it, too.

Danger. Heeding her internal alarm, she straightened her spine and breathed in.

"Would it help or hurt my case if I called Sam and asked him to talk you into handling it personally?"

To her surprise, her mouth twitched in amusement as she tried not to laugh. Normally, she'd find this kind of thing—going to the old sheriff to try and coerce the current sheriff—annoying. Maybe it was the fact that Parker was so open about it. And so hopeful. His sexy masculinity didn't hurt, either.

Sheriff, she reminded herself. She'd worked damn hard to get where she was. She loved her life here in Getaway. She'd made a home for her daughter and her mother. She couldn't let herself risk it because of a gorgeous bad boy with bedroom eyes.

Something of her inner conflict must have shown on her face.

"Same here," he drawled. "You're a distraction I can't afford, Rayna Coombs. Not right now. But when the time is right, I promise you we *will* explore this thing between us. No matter how far down that road that might be."

Desire made her lower body tingle. She looked down at her desk, working on breaking the spell of longing he aroused. She waited until her heartbeat slowed, until she could think and see past the cloud of need that his declaration brought.

When she spoke, her voice would be steady and professional. And she'd change the subject.

"You know, I worked on the case the first time," she pointed out, as if he'd never spoken. "I'm thinking it will be better to have fresh eyes. Larry might find something I overlooked."

Now it was he who fought the urge to smile. She could tell by the quick spark of laughter in his eyes and the way one side of his mouth curved in the beginning of a grin.

Yet when he spoke, he matched her cool tone. "While you do have a valid point," he said, leaning forward in his chair, "let me ask you something. If the missing girl was your family member; your mother, your sister or, God forbid, your daughter, would you rather look for them yourself or trust Larry?"

He paused a moment, clearly letting that question sink in, before he continued. "I don't know you yet, Rayna Coombs. But I'm betting you'd look over and over and again, as many times as you had to. I suspect you wouldn't rest until you had answers."

He had her there.

"That's how I feel," he said. "I've known Nicole Wilson for the last five years, since she was a thirteen-year-old tomboy. She's my best friend's baby sister and he loves her more than anything on this earth." He took a deep breath. "He's dying, Sheriff. Barely hanging on. He served our country at the same time I did. I hope and pray that I can bring Nicole to see him before he goes. Is that too much to ask?"

Of course it wasn't. Her heart melted, just the tiniest bit.

"Let me see what I can do," she relented. "I can take point on some of the investigative work."

"Thank you." Though he calmly nodded, the relief shining in his eyes told her how much her decision meant to him. "I'd like to go with you, if you don't mind."

"That's not a good idea," she began, ignoring the way her heartbeat kicked up a notch. "Civilians and police work—"

"Sheriff." Larry pushed her office door open and poked his head in. Behind him, she saw Mary twisting her hands together, her expression alarmed and worried. "Could I have a word with you?" Larry's voice shook.

"What is it?" she asked, pushing to her feet. Larry glanced at Parker.

"It's okay. We're about finished," she assured her officer. "What's going on?"

"Skeletal remains were found in the cornfield near the Ramsey's farm," he said, swallowing hard. "I've called for the county ME to get out here and sent Scott out to guard the scene until he arrives. But I thought maybe you should take a look."

Parker had gone utterly still. "Were they able to determine if this was a male or a female?" he asked. The agonized look in his eyes told her he thought he already knew.

"Not yet," Larry answered, pity in his gaze. "Judging from the size of the remains, they're thinking female. But we won't know for sure until the ME takes a look."

"I want to go out there," Parker said, his eyes locked on Rayna. "Now."

"I understand," she said, shooting a quelling look at Larry when he opened his mouth to speak. "You can ride with me."

Parker wished he'd taken his motorcycle and followed the sheriff instead of riding shotgun in her patrol vehicle. He'd never liked letting someone else drive anyway—something about the lack of control. Especially in times like this, with his adrenaline pumping and hope battling...sorry, he wanted—no, *needed*—to feel his powerful bike underneath him.

If the body turned out to be Nicole—and really, who else could it be?—he didn't know how the hell he was going to break the news to John. Barely an hour ago, John had texted him, asking if he'd had any luck yet locating her. Because of the way Parker had phrased things, John thought Nicole had merely taken off to explore the countryside before coming to see him in Dallas. He had no idea his baby sister had truly gone missing. And Parker had done everything he could to keep things that way.

John had enough to worry about, battling for his life. Though he'd begun to suspect something might be wrong, John hadn't enough energy left in him to probe deeply.

Plus, he trusted Parker. If you couldn't trust the man who'd saved your life, then who could you trust?

Parker despised the thought of letting his friend down.

With the radio crackling various calls, Rayna drove down the same road he'd taken on his bike the day before. Past the stock pond where he'd considered skinny-dipping, turning onto an old dirt track between two fields. As they turned a corner, he saw the flashing police car lights ahead.

His stomach clenched. Swallowing hard, he tried to prepare himself for the worst.

"Depending how long the body's been out here, you won't be able to tell much from just looking at it," Rayna cautioned. "From what Larry said, I think it's mostly just bones."

He nodded. "How long would it take a corpse to get like that?" Praying she'd say far longer than Nicole had been missing.

"That depends," she allowed, her expression thoughtful. "If wild animals happened along or not, whether the body was in water or dirt or something else. That's one of the reasons why the medical examiner is needed."

"I see." He got what she was trying to tell him. Didn't like it, but knew she was right. Until they knew more, all he could do would be to sit tight and wait.

If not Nicole, then who? While he suspected in his heart that she was dead, he refused to accept it as truth until positive ID had been made. Even if the odds seemed stacked against him.

"Does a county this small even have a medical examiner?" he asked. He remembered reading somewhere that Kent County was the sixth-least-populated county in the entire state of Texas.

She glanced at him. "We send to Abilene. Taylor

County sends someone. Kent County, like all the other smaller counties, uses a regional ME."

Which meant getting results back might take longer.

Glancing at Rayna, who'd driven with quiet competence and single-minded intensity, he noted the tense set of her jaw. Naturally, she didn't like this. Who would? But to her, it was more than an isolated crime. Someone—maybe Nicole—had been killed in her town, *on her watch*.

"It's not your fault," he heard himself say, inwardly wincing.

"I'm aware of that," she responded tersely, barely glancing his way. "It still pisses me off. Unless this victim died accidentally, this means we've got a murderer in our town. While it might have been someone just passing through, it's much more likely to be a resident."

Which meant she'd have to find out who.

She pulled over behind one of the other vehicles and parked. Turning to Parker, she unclicked her seat belt. "You can stay here if you don't want to see the remains," she offered.

"I want to see."

One small dip of her chin to show she understood. "Fine. You can come with me. Stay close to me and out of the way, all right?"

He agreed. *Please don't let this be Nicole* ran on repeat inside his head. He kept close to Rayna, and they picked their way across the uneven dirt until they reached the small group of people clustered around what appeared to be a shallow grave in the middle of a field. Yellow crime scene tape had already been placed in a large rectangle around the area.

At the edge of the tape, Rayna stopped so abruptly

Parker nearly collided with her. "Wait here," she ordered. "Don't cross into the crime scene."

If he stayed put, he'd see nothing. Several people in uniforms blocked everything from his view.

He thought for a split second, and then went after Rayna. Focused on her colleagues, she didn't appear to notice. Everyone else seemed too intent on their tasks to pay much attention to a stranger following the small-town sheriff.

The clustered group moved apart as Rayna approached. A couple of people greeted her by name.

And then Parker saw it. Partially obscured by dirt, a skeleton. As far as he could tell, precious little flesh remained. Just from looking at it, he couldn't tell definitively if it was Nicole or not.

Had he really expected he could?

Stumbling slightly, he bumped Rayna. She turned and glared at him, silently chastising him for not doing as she'd asked. But she was all business here, and returned her attention to the others.

From what he could tell, mostly they all appeared to be waiting on the ME. No one wanted to touch anything. Couldn't disturb the crime scene until Forensic could gather their evidence. Parker had watched enough TV shows to understand doing that would be taboo.

Moving away from the others, he walked around the very edge of the tape. Someone had found what appeared to have been a shallow grave. He couldn't tell if wild animals had unearthed the bones or if the elements might have played a part. Right now, that wasn't his concern. He wanted to see if there were any personal belongings like jewelry that might be an identifier.

Disappointed, he realized if there was, right now the dirt and earth obscured it.

"What are you doing?" Rayna muttered. "What part of 'Don't disturb the crime scene' did you not understand?"

"I'm being careful," he replied. Still, now that his curiosity had been satisfied, he moved deliberately back, away from the crime scene tape and the others.

Rayna went with him. "It's going to be nothing but waiting," she said. "We can't do anything until the Taylor County ME gets here. And since that's a bit of a drive..."

They could be waiting hours. He winced.

"Do you want me to have one of my people run you back into town?" she asked. "There's no reason you should stay. There won't be any immediate determination of anything, I promise you." She glanced back at the others. "I have to stay here. It's my job."

Briefly, he considered. "Thank you, but I'd rather stay. If that is Nicole, I can't abandon her now that she's been found."

Eyeing him, she opened her mouth and then closed it. Her expression finally softened. "Understood. But, since we don't normally allow civilians at crime scenes, I'm really going to have to insist you stay out of the way. Understood?"

"Got it. Just so you know, I was only trying to see if there was a necklace. Nicole always wore one with a state of Texas charm and a heart. She never took it off."

"I didn't see a necklace," she said. "But I can't brush the dirt away. I'll tell the ME to keep an eye out, though."

"Thanks. I'd appreciate it." And then he moved

back, putting several feet between him and the crime scene tape.

She watched him go and then turned back to rejoin her colleagues.

Chapter 3

Word traveled fast in a small town. All everyone talked about in the café the next morning was the body found in the field. By now, people had embellished and exaggerated, so half of what people asked Rayna bore absolutely no resemblance to the truth.

"We don't know yet," she replied so many times that she asked for her coffee and breakfast sandwich to go. The general consensus seemed to be that the body was Nicole. She tended to agree with them, but of course she would have to wait like everyone else for the ME's report.

Just as the waitress handed over the brown paper bag, someone tugged on Rayna's arm. She turned, swallowing her alarm when she saw Serenity Rune standing in front of her, an expectant look on her cherubic face.

"They're wrong, you know," Serenity said, her soft

voice pitched so low that Rayna had to strain to hear her. "Nicole Wilson is alive. I can feel it."

Rayna nodded her thanks. "Larry told me you'd said that. I can only hope that you're right."

Driving to the sheriff's office while eating her breakfast sandwich, Rayna thought about Serenity. Most people believed her harmless, an oddity who brought her own special brand of vibrance to the small town. Rayna had dealt with her more than a few times, always on unsolved cases. On those, Serenity had been right about three-quarters of the time, maybe more. Enough that Rayna listened whenever the older woman spoke. If Serenity said Nicole was alive, then Rayna could only hope she was once again correct.

Which would mean the bones belonged to some other unlucky young woman or girl. The ME's office had confirmed they definitely belonged to a female. Now they were all waiting for cause of death, the time and date of death and hopefully a positive identity. That was the hard part, the waiting. Because unlike on television, getting results back from an overworked medical examiner's office took time.

Luckily, Parker seemed to understand that, even though time apparently was the one thing his terminally ill friend didn't have. She felt bad for him, having to wait around for answers. So much that she pulled every string, called in every favor she had to get the results back quicker.

The phones never stopped ringing, not once, all day long. Poor Mary couldn't keep up with the volume of calls so both her backups were called in to assist her.

Rayna left strict instructions that they were to respond to all media inquiries with a stern and simple *"No comment."* They could follow that up with the news that Rayna would do a press conference once she learned anything definitive, but that could take some time.

In addition to the onslaught of phone calls, people started stopping by. With every ounce of her time occupied dealing with phone calls, Mary wasn't able to fend off the numerous visitors. Most of them simply managed to make their way back to Rayna's office, full of questions and concerns about the body.

By the time the day was over, Rayna knew she'd be stopping by the Rattlesnake Pub for a drink before heading home. Of the two bars in town, she favored the Western atmosphere of the RP more than the ultramodern hipster decor of the newly opened place called the Bar. While she understood the owners, Mark and Shirley Prescott, trying to pull in some of the same trend seekers who traveled to Marfa to see the lights and stayed and opened art galleries, she wondered if they'd soon realize they weren't in Marfa or Austin and realize what kind of clients they needed to cater to here in Getaway. Farmers and ranchers, cowboys and tradespeople, housewives and young parents: these were the kinds of hardworking people who lived in Getaway.

Naturally the younger ones, the kids who came home from college for the summers, would love the place. Everyone else mostly went to RP.

The bar was still half-empty when Rayna pulled into the lot. Good. After parking, she sent a quick text to Wanda to let her know she wouldn't be home for dinner. Then, she began to make her way toward the entrance when she spotted the Harley. Shiny black and chrome, customized. Parker's bike. Immediately, her heartbeat accelerated.

Once inside, she stopped for a moment, blinking as she let her eyes adjust to the dim light. Several of the tables were occupied, as were a couple stools at the bar. She spotted Parker on one of the stools. The instant their gazes met, he waved her over.

Despite the alarm bells going off inside her head, she went, taking the empty stool next to him.

"Rough day?" he asked.

"You might say that." She signaled to Tony behind the bar that she'd like her usual, a tall glass of wheat beer with a slice of orange. "Everyone in town is speculating..." Aghast at herself for what she'd been about to say, she stopped.

"I know. I've hung out downtown all day," he said glumly. "I had lunch at the Tumbleweed Café. Evidently, enough people figured out who I am and why I'm in town. I ended up stuck at a table with about ten strangers, all of whom wanted to tell me their pet theories about what happened."

She grimaced. "That's rough. I'm sorry. It was pretty much like that at the station today."

Her beer arrived, the tall glass sweating. She accepted it gratefully and took a long drink.

"Are you going to eat?" he asked. "I'm starving and I'd love the company."

Considering, she nodded. "Sure."

"Do you want to eat here at the bar or get a booth?" he asked.

"A booth," she replied. "They have really good chicken wings and their burgers are good, too."

Two booths remained empty near the bar area, and they simply moved over to one of them. Parker waved to the server to make sure she understood they'd moved.

With a wide grin, she brought them menus, barely even glancing at Rayna. Only when Parker looked away did she appear to realize she'd been standing there, entranced. She blushed, bit her bottom lip and rushed off toward the kitchen.

Rayna briefly considered teasing Parker, but decided she didn't know him well enough and he hadn't noticed his admirer anyway.

They ordered cheeseburgers and fries, not the healthiest options, but Rayna was too hungry to care. She shared an easy camaraderie with Parker and thought that under different circumstances, they might have been friends. If she could get past her nearly overwhelming attraction to him. She could kind of sympathize with the waitress. She got exactly how the other woman felt, only she was better at hiding it.

Mellowed a bit by the beer, her belly full, she allowed herself to relax and feel warm and fuzzy. Parker was good company, amusing and knowledgeable about a wide variety of subjects, so much so that she jokingly told him he ought to play the bar trivia game they ran every night at seven. Which was in ten minutes.

"I like that idea," he drawled. "How do you play?"

"We have to go back to the bar," she replied. "They have these connected electronic tablet things there."

"Let's do it." He signaled for the check. When she reached for her wallet, he waved her away. "This one's on me. You can get it next time."

Next time. Blinking, she gave an internal shrug and allowed herself to bask in his magnetism.

Once he'd settled up, they took their beers and wandered back over to the bar. The place had grown a little more crowded and there was only one empty stool.

Parker told her to take it and he'd stand behind her. Heaven help her, but she liked the way she felt with his strong body pressed right up against her back.

The trivia challenge started in five minutes. Parker ordered a second beer, asking her if she wanted one. Since she still had half a glass left, she declined. She couldn't believe how excited the thought of watching him play trivia made her. She loved trivia, though she'd never been very good at it. She had a feeling Parker might be. Even better, the person at the barstool next to her got up, allowing Parker to have the seat.

When the game started, she scooted in close. She and Parker sat shoulder to shoulder, which gave her a pleasant sort of thrill. She couldn't resist glancing over at his muscular arms and wondering how they'd feel under her fingers.

Parker won the first round handily, answering questions about bugs and birds and landmarks. "I'm seriously impressed," she told him. "You're really good."

"I have a wealth of useless knowledge," he said, shrugging. "I enjoy learning new things, even if the only time that comes in handy is in a game of Trivial Pursuit."

The next three rounds seemed easy for him, too. As more and more players dropped out, Rayna glanced across the bar and spotted Scotty Randolph, Getaway's only CPA. He continued to play, occasionally shooting a glowering glare at Parker. Which meant Scotty was Parker's main competitor.

Since Rayna had gone on a couple of dates with Scotty before realizing he was an insufferable know-it-all, she sincerely hoped Parker could beat him.

By round six, Parker and Scotty were the only two

still playing. A small crowd had gathered behind each man, and the bartender brought them both another beer on the house. Since Rayna had finished her beer and Parker still had most of the one he'd ordered earlier, he slid it over to her. She sipped occasionally on his instead of ordering another.

In which country was Julie Christie born? Parker paused, studying the choices. "India," he muttered, selecting that. Scotty chose England. And just like that, Parker became the Rattlesnake Pub's new trivia champion. Tony flashed the lights above the bar and rang a huge dinner bell that had been installed there just for that purpose. "We have a new champ," Tony announced. If Rayna remembered right, Scotty had held the title for a little over two years. She hoped he wouldn't take the loss badly.

The crowd went wild, whooping and yelling their congratulations. To cheers and applause, Parker accepted his prize—a gift certificate for a meal for two. Grinning, he thanked Tony and eyed Scotty across the bar.

"Do you think he's pissed?" he asked Rayna, low voiced. "He looks pretty mad."

"Give him a second," she advised. "He's got kind of a high-profile job in town, so I'm sure he won't do anything to jeopardize that."

Parker tilted his head, apparently intrigued. "Oh, yeah? What exactly does he do?"

"Everyone's taxes and payroll. He's a CPA."

"Ah." Parker nodded. "I see."

"Hey, I didn't say it was glamorous." She laughed. "Just that everyone knows him."

Moving stiffly, Scotty finally got down from his bar

stool and came over to shake Parker's hand. Faintly relieved he hadn't turned out to be a sore loser, Rayna nodded a brief hello. Instead of nodding back, Scotty pointedly ignored her.

"You're new in town," he said, eyeing Parker quizzically. "Where'd you get so much trivial knowledge?" Shorthand for *How does someone who looks like a biker know so much?*

Rayna laughed. Scotty ignored her. Somehow, Parker managed to keep a straight face. "I read a lot," he replied, with a casual shrug. "How about you?"

"Oh, I read of course. I also have numerous degrees from Tech. I loved learning so much that I just kept going back and getting degrees in something else."

Rayna braced herself. So help her, if Scotty asked Parker if he had any degrees, she might just have to intervene. In their small community, many of the hardworking ranchers and shop owners had only finished high school. Scotty had long lorded his prestigious education over them and wasn't well liked for it.

She glanced at Tony, who was too busy waiting on customers to intervene. If she got involved, she knew Scotty wouldn't appreciate it and most likely, neither would Parker. She decided to sit back and simply observe.

"What degrees do you have?" Scotty asked, his smug voice making her aware he thought he already knew the answer.

"None," Parker answered easily. "After high school, I enlisted in the Marines. I did two tours of duty in Afghanistan."

Just like that, Parker won again. There was nothing

the citizens of a small Texas town respected more than someone who'd served their country.

"Thank you for your service," Scotty managed to say. He turned away and hightailed it back to the other side of the bar.

Rayna and Parker looked at each other and burst into laughter. "This town is full of characters," he mused. "Even more so than I remember when I came here as a kid."

"Did you stay with Sam?" she asked. "I imagine he was a wonderful uncle."

"Yes, and he was." Regarding her curiously, he smiled. She felt the impact of that slow smile all the way down to her toes.

Distracted, she glanced at her watch. "I'd better get going," she said, not without regret. "My mother is watching my daughter, and I like to make it home before Lauren's bedtime."

"I'll walk you to your car." He dropped a ten-dollar bill on the bar and took her arm.

Part of her wanted to shake him off. The other part wanted to lean into his strong body, breathe in his scent and enjoy her brief moment of good fortune.

Clearly, she would never learn.

Outside, the night air still hot from earlier. They walked in silence to her car. The parking lot had gotten full, though most everyone had already gone inside.

"I don't know how I'm going to tell John that his baby sister is dead," he said. "He's fighting for his life. I'm afraid this might kill him." Expression miserable, he swallowed hard.

She touched his arm. "I suggest you wait until the DNA results are back. We don't know for sure it's her."

Gazing down at her, he appeared to be struggling to speak. And then he covered her mouth with his and kissed her.

Shocked, stunned, and yes, aroused, she kissed him back, helpless to resist. Her arms somehow found their way around his neck, her body full up against his with her back against her car.

Somehow, they made it inside the car. Apart, no longer locked together like a couple of horny teenagers. A good thing, she thought, trying to catch her breath. Because if someone had seen them, she'd have been the topic of gossip for the next several days.

"That was…" She struggled to express herself.

Parker simply gazed at her, his expression hidden in shadows. "I want you," he rumbled.

Oh, hell. She knew she should manage to say something polite, maybe thank him, and then ask him to get out of her car so she could go home. But with her entire body thrumming with need, she couldn't even find the right words. Or any words.

He kissed her again. This time, she tried to resist. Okay, maybe half-assed, because somehow she ended up straddling him in the front seat of her car. When she realized, her entire body blushed. "At least we're still fully clothed," she said, climbing off him and moving over to the driver's seat.

"We can change that," he said, his voice silky with invitation. And just like that, she knew what she wanted.

"Not here, not in my squad car, where anyone could see us."

"My motel room."

She nodded. "The Landshark Motel, right?"

"Do you want me to drive?" he asked. For a second,

she thought he meant to follow her there. Part of her hoped he would, because once his physical presence was out of her vicinity, she might be able to summon up the willpower to resist him.

"Um…" Warring with herself, not sure how to answer, she simply gazed at him, letting all her desire show in her eyes.

He groaned. "Never mind. You drive. I'm so hard, I can barely move."

Damn. Any hope for resisting had just flown out the window. Mouth dry, she started up the car and drove them to the motel.

Once there, they spilled from the car, moving as though drunk on lust. At the door to his room, he fumbled with the key but got it unlocked. Once he'd pushed it open, he pulled her inside.

Now would be the time, she thought wildly, her entire body aching. Now would be the time if she was going to back out, to do it. But she wanted him, with his sexy hard muscles and come-to-me eyes. Oh, how she wanted him.

He touched her then, pulled her close and kissed her. Head swimming, she allowed herself to drown in that kiss.

Mouths locked together, they each helped the other shed their clothes. For a split second, she worried about whether or not she'd worn one of her good bras and prettier panties, but then he slipped his finger inside her and she no longer cared.

"You're so wet." His voice was a husky murmur, the movement of his fingers driving her wild. Frantic to touch him, she reached out, found the thick bulge of his arousal and freed it from his briefs.

"Wow," she murmured, wrapping her hand around him and moving it up and down the satiny shaft. She bent, intending to take him into her mouth, but he stopped her by twisting away.

"Come on." Pulling back the awful yellow-and-orange bedspread, he tugged her down with him onto the sheet. "I want to be inside of you."

Her entire body quivered in anticipation. His hands resting above her, she arched her back, wanton and shameless, beyond caring. "I want you inside me. Now."

Using her hands, she tried to pull him down to her, but he resisted, despite the force of his arousal. "Wait," he rasped. "I want our first time to be slow."

"Not me," she countered, taking him in her hands. "I want wild and fast and hard. And now."

He muttered something—either a curse or a prayer—and covered her with his body. So big, so hard, so damn sexy, she almost came just then.

Ah, but she clenched herself, holding back. Because she wanted more. She helped guide the already moist tip of him, right against her. And then, in one quick move, he pushed the entire swollen length of him inside her.

This. He filled her up, holding still while her body adjusted. She'd forgotten how good sex could feel. And then he started to move.

Whatever he'd expected to find when he came to Getaway again, it hadn't been this. Cradling a sensual armful of woman, Parker wondered if their lovemaking had shaken her to the core. It certainly had him. There was satisfying and great and then there was… this. The depths of passion they'd reached defied rational explanation.

Despite that, his body stirred, already wanting more.

Ever since he could remember, women had wanted to be with him. He hadn't been a jock in high school, or particularly brilliant or talented. One of his girlfriends had told him he gave off some kind of bad-boy vibe, though damn if he'd ever understood what she meant. At the time, he hadn't particularly cared.

The first time he'd been without women had been his stint in the military, specifically when he'd been stationed in Afghanistan. Like all the other guys, he'd spent more than a few nights with a magazine and his hand. But the period when he'd been in the desert had also brought him a time of great clarity, when he'd realized there just might be more to life than a series of one-night stands.

Honorably discharged and stateside, he'd gone to great lengths to avoid exactly this kind of thing.

Then why...?

Rayna was different. She could be more.

Stunned, he considered. He'd had no plans other than to find Nicole and attempt to make John's final days the best he could.

Shaking his head at his own deep thoughts, he knew he couldn't even think about getting emotionally involved with someone right now. No, he had to do what he'd planned, find John's kid sister and drag her happy ass back to Dallas.

Maybe once all that was settled... He shied away from the thought, unwilling to face how much his world would change without John in it. This, what he'd done, what he and Rayna had done, was completely unfair to her. She wasn't a one-night-stand type of woman. And right now, he couldn't give her more. No matter how much he might want to.

He'd made a mistake. He'd been thinking with the wrong head. All the trite excuses and rationalizations went around and around inside his head, but the truth was, Rayna Coombs had gotten under his skin.

Worse, he had no idea how she felt. She sighed, stretched and then eased out of his arms. Completely confident in her nakedness—and why shouldn't she be with a body like that?—she'd gotten up, cool as a cucumber, gone to the bathroom to wash up, come back and put on her clothes and then offered to drive him back to his bike. With him still flat on his back in the bed, wanting her still.

Bemused, he'd agreed and pulled on his clothes.

Rayna acted as if nothing unusual had happened. She was back to the brusque, efficient sheriff of few words as she drove. Still sexy as hell, but now she'd returned to being remote and polite. As if she hadn't just come apart in his arms. He wasn't sure how to react to that, so he didn't.

When they reached the parking lot, now packed with numerous cars circling looking for spots, she pulled up behind his Harley and put her cruiser in Park. "Drive safely," she said, her pleasant smile untouchable.

He had a sudden urge to pull her to him and kiss that smile right off her face, but the Rattlesnake was now hopping and a constant stream of people spilled out into the parking lot.

"I will, thanks." Equally pleasant, he got out with a wave.

She drove off and never even looked back.

Aching, Parker climbed on his bike, well aware he

couldn't follow her. He toyed briefly with the idea of going back inside and having another beer, but decided against it. Instead, he headed back to the motel, aware his room would smell like sex and Rayna, and wondering what the hell was wrong with him.

When he woke the next morning, his head was back where it needed to be. Since finding out if the bones belonged to Nicole would be a waiting game, he decided to see what he could do to retrace her steps from the moment she'd arrived in Getaway. Starting with the Welcome to Getaway sign.

Surely with all the research the sheriff's office had done previously, they'd have some idea of where she went after that. But then he remembered Rayna saying they had no evidence of Nicole being in town. Nothing on camera, no witnesses who'd seen her, absolutely nothing. He'd doubted that then and also now, but their assertion that something possibly happened to Nicole before she ever reached the city limits could be correct.

Taking that at face value, he knew he needed to find out where she'd gone after taking the selfie at the welcome sign. If only they'd located her phone, they could use the GPS tracker to pinpoint her journey.

Since her phone—actually, none of her belongings, including her vehicle—had ever been found, he didn't have a whole lot to go on.

Once he reached the Welcome to Getaway sign, he pulled over to the side of the road. For the most part, west Texas was supremely flat, and from this slightly elevated spot, he could see for miles in all directions.

Toward the west, he could see some of downtown, even though the tallest building was only three stories tall. East were fields, some dotted with cattle, others crops. Way, way off, he spotted a farmhouse and barn, both with red roofs.

He turned slowly, and north and south had views similar to what he saw looking east. More fields, more crops and livestock, and a couple more ranch houses and barns, some of them just specks in the distance.

He imagined the sheriff's office would have started there, interviewing the occupants, asking them if they'd seen anything unusual.

Turning his bike around, he headed into town. He'd stop at the sheriff's office and find out exactly what they'd investigated and how.

He had to admit, the thought of seeing Rayna again filled him with anticipation.

When he strode into the small building, Mary looked up from her desk, holding up her hand to let him know she was on the phone. She wore a headset on one ear and appeared to be asking the caller several pointed questions.

Parker glanced past her, trying to see if Rayna might be inside her office. But due to the way the cubicles had been arranged, he couldn't see past the front row. He suspected this might be deliberate, one of Sam's safety measures in case a bad actor came in with the intent of hurting cops.

Finally, Mary finished up with her call. "What can I do for you today, Mr. Norton?"

Since he'd already learned he couldn't get past her, he outlined what he hoped to learn.

"You'll have to talk to Larry about that," she said, her eyes narrow slits behind her eyeglasses. "I know you want to see Rayna, but she's on a conference call with Abilene and can't be interrupted."

"Abilene?" he asked. "Do you mean with their medical examiner's office?"

"I have no idea." Her sharp tone told him she felt it was none of his business.

"Fine. I'd like to talk with Larry," he conceded.

"Then come back after lunch. He doesn't come in until one."

He didn't even have to consider. "I'll wait for Rayna." He took a seat in one of the chairs. "Surely her teleconference can't last too long."

Chapter 4

Mary popped into Rayna's office, opening the door slowly. When she realized Rayna wasn't on the phone, she came all the way inside, closing the door behind her.

"That man is here again," she said, her mouth turning downward. "At first, I thought I had him talked into discussing the case with Larry, but Larry's shift doesn't start until one. Even though I told him you were on a teleconference, he's insisting on waiting."

Rayna managed to conceal the way her entire body came awake. She didn't have to ask which man Mary referred to. Parker. The man with whom she'd made mad, passionate love last night. And whom she ached to make love with again.

Apparently once hadn't been enough. Giving herself a swift mental kick in the butt, she pushed to her feet. "It's okay, Mary. Go ahead and send him back."

Though disapproval sparked in the older woman's eyes, she turned on her heel and headed back up front. At least she hadn't argued. Rayna supposed Parker's rough biker look must have put Mary off. She wished he affected her that way. Instead, everything about him turned her on.

Tap, tap, and then her office door opened. Parker stood in the doorway, larger than life and sexier than hell. His brown eyes glowed with warmth, making her remember how he'd looked at her last night, during and after...

Hells bells, but she blushed. "Parker." Despite her rosy complexion, she tried to act as if nothing had happened between them. She kept her tone professional and held out her hand for him to shake.

Though this appeared to briefly startle him, he finally enveloped her fingers with his large hand. If he held on a bit too long, she pretended not to notice. Even if she wanted to tug on his hand and pull him close to her.

"What can I help you with?" she asked.

Finally releasing her, he nodded. "I'd like to review the records and see what y'all turned up when you completed your investigation."

She considered his request, thinking of the bones in the shallow grave and the look of devastation on Parker's chiseled face. "I think I can arrange that. Larry's not due to come in until after lunch, and he's been looking into everything. Most of it should be in files on his desk. You're completely welcome to look through them."

He stared at her for a moment, making her wonder if her agreement had surprised him. "Thank you," he said.

She took him back to their small but adequate interrogation and conference room and brought the files to him. The utilitarian ten-by-twelve-foot space contained a long metal-and-wood conference table and six battered metal chairs. "The coffeepot is over there," she said, pointing. "And the restrooms are down that hall. Let me or Mary know if you need anything else."

Already intent on flipping through the first manila folder, he nodded. "Thanks again."

She left him then, closing the door quietly behind him. She couldn't help but hope the unidentified remains belonged to someone other than Nicole. Of course, if that turned out to be the case, it would open up an entirely new set of problems. As in, who did the bones belong to, how long had they been there and were there more?

Worried, she put in a call to Sam. Not only was he always the voice of reason, but his long career spanning decades working in law enforcement provided him with valuable insights.

Sam listened as she explained what they'd found.

"How's Parker holding up?" he asked, once she'd finished telling him everything.

"As well as can be expected. He's here right now, going over the case files from the first investigation."

"I'm not surprised." Sam sighed. "You do know, whether this turns out to be Nicole or not, you've got to consider the very likely possibility that there's a killer in Getaway."

"I have," she replied. "And I've also considered that it might have just been someone passing through."

"True, but Getaway isn't exactly on a well-traveled route to anywhere. Nor is it exactly a tourist destination. It's much more likely to be someone living right there in town."

She groaned. "We don't have any people who've been reported missing, other than Nicole. She was just passing through on her way to Dallas from Texas Tech. The rare times we had a crime problem, it always turned out to be someone on their way to somewhere else."

"I know." Sam chuckled. "Some things never change. I hope for Parker's friend's sake, those remains aren't Nicole's. Even if they are, you've got to start looking for the killer."

"Which will be like trying to find a needle in a haystack," she groused. "I know just about everyone in this town. I can't imagine any of them doing something awful like that."

"True. Anybody new move there recently? Someone that keeps to themselves, avoids socializing?"

She thought for a moment. "Not that I'm aware of, but I'll check."

"Have Larry do all of that. He loves poking his nose around in places it doesn't belong." Sam laughed, making Rayna remember how he and Larry used to joke about who was actually the nosiest. This memory, combined with the knowledge that Sam was all the way down at the Texas coast, over five hundred miles away, made her sad.

"Are you sure you're not ready to come back here for a visit?" she asked, ever hopeful. "It's been a few years since you retired and moved to South Padre."

This made him laugh again. "Not yet, Rayna. Not yet. Visiting now would be the definition of bad timing."

He had her there. They chatted a bit more about family. She told him Wanda and Lauren were fine and he discussed his wife's continued remission from breast cancer.

"I'm going to put a call into the Taylor County ME's office," Sam finally said. "Cherry and I go way back. I'll see if she can put a rush on this for you."

Once again, Sam came through. She thanked him, hoping as usual, his personal touch would get things moving. She really didn't know what she'd have done without Sam having her back. She'd learned so much since coming to work here, and all of it made her not only a better law enforcement officer but a better person.

When they finally ended the conversation, for the first time she felt more at ease since getting the call about the remains. She stood and walked to her door, fighting the urge to head down to the conference room and check on Parker.

"There you are!" Mary exclaimed. "I didn't want to interrupt your phone call. It's lunchtime. I was about to run down to Mickey D's and grab a salad. Do you want me to get you one?"

Glancing at her watch, Rayna saw it was nearly one. Larry would be in soon. "Sure," she replied, going back for her purse and extracting a ten. "I'll have a sweet tea, too, please."

Mary accepted the money and then glanced toward the closed conference room door. "What about him? Should I see if he wants me to pick him up anything?"

"Sure." Touched by Mary's thoughtfulness, she smiled. "That's really nice of you, Mary."

"He's easy on the eyes," Mary drawled, playing off the compliment by teasing. "I see the way you look at him."

Rayna's heart stopped for a second. Swallowing, she managed to shrug, hoping to play it off. "Hey, I'm female and human, right?"

"Right." Oblivious to the turmoil inside her boss, Mary stepped over to the conference room and knocked.

Rayna slipped back into her office and closed the door before Parker answered. Mary's comment on the way she looked at Parker touched a raw nerve. After all, she'd heard similar remarks before when she'd started dating Jimmy Wayne, a local politician in Conroe. Unbeknownst to her, he'd also been under investigation by the FBI for various criminal activities. She'd been a police officer. When he'd been arrested, there hadn't been many on the force who hadn't thought her crooked.

But she hadn't known. The one time she'd thought it safe to abandon her work persona and enjoy life, she'd had the wool pulled over her eyes. Not only did his arrest almost cost her the job she loved, but Jimmy Wayne had believed that she'd somehow been behind the entire investigation.

Blinking, she reminded herself that the past was exactly that. Jimmy Wayne was no longer a threat, and she'd vowed that she'd never again be played for a fool by a man. Clearly, she had a thing for bad boys. Jimmy Wayne had been one. And Parker Norton another.

Part of her protested—already!—that Parker was nothing like Jimmy. But up until the moment the Feds had come for him, she'd thought Jimmy Wayne was just about perfect. Sure, Wanda hadn't liked him and had made no bones about telling Rayna exactly what she thought, but Rayna had simply believed it had been a case of "no one is good enough for my daughter." Turned out her mother had been correct. Jimmy Wayne had been a liar and a cheat and a criminal. And she'd been a cop, too blinded by love to see the truth.

Again with the past. Shaking her head, she exited her office just in time to see Larry arrive. Since she knew how possessive he could be about "his" files, she hurried over to his desk to let him know they were with Parker in the conference room.

Just as she finished explaining, Mary got back with their lunches. "I'm taking them in the conference room," she said as she breezed past. Since their small station didn't have an actual break room, they often ate there. "I got Parker lunch, too."

Larry, who'd been on the verge of getting indignant over his missing files, now appeared crestfallen. "Wonder why she didn't bring me lunch."

"Probably because you always eat before you come in." Rayna pointed to the sub shop cup on his desk. "Looks like today was no exception."

Though he rolled his eyes, he had no choice but to agree with her. "By the way," she continued, "I'm permitting Parker Norton to review the files on Nicole Wilson. I'll make sure they're back on your desk once he's finished."

Larry stared. He opened his mouth as if he wanted to protest, and then apparently decided not to. "Okay, boss."

She actually wanted to thank him for not making a big deal out of nothing. Instead, she simply nodded. "I'm going to go back there and eat. Let me know if anything comes up."

"Will do."

Steeling herself, she turned to go back and try to choke down her lunch around the one man she needed to resist. Doing so really didn't sound appetizing at all. She briefly considered grabbing her lunch and taking it to her office to eat, but if she did, she knew Mary would comment. Her entire staff had been on her the first time she'd done that, telling her how Sam had always said it was important to take a real break from the job. And they'd been right. Sam had always either eaten in the conference room or gone out for his meals. He'd always made a point to never eat in his office at his desk. So even now, there was no way she could.

At the doorway she paused, took a deep breath and opened the door to the conference room. When she stepped inside, trying to act like her heart wasn't about to pound out of her chest, Parker or Mary didn't even look up. They scrolled on their phones while eating.

One of her pet peeves. Yet she, too, had been guilty of the same thing. As she pulled out her chair and took her seat, she reconsidered. Maybe she wouldn't have to engage in small talk with Parker and Mary, all the while secretly wanting him inside her.

This could be a good thing.

She grabbed the bag containing her salad as quietly as possible. Mary, she saw, had already finished. And Parker had eaten a burger, though he still worked on his fries while intent on his phone.

The lack of attention enabled her to relax somewhat and enjoy her salad. Still, she kept her head down and ate quietly, not exactly rushing, but not taking her time, either.

Once finished, she got up. Carrying her bag to the trash, she strode to the door. She didn't want to appear to be in a hurry, but did want out of there as quickly as possible.

"Wait up," Mary said. "My lunch break is over. That way we can both leave Mr. Norton here to go through his files in peace."

Rayna nodded. As soon as Mary pushed past her, she closed the door, exhaling silently in relief. Maybe now, with an actual physical barrier between them, her head would clear and she'd be able to think. Perhaps the persistent ache of needing him would fade away. It had better, because she needed to focus on her job instead of the muscular, sexy man in her conference room.

Parker could tell Rayna felt uncomfortable around him in her work environment. Almost as if she regretted what had happened between them. If they'd been alone, he might have teased her, told her not to worry, that he wasn't the type to combine business with pleasure. And he almost could make himself believe that, despite the way every single time he even glanced at her, he had to fight memories of her soft skin under his hands. Or how good she tasted, and how damn bad he wanted to be inside her again.

He didn't know what it was about this woman, but he'd wanted her from the moment he'd first laid eyes on her and still wanted her.

Even when he couldn't allow himself to lose focus.

Like now. Glancing at her outside the glass wall, he dragged his gaze away from her shapely rear and back to the slender stack of file folders in front of him. Nicole was what mattered now. He'd deal with this attraction to Rayna later.

He made careful notes of all the names mentioned in the case files. People who had been interviewed, and why. Some of them he labeled as possible suspects, mainly due to the character notes he saw written there. A man named Orville Mexia who pretended to be homeless. Another, simply called Old Man Malone, who wandered around downtown with a metal detector.

Parker decided he'd talk to these two first. After that, he planned to interview a rancher named Ted Sanders, whose ranch was out near where the unidentified remains had been found.

Unidentified remains. Safer to consider them that, rather than worry they might be Nicole's. No. He refused to even consider that possibility. Hopefully, Rayna would hear from the medical examiner's office soon.

Once he'd finished making his list, he tucked his small notebook in his back pocket and carried the file folders back to Larry's desk.

Larry leaned back in his chair, arms behind his head, and studied him. "You do know that you can't mention to anyone that you've reviewed these files, right?"

Parker hadn't known, but he went ahead and nodded. "That makes sense. I'm still thinking I might talk to a few of the people who were interviewed previously."

"Why?" Larry grimaced. "Right now, we're in a holding pattern until those bones are identified. There's no point in stirring things up."

Parker mustn't have looked convinced because Larry jerked his thumb toward Rayna's office. "Go talk to her. She'll tell you the same thing."

Partly because he didn't want to do the wrong thing, and partly because he just wanted to see Rayna again, Parker nodded. "I'll do that," he said, heading for Rayna's office.

She'd left her door open, but even so, he tapped lightly on it before entering. Engrossed in something on her desktop, she looked up. When her gaze met his, she froze.

And blushed. Which meant he affected her as strongly as she did him. Good to have confirmation.

Focus. Clearing his throat, he outlined what he and Larry had discussed. The dazed look in her eyes cleared as she realized why he'd stopped by her office. He could have sworn a quick flash of disappointment crossed her face, but that might have been wishful thinking on his part.

"Technically, Larry is correct," she said, after hearing him out. "Right now, all of Getaway is in a frenzy about those remains. People are talking serial killer and we're trying to squash that. At least as long as we only have one body."

"Do you think there might be more?" he asked, before he could help himself.

"I don't know." Though frustration shone in her eyes, her tone remained level and calm. "Let's take this one step at a time. I am opening a new investigation, of course, but it will be helpful to get an ID on the victim."

"But why wait for that?" Unlike her, he could barely keep his frustration bottled inside. "If it takes several weeks to a month, that gives the killer that much time to either disappear or cover his or her tracks."

"I know."

Her rapid agreement startled him. "Then why—?"

She held up a hand. "I'm going to be blunt. Questioning people is law enforcement's job, not yours. I understand you want to help, and I can appreciate that. Don't make me regret letting you review our case files."

Though he really wanted to argue, he knew she was right. "I feel like I have to do something," he finally said. "I told John I'd bring Nicole back to see him before he dies. I'm not in the habit of breaking my word."

"This is beyond your control." Now a trace of anger leaked through her steady voice. "There hasn't been a murder in Getaway in over thirty years. The entire time your uncle was sheriff, no life was lost. None. I've barely been sheriff two years. How do you think it makes me feel, knowing this happened on my watch?"

He threw her own words back at her, knowing she needed to hear them as much or more than he did. "That's beyond your control. But at least you have a chance to rectify that. You can catch the killer, bring him or her to justice. That's what you can do." He took a deep breath, lowering his voice. "And if that body turns out not to belong to Nicole, you can help me find her."

After listening intently, she nodded. "Sounds like a good plan." And then she smiled at him. "Do you feel better now?"

Better? The beauty of her smile took his breath away. All he could think about was how badly he wanted to kiss her lips. Through a haze of desire, he heard the humor in her voice and realized she was teasing him.

"Of course, I plan to do everything you mentioned," she continued. "That's my job, after all."

"Point taken." He sat back in his chair. "Will you let me go with you? Maybe not all of the time, but sometimes?"

Her smile faded. "You're a civilian," she pointed out. "I honestly don't think that's a good idea."

"I could be a silent observer," he pressed. "I know that's allowed, because one of my friends and his wife participated in their city's citizen's police academy."

Gaze locked on his, she considered. "Silent? You'd give your word you wouldn't interfere in any way?"

"Yes." Leaning forward, he held her gaze. "I give you my word."

"I'll consider it." She finally looked away.

"Thank you. It would mean a lot to me."

"I get that." With a sigh, she dragged her hand through her hair. "We need to talk about what happened last night."

"Do we?"

"Yes." Doggedly, she continued. "Because you need to understand it can't happen again."

"Agreed," he replied immediately, even though every instinct inside him clamored for the opposite. "All that would do is cloud my judgment."

She grimaced. "*Your judgment?* I'm the one who has to be careful."

Though he considered asking her why she felt sheriffs weren't allowed to date, he held back. He didn't want to say or do anything that might jeopardize her taking him along while she questioned potential witnesses or suspects.

"We'll head out first thing in the morning," she finally said. "I'll swing by and pick you up at the motel around eight."

"Thank you." He got up and turned toward the door with the intent of getting out of there before she changed her mind.

He strode through the small room like a man on a mission, lifting his hand in a casual wave to Mary on his way out the door. Once outside, the bright sunlight and brutal heat hit him like a slap in the face. Pausing, he went to his bike and put on his helmet.

Damn if he wasn't regretting agreeing with her statement about keeping things platonic from here on out. They'd fit together as if their bodies had been made for each other. And even if he never touched her again—a thought that made his entire being ache—he'd never stop wanting her. Rayna Coombs would be a distraction no matter how hard she tried to remain aloof.

Instead of going back to his motel, he cruised slowly down Main Street. The heat and the sun made the town look sleepy. Everyone appeared to have wisely chosen to remain inside, under the air conditioner or a fan.

Once he left Main, he continued past the train tracks and old oil rigs that no longer worked. He passed the old haunted farmhouse, still boarded up and spooky, even in the bright sunshine. Slowing, he pulled over and stared. As a kid, he'd used to imagine how the place might have looked back in its heyday, when a family had lived there and fresh and new paint covered it. He'd even told Sam once that someday he intended on buying the place and restoring the farmhouse to its original splendor. Sam had laughed and told him the only value there was in the land.

Now Parker understood. Sam had been correct. The farmhouse had long ago fallen into disrepair and now, so many years later, it was long past the point of being anywhere near salvageable. It would need to be torn down and a new house built in its place, assuming someone would ever want to live there again.

Shaking his head, he pulled away. Nostalgia wouldn't help him find Nicole. And despite all evidence to the contrary, he clung to the hope that John's little sister was still alive.

The next morning, when the Getaway sheriff's office car pulled in front of his motel room, he was ready and out the door before she even put the transmission in Park.

Even though he'd prepared himself, his first sight of her sent a jolt through his entire body.

"Mornin'," she drawled. "I picked us up a couple of cups of coffee on the way over here. I hope you drink yours black."

"I do." Smiling at her while he secured his seat belt, he reached for the foam cup. "Thank you. I appreciate it."

She blinked, her gaze skittering away, almost as if she was nervous. "You're welcome. I figured this would be a lot easier if we were both wide-awake."

Taking a sip, he nodded. The coffee tasted good, strong and rich and hot. Just what he needed.

Putting the car in Drive, she exited the motel parking lot and turned left on the road, which meant they were heading out of town.

"First stop today is Ted Sanders's ranch," she said. "He's a good guy, raising two twin girls on his own. They just got their driver's licenses, so he's got his hands full."

"I remember the name from the previous investigation. His ranch is pretty close to where the remains were found."

"Exactly. That's why we're talking to him first." Glancing at him, she flashed a smile. He wondered if she realized how beautiful she was.

As she drove, they sipped their coffee in companionable silence. He appreciated the fact that she didn't need to fill the quiet with chatter. Instead, they watched the sun, still low on the horizon, color the sky with purples, pinks, reds and oranges. He couldn't believe he'd nearly forgotten the stark beauty of a west Texas morning sky.

They passed the spot where the remains had been found. Yellow crime scene tape fluttered in the dry breeze. Quickly, he averted his gaze. Even though there hadn't been a positive ID yet from the medical examiner's office, the spot still felt too personal, his emotions too raw to discuss it yet.

Luckily, Rayna didn't even glance toward the crime scene.

After traveling half a mile farther, they turned down a gravel road, bordered on both sides by fields. "Ted Sanders is a really nice guy," she said, a hint of warning in her tone. "I wanted to make sure his daughters would be in school when we stop by. I don't want them to panic."

It took a second before her meaning sank in. "You think there's a possibility they might be in danger?"

Her shrug seemed a bit too studied, too casual. "There's always a possibility of that. My job is to keep the people in this town safe. If warning Ted might help do that, then I'll warn Ted."

"So we're not actually going out there to question this guy?"

"He's already been questioned. I might ask a few follow-up questions, like if he's seen anything out of the ordinary. But mostly I want him to be aware that there might be a killer out there targeting young women. Yvonne and Yolanda just turned sixteen. There's no sense in taking any chances."

He had to agree with her there.

The road came to an end at a large metal gate. Rayna

parked and got out, opening it. She climbed back into the car, drove through and then got out again to shut it.

"He doesn't keep it locked?" Parker asked, genuinely curious.

"Nope. There's never been a need to before." She swallowed and made a wry grimace. "Until now, there actually hasn't been much crime in Getaway. What little we had was the result of people passing through."

A long ranch house came into view. While judging from the style, it appeared to have been built in the late sixties or early seventies, the place appeared well tended.

Rayna parked and killed the engine. "Ready?"

He nodded. As they got out of the car, a tall, lanky man came striding toward them. He wore a cowboy hat, jeans and muddy work boots. "Rayna!" Grinning, he enveloped her in a bear hug. "What brings you all the way out here?"

Parker told himself he wasn't jealous. Just because this rancher looked like an actor playing one, with his chiseled jaw and bright blue eyes. And single, too, according to Rayna.

Finally, Rayna stepped away from the other man's embrace. Expression grave, she eyed him. "Ted, I take it you haven't heard, then?"

Frowning, he shook his head. "Heard what? You know I haven't got time for all that gossip folks in town like to spread around like manure. What's going on?"

"Unidentified remains were found in a field up the road."

Parker half listened as she told Ted the rest of it, including that Nicole was missing.

"Your sister?" Ted asked, pity in his gaze.

"My best friend's," Parker answered. "She was—is—a sophomore at Texas Tech. She was passing through on her way to Dallas to visit her brother."

"We don't know for sure the remains belonged to her," Rayna hastened to say. "And that's partly why I came out here to talk to you. If there is some sort of killer in this area targeting young women, there's a possibility that your girls might be at risk. Just for now, let's keep this between us. I don't want to start a panic in town. But be extra vigilant, okay?"

Ted's jaw tightened. "Thanks for the heads-up. The twins already claim I'm too strict. But until this thing is solved, I'll be watching them like a hawk."

Chapter 5

Rayna could relate to the quick flare of panic she saw in Ted Sanders's eyes. She understood all too well the worry that came with being a parent. Especially when it came to something dangerous like this.

Parker stood quietly behind her, not interfering, as she'd asked. But she could sense his impatience. He wanted her to ask Ted pointed questions about what he might or might not have seen. And she would, but out here there was a right way to do things. Going after somebody like a battering ram wouldn't work.

"You'll let me know if you see anything unusual, right?" she asked Ted. "I know you're out in the fields most of the day. Any strange vehicles or people, or anything, you just pick up the phone and give me a shout."

"Will do." He glanced at Parker. "And I definitely hope you find your friend's sister."

"Thanks."

Hands in his pockets, Ted watched as they got back in the cruiser and turned around.

When they reached the gate at the end of the drive, Parker jumped out and opened it, waving her through before closing it again.

He got back in the car and glanced back over his shoulder toward the ranch. "Ted Sanders seems like a nice guy."

"He is," she replied. "And you know he'll be watching for anything even the slightest bit off."

"I kind of got that." He swallowed. "I'm guessing he was never a suspect?"

"Ted?" Shaking her head, she had to laugh, just a little. "Not really. Though anything is possible, so if something happened that gave me reason to wonder, I'd look into it. It's the same with almost everyone else I'll be talking to. There's always a remote chance, and I keep my eyes and ears open, but until I have something concrete to go on, these people are the citizens I'm paid to protect."

After considering her words for a moment, he nodded. "I get that. Sam was the same way. He honestly considered half the town his family."

"Yep. Sam was like that. He was a guest teacher when I went to the police academy. For whatever reason, he befriended me and we kept in touch, even when I took a job in Conroe." And when Sam had heard through the grapevine that she was in trouble, he'd reached out and offered her a hand. As far as she was concerned, Sam had saved her life.

She told none of that to Parker. Not yet, maybe not ever. "Your uncle is a good man," she said. "Now we're going to meet a few other locals. If you came here as a kid, you might even remember a couple of them."

First stop was Serenity Rune's unusual store, with its colorful array of bright flower arrangements interspersed with metaphysical books, as well as rocks of all sizes and shapes, along with exotic, polished crystals. She also did psychic readings and tarot cards. Maybe diversifying her offerings enabled her to remain in business, because she appeared to be doing quite well. Her shop had been there since long before Rayna had come to Getaway.

"I remember this place," Parker said, gazing at the storefront window with its colorful and eclectic display. Rayna had to admit Serenity had a knack for decorating. Even people who were merely driving through town stopped at Serenity's shop, aptly named *Serenity*.

"Did Sam take you here as a kid?" Rayna asked. Though she couldn't think of any reason Sam might have done so, for all she knew Parker might have collected rocks. Or crystals, or whatever Serenity called them.

"No," Parker replied. "But I used to walk by and look at all those rocks she had on display in the window. For whatever reason, I found them fascinating."

"Just wait until you meet Serenity," she said, grinning.

Parker raised one brow, but didn't comment.

The instant they stepped inside the shop, the mingled scents of eucalyptus and strong incense made her sneeze. "Dang it," she said, modifying a curse word since Serenity didn't like them. "My allergies are going nuts."

"Just a minute, dear," Serenity's always cheerful

voice sang out. "Let me extinguish everything and turn on a fan. I can get rid of the scents in no time."

Tempted to wait outside until mission accomplished, Rayna tried to buck up and tough it out, though her now streaming eyes and constant sneezing ruined that.

Parker took her arm and steered her out the front door. "Is it always like that?" he asked, coughing.

"No." Wishing for a tissue, she swiped at her eyes with the back of her hand. "Only every once in a while, from what I'm told. I don't go by there very often."

The front door opened and Serenity poked her head out. "Just a few more minutes," she explained, her gaze traveling from Rayna to Parker.

"Do you mind if we talk out here?" Rayna asked, her voice hoarse. "It won't take more than just a minute."

But Serenity didn't appear to be listening. She'd fixed all of her attention on Parker, even moving closer so that she stood maybe three feet away. Her long, dangly earrings swung in the hot breeze, and the brightly colored headband she'd used to keep her mass of curly hair away from her face gave her a Bohemian appearance.

"You." She jabbed her finger at his chest. "I have a message for you. Nicole Wilson is still alive."

Parker's only response was a slight narrowing of his eyes.

"Thanks, Serenity," Rayna put in, sneezing again. "That's actually what I wanted to talk to you about. I know we've discussed this before, and maybe even Larry has come by to talk to you about it, but have you seen anything—or *anyone*—unusual?"

"When?" she asked, fiddling with her gauzy long

skirt. "I mean, you and I might have different definitions of *unusual*."

"True. But you told me you can see auras. Or people's true natures," she explained, for Parker's benefit. "Have you seen anyone come through town, new or regular, who gave off—"

"Evil?" Serenity interrupted. "No. You can bet your sweet patootie if I do, I'll be right up to the sheriff's office to point him or her out. Why?" She peered at Rayna, her pale blue gaze intent. "What's going on?"

"Nothing yet." Rayna hated to mention it, even though she knew she had to. "Just thinking ahead to once we get an ID on those remains we found in the field. I don't suppose you saw anything relating to that?"

Serenity started shaking her head no before Rayna even finished the question. "That caught me by surprise," she admitted. "But I'm only given to see what I'm supposed to. Clearly, I wasn't meant to see that one."

"I wish you were." Rayna turned to Parker. "Serenity sometimes helps us solve open cases," she admitted, aware he probably thought she'd lost her mind.

"I do." Proudly lifting her chin, the older woman preened. "And I promise you, if I see anything about that poor soul buried in that shallow grave, you'll be the first one I call."

"Fair enough." Rayna stuck out her hand, but Serenity only used it to pull her in for a hug.

"You've got this," the older woman whispered loudly in Rayna's ear. "All of it. Do you understand me?"

Not entirely sure what Serenity meant, Rayna nodded anyway. "All right, then. We've got to go. Please be in touch if you see or hear anything."

"I always am," Serenity chirped. "Take care." She

fixed her gaze firmly on Parker, though she lifted her hand in a quick wave as Rayna turned to go.

Parker grabbed her arm before they got to her car.

"Do you think she's right?" he demanded, the hope in his gaze warring with the skepticism in his voice. "About Nicole, that is?"

"I don't know," Rayna answered honestly. "But I will tell you this. She often comes by the sheriff's office with information she 'saw.' So far, she's been right most of the time."

The hope that lit up his face twisted her gut.

"But there's always a first time," he said. "Right?"

"Sure. But right now, let's try to think positive. As soon as we hear back from the ME, we'll know more."

Ahead, she spotted Old Man Malone, doing his thing. She pulled over to the curb and parked. "Rain or shine, hot or cold, he's always out here with his metal detector."

Parker studied him curiously. "What's he looking for?"

"I have no idea. Money, most likely. He calls himself Old Man Malone. We're going to talk to him next. If anyone was going to see anything out of the ordinary, it would be him or Orville Mexia." She opened her door. "Come on."

Old Man Malone looked up as they approached. "Hey, Sheriff." He frowned at Parker. "What's up?"

"Just checking in to see how your money search is going," she answered, keeping her tone light. "Are you rich yet?"

He chuckled. "Not hardly. Orville does much better than I ever could."

Rayna let that one slide. "Listen, you know I rely on

people like you and Orville to let me know if you see anything unusual, right?"

"Of course." He lifted his chin. "You know you can rely on me. I'm the eyes and ears of Getaway."

She nodded. "I take that to mean you haven't noticed any strangers in town, male or female?"

"The only stranger I've seen around here lately is that feller." He pointed at Parker. "What's he want anyway?"

Parker spoke up before she could answer. "I'm looking for my friend's little sister. Getaway was the last place she was seen."

Just like that, Old Man Malone's outright hostility changed to instant sympathy. "I'm really sorry, man. I sure hope she wasn't the body that was found a couple days ago."

"Me, too." Parker cleared his throat. "But until we find out, I'm going to believe that wasn't her."

"Me, too." Dropping his metal detector, the older man reached out and clasped Parker's shoulder. "I'll be praying."

"Thanks."

Rayna stayed quiet until they were back in the car with the doors closed. "He'll be especially vigilant now. Next up, we'll try to find Orville Mexia."

"What do you mean, 'try to find'?" Parker asked. "Are you saying you don't know where he lives?"

"Not at all." She grinned at him, "How long ago did you say it's been since you visited Getaway?"

He thought for a moment. "It was before I joined the Marines, and I did two tours, plus I've been out awhile...so at least ten years. Why?"

"If it had been more recently, you probably would

have known Orville Mexia. He panhandles all over town."

"Is he homeless?" Parker sounded shocked. "Here, in Getaway?"

"No, he's not homeless," she replied. "He just likes to pretend he is. He lives with his brother out on Pine Road."

Parker gave her a quizzical look. "Then why do you allow him to panhandle? Or don't you have laws against that sort of thing?"

"Welcome to life in a small town. Everyone knows about Orville. All the money he collects goes to the Taylor County animal shelter."

This finally made Parker laugh. "I like it," he said, shaking his head. "Actually, that's pretty cool."

They shared smiles for a second before Rayna returned her attention to the road. "This time of the day, Orville likes to stay in the shade. So he's either near Roseville Park or near the lumberyard. He enjoys lunch at the food truck that stops by there."

Sure enough, they found Orville sitting on the curb under a huge live oak tree with some of the workers, munching on a big greasy taco. He looked up at the sheriff's car, but made no move to get up. Rayna saw he kept his trusty old coffee can close to him.

"Afternoon, Orville." She greeted him and his companions with a friendly smile. "Do you have a second to have a word in private?"

As she'd known it would, her question made Orville perk up. He lived to be of service, which was why not only did he go around collecting money for the animal shelter, but he could often be found lending a hand to anyone who might need it.

"Definitely," he replied, cramming the last of his taco into his mouth and chewing rapidly. He climbed to his feet and hurried over, swallowing right before he reached the car. "What's up?"

She outlined things the same way she had with Old Man Malone. Orville's happy smile dimmed when she introduced Parker, and he offered the same hope that the remains that had been found didn't belong to Nicole. He too promised to keep a lookout and report anything unusual.

Satisfied, Rayna rolled up her window and drove off. This time, Parker stayed silent, clearly lost in thought.

Which meant, of course, that Rayna kept glancing sideways at him, as if trying to memorize his features. She wanted to kick herself in the butt, but she couldn't seem to help herself.

Though she'd finally managed to relax somewhat, taking Parker with her to talk to people felt like a form of sensual torture. While she managed to stay professional, she remained hyperaware of the sexy beast of a man sitting next to her.

Sexy beast. Listen to her. They'd shared one night of amazing sex and still she wanted more. Even though they'd agreed that wasn't going to happen again.

The fact that he'd so readily agreed with her no-more-sex decision actually wounded her. She wasn't sure why. Maybe she'd hoped he'd put up more of a fight.

If not for the constant sexual tension, she would have really enjoyed his company.

So far, Parker had been a great companion, once she took desire out of the equation. He kept his word and stayed quietly in the background while she talked to people. Then, when they were back in the car, his comments and questions were insightful and intelligent. He was fun to talk to, as well as easy on the eyes.

The more time she spent with him, the more she actually liked him. All while fighting the urge to jump his bones. Definitely not professional. She knew all too well how dangerous following that path could be. Though it grew more difficult every day, she needed to keep her attention focused where it belonged—on the case. Finding Nicole, whether dead or alive, had to be her only priority. The rest would have to sort itself out later.

The more time he spent with Rayna Coombs, the more Parker found he admired Getaway's sheriff. Sam had clearly chosen the best person to succeed him. The townspeople loved her, and she exuded authority without arrogance, and a quiet competence he found wildly attractive.

In addition to that, the one night of lovemaking they'd shared had only whet his appetite for more. Sitting beside her while she drove, he found himself sneaking covert glances at her profile, the curve of her shoulder, the base of her neck and the way stray tendrils of her vibrant red hair escaped from its bun.

He hadn't been this in tune with a woman in a long time. Maybe ever.

Talk about bad timing. He couldn't get involved with anyone right now. Not until he'd taken care of finding Nicole and getting her to John. After that, all his time would belong to John, for however long his friend had left. There could be no distractions. Especially not a curvy redhead with vivid green eyes.

Damn. There he went again, craving her. When he

should be worrying about Nicole. Who had to be alive, somewhere out there. They just had to find her.

While he knew Rayna no doubt had already thought of this, he wondered what would happen if the ID on the body turned out to be someone besides Nicole. What would that mean for Getaway? Would it open the possibility of a serial killer operating in these parts? He figured Rayna would have to investigate that, as well as continue to search for Nicole.

Which brought up the question, if Nicole were alive, then where had she gone? He'd already run through numerous scenarios in his mind. A car accident, driving off a ravine, into a lake—all of these would explain why neither her car nor cell phone had been found. Luckily, college was out for the summer, so she wasn't missing any of her classes.

Spending this morning driving around town with Rayna had shown him he'd been wrong, too. He'd been thinking of everyone as suspects and had planned on taking an adversarial approach to questioning them. Watching Rayna handle it in a low-key, friendly way clearly pointed out why Sam had always had faith in her.

"Do you want to grab lunch?" she asked, startling him out of his reverie.

He glanced at the dashboard clock, surprised it was already eleven forty-five. "Sure," he answered, glad to spend more time with her.

"Seeing Orville munching on that taco made me realize I haven't had anything to eat since yesterday," she confessed.

This made him grin. "Same here. Where's the closest Mexican restaurant? I know every Texas town has one."

She laughed. "Of course. Getaway has two. One is

fast food and the other is a sit-down place. I'd like to sit and eat, if that's okay with you."

"Sure." He shrugged. "It's not like I have anywhere else pressing to be." The instant the words left his mouth, he realized how they sounded. "I didn't mean it like that," he said, chagrined.

To his relief, she simply smiled. "I get you. It's all good."

A few minutes later, they pulled in front of a building that appeared to be a former gas station. It hadn't been remodeled enough, though, to disguise its original purpose. A huge, gaudy sign proclaimed the name— Tres Corazones. Three Hearts.

"It's owned by three siblings," she clarified. "Two sisters and a brother."

"It's certainly bright," he commented. "Like when they started painting it, they couldn't decide on a color."

Still smiling, she nodded. "I like the purple. Though the flamingo pink is a close second."

"What about the yellow and orange? Or the blue and green?"

"I like them, too. It's very festive, for sure. They also have good food. And even better margaritas. I've had more than a few girls' nights out here."

He could definitely picture her, hair down, relaxed and happy, slightly buzzed, laughing with her friends. His body stirred. He shook his head, pushing the image away.

Inside, the restaurant smelled like fajitas and home-made tortillas. The woman at the front desk beamed when she saw Rayna. "So good to see you," she said, eyeing Parker curiously. "Table for two?"

"Yes, please. A booth if you have one."

"Of course we do."

They were seated in a booth by the big front window,

with a view of the parking lot and her cruiser. Immediately, someone brought a bowl of tortillas chips and two smaller ones of salsa. Rayna smiled, causing his heart to skip a beat. With the sunlight making golden waves in her fiery hair, she managed to look both ethereal and sexy, like an angel freshly fallen from the sky.

Wincing at his own lame analogy, Parker shook his head and checked out the lunch menu, looking for his favorite carnitas tacos or enchilada. Relieved they had it, he glanced over at Rayna, who hadn't even picked up her menu.

"I eat here a lot," she admitted. "And I know what I want. Brisket tacos. They're the best."

Right then, he changed his mind about what he'd eat. "Thanks for the recommendation. I'll try them, too."

The waitress came and took their order, stopping to chat a bit with Rayna before moving away. Rayna looked up and caught him watching her.

"What?"

He said the first thing that came to mind. "You seem well liked in this town."

Though she ducked her head, he could tell his words pleased her. "I truly care about the townspeople," she said. "Being sheriff is more than just a job to me. I think they know that and respond in kind."

"Maybe," he agreed. "Sam was like that, too. This was his town, his people. I admit, I was kind of shocked when he decided to move to the coast."

"He knew if he stayed here, he wouldn't be able to let go of the job," she said. "That's why he decided he needed to become a beach bum. I tease him with that nickname whenever I talk to him." Her green eyes sparkled.

Unable to help himself, he reached across the table

and covered her hand with his. "You're so beautiful," he told her softly, wishing he could find the right words to convey the mixture of desire and admiration he felt.

Their gazes locked and held. Her smile faded, though her mouth parted. She knew, he realized. Without him having to say a single word, she knew his thoughts.

Now so damn hard he could scarcely move, he swallowed. He considered himself lucky that they hadn't eaten yet, because there was no way in hell he was walking out of here like this.

Rayna shifted in her seat, wrenching her gaze away from him. "Casual lunch," she muttered, just loud enough for him to hear. "I have to go straight back to work after this. I hope you don't mind, but I'll just drop you off at your motel."

Though disappointed—he couldn't help but hope she'd be able to make a pit stop inside his room—he nodded. "That's fine. You're busy. I get it. Maybe we can get together another time."

Relief and some other, more complicated emotion flitted across her mobile face. "Of course," she said, her voice a tiny bit too bright. "Another time."

"Here we are." The waitress set their plates down. "Is there anything else I can get you?"

Both Parker and Rayna shook their heads. As soon as she left, they dug in, eating with single-minded intensity, apparently determined to ignore the sexual tension swirling around them.

By the time the check arrived, Rayna felt relatively normal, much more composed. She drove Parker back to his motel, chatting about inconsequential things like the town's annual Fourth of July parade. When she pulled up and parked, she kept her hands on the wheel and the engine running, not trusting herself if she got out of the car.

She'd end up in his bed and, while she wanted to so badly, she needed to maintain a bit more discretion.

Still, her entire body ached as she watched him walk away.

Back at the office, she managed to keep busy enough to put Parker out of her mind. Finally, the workday ended. She hurried away, eager to get home to her family and some sort of routine.

When she walked into the house, she went straight for the kitchen, aware that was where she'd find her mother.

"Hey, Mom." Sniffing the air, she stood in the doorway, trying to ascertain what Wanda might be making for dinner. "Smells great."

"Thanks. Katy saw you at Tres Corazones at lunchtime today," Wanda said, not looking up from the pot she stirred on the stove. "She said you were with some handsome biker. Is there anything you might have forgotten to tell me?"

Though her face colored, Rayna shrugged. "Not really. His name's Parker Norton. He's Sam's nephew. He's here because his friend's sister is the girl that disappeared."

Wanda gasped, turning to stare. "The one you found in the shallow grave out in that field?"

"We don't know that yet, Mom. We haven't received any kind of ID."

"Still…" Wanda shook her head. "That poor man must be so distraught. I'm guessing you're not dating him, then?"

She sounded so disappointed that Rayna had to laugh. "Not really, Mom. You remember what happened in Conroe with Lauren's father. I seriously can't risk anything like that happening again."

"It won't." The certainty in Wanda's voice touched Rayna's heart. "Sweetheart, you can't live your life afraid to take a chance with a man ever. If this new guy is as handsome as Katy said, maybe you should try."

"Try what?" Rayna loved teasing her mother.

Now Wanda blushed. "You're a grown woman. Don't pretend like you don't know what I mean."

"We're just friends, Mom." Rayna saw no reason to mention the one amazing lovemaking session she and Parker had shared. Friends with definite benefits.

"Invite him for dinner," Wanda ordered, her green eyes sparkling, almost as if she knew. "I want to meet him."

"Dinner?" Rayna stared. "Why?"

"Why not? It's been a long time since you've been interested in a man."

She didn't lie to her mother, ever. So, she couldn't say she wasn't interested in Parker. "If I do that, he'll think it's something more than it actually is. Plus, if word gets out, I'll never live it down. You know how this town gossips."

Wanda gave her a hard look. "Since when have you cared about gossip? You're allowed to have friends who happen to be men, you know."

When Rayna remained silent, her mother came over and wrapped her up in a big hug. "Honey, you don't have to be afraid. What happened with Jimmy Wayne wasn't your fault. You didn't know. And the likelihood of that happening again… Well, that's impossible."

Hugging Wanda back, Rayna finally pulled away.

"He's only in town to find his friend's sister. Once she's located, he'll be gone."

"Which could be mighty soon."

"Exactly," Rayna agreed. "I mean, we're all hoping those remains don't belong to Nicole, but it's highly likely they do."

"Invite him to dinner," Wanda repeated. "Especially since his time here is limited. A brief romantic fling might be just what you need."

Later, after Lauren had been put to bed and Wanda had planted herself in front of the television watching some reality show, Rayna poured herself a glass of wine and walked outside. Gazing up at the cloudless, starry night sky, she pulled out her phone. Did she really want to do this? If she asked Parker to meet her family, wouldn't that give their relationship—if that was what it even was—way more significance than it called for?

Her text message alert chimed. Parker. She stared, wondering how he'd known exactly the right time to text her.

Are you busy?

Heart skipping a beat, she texted him back.

No. I'm sitting out in the backyard sipping a glass of wine.

Wish I could join you.

She hesitated for a second. Me, too.

Let's go out to dinner tomorrow night, he sent. My treat.

Now or never. Taking a deep breath, she typed:

I have a better idea. How about some home cooking? My mother is a fabulous cook and she loves meeting new people. Would you like to come here to dinner tomorrow night instead?

After she hit Send, she waited. If he said no—and really, she couldn't blame him—at least she could tell her mom she'd tried. Still, she hadn't realized how badly she'd hoped he'd say yes until this very moment, while he mulled over her invitation.

I'd love to, he sent back. What time?

Since she tried to be home from work so they could eat by six, she told him six.

Great. See you then.

Though she really wanted to continue the chat, she simply responded with a thumbs-up and let it go. If she'd had her way, she'd have dialed his number and talked to him in person, just so she could hear his voice. Instead, she sat back and continued sipping her wine, delaying the moment when she had to tell her mother. Wanda would not only go on a cleaning frenzy, but she'd begin frantically planning the dinner menu, too. Rayna decided she'd tell her either right before she went to bed or first thing in the morning, as she left for work.

When Rayna finished her wine, she went inside and in search of her mom. She found Wanda asleep in front of the TV, a half-eaten bag of popcorn in her lap. Heart full, Rayna stood for a moment and studied her mother. Slender, with the same wild mane of fiery waves she'd bequeathed her daughter, Wanda didn't look old enough to be Rayna's mother. She was, Rayna realized, beautiful. While Wanda apparently worried about fixing her daughter up, maybe Rayna should have been trying to do the same for her mother.

Something to think about.

At least her decision of when to tell her mom about Parker coming for dinner had been made for her. She'd tell her in the morning, while on her way out the door.

The next morning, she did exactly that. Dropped a quick kiss on her daughter's cheek before doing the same to her mother. "Oh, by the way, Mom. Parker is coming to dinner tonight. He'll be here at six." And then she hurried away, got into her squad car and drove off, hoping her mother wouldn't be too upset.

When she got to work, she saw a text message from her mother. I'm thrilled! And Wanda had followed that up with a bunch of heart emojis. Rayna grinned. Well, that answered that. Now she could go to work with a clear conscience.

For the first time in a long time, the day dragged. Rayna found herself constantly checking her watch, willing the day to end. She had so many butterflies in her stomach she could barely choke down the barbecue sandwich Mary brought her from home. And Mary's chopped-barbecue sandwiches were legendary.

"Are you okay?" Mary asked, eyeing her half-eaten sandwich with concern. "You usually devour these when I bring them."

"It's delicious." Rayna managed a smile. "My stomach is a bit wonky today, so I might just wrap this up and put it in the fridge for tomorrow."

"Okay." Mary shook her head, the slight frown creasing her brow letting Rayna know she felt offended. For a second or two, Rayna considered telling the other woman the real reason why she had no appetite, but since Mary loved to gossip, decided silence would be better.

Finally, the clock inched past five. She closed down her computer, striving for casual even though her heart beat way too fast. She usually didn't leave until five-ish, but had the stomachache excuse if Mary or someone else asked.

Busy on the phone, Mary barely looked up as Rayna walked past her. Perfect. Now all she had to do was get home and freshen up before Parker arrived.

Chapter 6

Getting ready for dinner, Parker told himself Rayna was just being kind. Nothing more than a friendly invite to share a meal. With her and her family. Normally, something like that would scare the hell out of him. But this was Rayna, who wanted to keep things casual like he did. A polite gesture, nothing more, and one he needed to accept in the same spirit it had been offered.

Then why did he feel so damn nervous?

He'd gotten up and gone down the street for breakfast, lingering over his meal and listening to the ebb and flow of the conversation around him. Then, too restless to sit still for long, he'd taken his bike and gone for a long, meandering ride. He'd headed west, his favorite direction, and spent some time in a few of the little towns between Abilene and Midland. He'd hit Sweetwater and Colorado City, stopping in Big Spring before heading north to Lamesa, then east to Snyder and Anson before pulling back in to Getaway shortly after four.

At least he felt better than when he'd left.

He left the motel again at exactly five forty-five and pulled up in front of Rayna's house in seven minutes. Parking his bike at the curb, he sat for a moment eyeing the neat little frame house. Roses of every color bloomed in carefully tended flower beds in front, adding to the warm, inviting appeal.

Walking up the sidewalk, he realized too late he should have brought flowers or a bottle of wine. Kicking himself mentally, he shook his head and pressed the doorbell.

Rayna answered it, smiling warmly. She'd changed out of her sheriff's uniform and wore a formfitting, long floral dress. She wore her wavy red hair loose and flowing down her back. She looked so beautiful, his chest ached.

"Welcome," she said, stepping aside. "Come on in and meet my mom and my daughter."

Suppressing the urge to pull her close and kiss her, he came inside. As she turned to shut the door, she brushed his arm, making him realize she smelled like the roses out front.

They'd barely taken two steps when a small girl came barreling down the hallway, throwing herself at Rayna. "Mama, Mama! I want to play!"

"Not now, Lauren," Rayna said firmly. "We have company and we're about to eat dinner. Say hello to Mr. Norton."

Lauren went still, peeking up at Parker from behind her mother's dress. "Hello," she finally said. "Are you Mama's friend?"

"I am." He smiled at her, hoping he looked friendly rather than intimidating.

"Is that a bird on your arm?" she asked, pointing at one of his tattoos.

"A dragon," he answered.

"Well, hello there," another feminine voice drawled. He turned around to see an older version of Rayna standing in the kitchen doorway, smiling. "You must be Rayna's friend Parker."

They shook hands. She eyed him in a way that told him she knew how awkward he felt.

"Parker, this is my mom, Wanda. Mom, this is Parker Norton, Sam's nephew."

"Come on in the kitchen and take a load off," Wanda said, turning and leading the way. "Would you like a beer? Or iced tea? I've even got some bourbon if that's what you prefer."

"I'd love a beer." He took a seat and managed to tear his gaze away from Rayna long enough to accept the longneck from her mother. "Thank you so much for having me. It's been quite a while since I've had a home-cooked meal."

"Really?" One perfectly shaped brow rose as Wanda looked from him to Rayna and back again. "Well then, you're in for a treat. I've made chicken-fried steak, gravy, mashed potatoes and fresh green beans with bacon. One of my specialties."

His mouth watered just thinking about it. "Those are all my favorites, ma'am."

Wanda ducked her head, clearly pleased. "Good. I'm glad to hear it."

"Is there anything I can do to help?" Rayna asked, grabbing her own longneck from the fridge.

"You just sit down with your friend and relax. We're going to eat buffet-style." Attention already returning to the stove, Wanda turned her back to them and got busy.

Rayna shook her head and took a sip of her beer, a smile playing around the corner of her mouth. "We only eat buffet-style on holidays," she murmured to Parker. "Wait until you taste Mom's food. I've been telling her for years that she ought to open her own restaurant."

"And I've been telling her I spent way too many years working in the food service industry to have any desire to go back," Wanda replied, all without turning around. "Now I cook for pleasure. My own enjoyment. I'd hate to have to do it for money."

"Were you a cook before?" Parker asked, genuinely curious.

"Nope. A waitress," Wanda and Rayna answered at the same time, which made Rayna laugh.

"We're always doing that," Rayna said. "We're a lot alike. We're lucky we don't get on each other's nerves."

"Who says we don't?" Wanda quipped. "Just kidding."

Lauren, who still clung to one of Rayna's legs, continued to stare at Parker as if he'd sprouted horns.

"It's okay, honey." Rayna smoothed back her daughter's hair. "You don't need to be frightened of Parker."

If anything, this made the little girl's frown deepen. "I'm not scared," she declared indignantly. "I'm brave. But you said not to talk to strangers, so I won't."

"Parker isn't a stranger," Rayna said. "He's my friend, and I invited him into our house to have dinner with us."

Silence while Lauren digested this. "Okay," she finally said. "He has pretty pictures all over his arms. I like them."

"Thank you," he told her, smiling. Surprisingly, most small children really liked his tattoos.

"Dinner is just about ready," Wanda announced. "Lauren, go wash your hands, please. Rayna, would you mind setting the table?"

Parker got to his feet. "What can I do to help?"

"Nothing." Wanda shooed him away. "You're a guest. Your job is just to enjoy the food."

Behind her, Rayna grinned. "And keep us entertained with your scintillating company, of course."

"Of course." Bemused, he grinned back. Damn if he didn't really like this woman. Even here, around her family, desire for her simmered just under his skin.

Lauren returned, her small hands still dripping water. Clearly anticipating this, Rayna handed her a dish towel and waited while she used it. One of the chairs on the side of the table closest to the wall had a booster seat, and Lauren climbed up in it. Though she still shot Parker the occasional curious glance, she now appeared much more focused on what her grandmother was doing with the food.

Parker inhaled, savoring the tempting aromas. "It smells delicious," he commented. I can't wait to try it."

Wanda grunted, clearly too busy to speak. A moment later, she turned around and pointed. "Food is ready. Grab your plates and fill them. Parker, you go first. You're company."

"Lauren, stay put," Rayna cautioned. "I'll fix your plate for you."

"I want extra gravy," Lauren said. "Please."

"I know." Rayna grabbed two plates and then looked at Parker. "What are you waiting for? We're all hungry."

This made him laugh. "I was brought up to stand back and let ladies go first," he said. "So that's what I'm going to do. I'll get my food once y'all have gotten yours."

Rayna shrugged and went past him, filling both her daughter's plate and her own. Wanda looked from her daughter to Parker, her gaze speculative. "Good manners, too," she mused. "I like you, Parker Norton. You seem like good people, just like your uncle Sam."

"Thank you, ma'am." He ducked his head. "As far as I'm concerned, there's no higher compliment you could pay me."

After Wanda had also filled her plate, Parker grabbed his and went over to check out the food. Perfectly cooked chicken-fried steak, creamy mashed potatoes, green beans with bacon, and a bowl of thick pepper gravy. A basket of fresh rolls sat next to a stick of yellow butter.

Once he'd taken a generous portion of everything, he joined Rayna and her family at the table. The instant he sat down, they all picked up their forks, but instead of eating, they watched him.

"No pressure or anything," Rayna joked. "My mom loves to cook for people."

He nodded, cutting off a piece of his chicken-fried steak and putting it in his mouth. As the texture and flavors hit his tongue, his eyes widened. Once he swallowed, he slowly shook his head. "You weren't kidding. That's amazing."

Wanda laughed, as did Rayna. The musical sound of their laughter made him smile. Lauren even looked up from her plate. "Everyone likes Gammy's food," she said.

While they ate, Parker not only allowed himself to enjoy the food, but the company. He felt at home, and only partly because of the gorgeous redhead he couldn't get out of his mind. Her mother and her daughter all made him feel like part of the family, an honored guest.

He could get used to this.

The thought floored him. Cozy get-togethers with his lover and her family were not even remotely in the cards right now, for Christ's sake. He shouldn't have to keep reminding himself, but he'd never expected to be longing for something like this, a woman like this. A life like this.

Realizing he'd managed to clear his plate, he went back for seconds. The others were still eating, though he caught the delighted look Wanda gave Rayna. He took a second helping of everything and sat back down. "It's amazing," he said, before resuming eating.

Once everyone finished, Wanda brought out individual strawberry shortcakes, which she topped with whipped cream. The sight of these made Lauren clap her hands and squeal with delight.

"Do you have room for dessert?" Wanda flashed a wicked grin. She looked so much like her daughter when she did that Parker cracked up laughing.

"I'm pretty full, but I think I'll manage," he responded, smiling.

Next to him, Rayna nudged him with her knee under the table. "Way to make my mom feel good," she murmured. "Thank you."

Gazing into her sparkling eyes, he nearly leaned over

and kissed her. At the last minute, he managed to rein himself in, just as Wanda brought them over their dessert.

Just like everything else, the strawberry shortcake was delicious.

"Best meal I've had in years," he proclaimed, pushing away his plate. "Thank you so much, Wanda. That was wonderful."

Wanda beamed at the compliment.

"Gamma's a good cook," Lauren chimed in. She fixed her direct green gaze on Parker. "Are you Mama's boyfriend?"

"Lauren!" Rayna flushed. "Mr. Norton is just my friend."

"He's a boy," Lauren insisted. "And your friend. Boyfriend."

This made Wanda laugh. "She has a point."

Rayna shook her head and began gathering up plates and carrying them to the sink. Parker pushed up and helped her. "I'll wash and you dry," he said.

"We have a dishwasher," she pointed out. "But thanks for the offer."

"Come on, Lauren." Wanda held out her hand. "Let's go see if one of your shows is on while they clean up the kitchen."

Though Lauren appeared undecided, shooting looks at her mother and at Parker, finally she nodded and took her grandmother's hand, allowing herself to be led out of the room.

Parker stacked the dishes neatly in the sink. Rayna rinsed them before placing them in the dishwasher.

"Thank you for inviting me," he said. "I can't even remember the last time I had a meal so delicious. It was restaurant quality, actually even better than restaurant quality."

"I know." Rayna glanced sideways at him.

Damn, he wanted to kiss her. He jammed his hands into his pockets to keep from touching her.

"You have a great family, Rayna."

Expression surprised, she nodded. "I know. Everything I do is for them. They're my everything."

And just like that, he fell a little bit more in love with Rayna Coombs.

After Parker left, Rayna gave Lauren a bath before reading her a story and then putting her to bed. As she tucked her daughter in, she answered Lauren's endless questions about Mama's new friend. Lauren found Parker's body art fascinating, and she wanted to know why Rayna didn't have any tattoos. Rayna told her the truth, that she actually did have one, a small vine with flowers, tattooed on her hip. Of course, then nothing would do but to show it to her. Lauren oohed and aahed, tracing the design with her small finger and stating she wanted to have one just like it.

"Someday," Rayna said, kissing her five-year-old on the cheek and pulling the sheet up to just under her chin. "Now it's time to go to sleep." She turned out the light. "I love you, baby girl."

"I love you, too, Mama." Lauren yawned loudly. "Night."

"Good night." Rayna closed the door and headed straight to her room. She wanted nothing more than to change out of her clothes and wash off her makeup. Then she planned to pour herself a glass of wine and carry it outside on the back porch to relax.

She'd barely finished cleaning her face, changing into a pair of soft running shorts and a tank top and slipping her feet into flip-flops when Wanda tapped lightly on her bedroom door.

"Come in," Rayna said, tugging her hair into a pony-tail.

"I like him," Wanda announced, leaning on one side of the door frame. "He's handsome, sexy and polite. Since he's Sam's nephew, you know he's good people. You did well this time, Rayna. Parker Norton is nothing like Jimmy Wayne. In fact, he's pretty much his direct opposite."

Wanda had never liked Rayna's previous boyfriend, despite the fact that he was Lauren's father. Rayna had often wished she'd listened to her mother. She could have avoided a lot of heartache. Of course, she wouldn't have Lauren then. Lauren was worth all the craziness and suffering.

"Don't let this one go," Wanda continued. "Seriously."

"Mom." Closing her eyes, Rayna took a deep breath before opening them again and meeting her mother's gaze. "We've already discussed this. Neither Parker nor I are looking for a relationship. We're just spending time together until his friend's daughter is found."

Arms crossed, Wanda shook her head. "So you've said. But girl, did you see the way he looks at you? Like you hung the moon and the stars."

Rayna shrugged the words off, pretending that her breath didn't catch in her throat at the thought. "We're friends. Nothing more. Please don't go making this more than what it is."

Though Wanda grimaced, she finally nodded.

"Whatever you say, Rayna. Seems a perfect waste of a good-looking man, but you're a grown woman." And then, as if Rayna had personally offended her, Wanda spun and flounced out of the room.

Rayna let her go. She sat down on the side of her bed and rubbed the back of her neck. *Perfect waste of a good-looking man.* Hah. Rayna didn't think so. She enjoyed Parker's company, she'd spent some amazing time with his body, but she couldn't let things go any further than that. Not if she wanted to keep her heart from getting broken. Because Parker had been up-front with her, making it clear that he planned to head back to Dallas as soon as Nicole was found.

Which might actually be a good thing. Especially since she wanted to keep her focus where it belonged— on her family and on her job. She'd let love blind her once. She didn't plan on making that mistake again.

The next day at work, they were surprisingly busy. One of their officers made a drug bust on a semitruck with a trailer full of produce that turned out to have a hidden compartment. The DEA had been called in and the county sheriff's office even stopped by, due to the size of the bust.

On top of that, Mrs. Smith on Seventh Street tried to put out a grease fire with water and nearly burned her house down. Though the volunteer fire department handled that call, Larry had gone out, too, just to make sure the elderly woman was all right.

There was a lost dog who caused a minor accident by running out in front of a car on North Main, which made one driver swerve into another. And someone called a bomb threat in to the high school, which not only resulted in all the schools being put on lockdown, but Jones County had to send one of their canine handlers over to search the high school just in case there actually was a bomb. There wasn't, and with a little investigative work the culprit was caught and arrested. He was a disgruntled student, shocked to learn what he'd done was a crime. Rayna had to deal with him and then his parents, who also appeared to be in complete denial about the seriousness of the situation. At least until their family attorney showed up and set them straight.

Every time Rayna turned around, something or someone else needed her attention. She barely had time to eat lunch, even though Wanda had packed her some leftover chicken-fried steak. When she finally escaped into the conference room, asking for fifteen minutes, she used the microwave to heat her food to just luke-warm so she could eat it quickly.

When she'd finished eating, she washed the entire thing down with a bottled water and took a deep breath. Hopefully, the remainder of the day would be better.

On her way back to her office, she stopped by Mary's desk and left instructions not to bother her unless it was a true emergency. Larry was there, and she had three other officers out working the streets. As sheriff, she needed to deal with paperwork and reports, so she'd like to work uninterrupted.

Mary nodded, unimpressed and exhausted. "It must be a full moon," she groused. "I hate when it gets like this."

"Me, too." Confident that she'd now have at least a couple of hours to herself, she closed the door and logged on to the internet. Nothing from the ME's office. She wasn't sure if they'd email or call, but she'd been resisting the urge to call them and just ask about the results up front. She knew Sam had promised to call in a favor, but had no idea if that would actually have any effect.

Hopefully it would. Soon. Sam usually got results.

The timetable was a mystery. Parker wanted the results yesterday. Truth be told, she did, too.

Despite her instructions not to be bothered, Mary knocked on her door. Before Rayna could speak, Mary pushed open the door and stuck her head in.

"The ME's office is on the phone," Mary said, refusing as she did most days to use the intercom. This time, Rayna forgave her. "Line three."

Damn. Willing her racing heart to slow, Rayna took a deep breath and punched the button for line three. "Rayna Coombs."

"Hello, Sheriff Coombs," a professional-sounding woman's voice said. "This is LaKesha Jones with the Taylor County Medical Examiner's office. I've gone ahead and emailed you what we found on your case, but I thought I'd place a courtesy phone call. The DNA did not match up with your missing person, Nicole Wilson."

Did not match up. The remains did not belong to Nicole. Serenity had, once again, been right with her prophecy.

Relief made Rayna's legs go weak. Good thing she was sitting down. But if not Nicole, then who? "Were you able to make a positive identification?" she asked.

"We're still working on that," LaKesha said. "I'll call you as soon as we have a definitive ID."

"Thank you." Couldn't ask for more. Hanging up, Rayna turned, planning to inform her staff and then decided to wait. Parker needed to be the first one to know.

"Well?" Mary poked her head in the door again. "What'd they say?"

"She'll call me as soon as she has a definitive ID," Rayna replied, sticking with a partial truth. She'd tell Mary and Larry and the others later, after Parker. For whatever reason, this felt important to her. The right thing to do.

"I've got an errand to run," Rayna said, standing. "I'll be right back."

Though Mary eyed her suspiciously, she stepped aside. She'd worked with Rayna long enough to know when something wasn't right. Her BS radar had to be working overtime. Rayna would definitely make it up to her later.

Getting into her squad car, she drove to the Landshark Motel, relieved when she spotted Parker's Harley parked in front of his room. Refusing to question her judgment, she knocked on the door.

A moment later, Parker opened it. He wore only a pair of workout shorts that rode low on his hips. A slight sheen of perspiration dampened his skin. "Rayna?" Stepping aside, he motioned her in. "Sorry, I was working out."

"Yoga?" she asked, eyeing the yoga mat on the floor. "Somehow, you don't look like a yoga guy."

This made him laugh. "Push-ups, actually. But just so you know, I've done my fair share of yoga, along with various forms of martial arts."

Since she could barely concentrate with his bare chest and muscular body so close, she swallowed and nodded. Fixing her gaze on his face, she inhaled. "I've got some news. The ME's office called. While they haven't gotten a positive ID yet, they have determined that the remains do not belong to Nicole."

He froze, searching her face. "Not Nicole," he finally said, grabbing her hands and pulling her in for a quick, jubilant hug. "Not Nicole. I can't tell you how relieved I am."

"Me, too."

"Thank you for coming to tell me in person," he said. His voice broke and she realized emotion had gotten the best of him. Because he needed someone to hold, she let him and even held on back. Knowing how guys felt about others seeing their tears, she pretended not to notice his.

Then he pulled back slightly, bent his head and kissed her, feelings still damp on his cheeks. The press of his mouth on hers began as a celebration, a release, and that tiny spark roared to life, flame becoming inferno.

This. Body to body. Skin to skin and mouth to mouth. She wanted him, needed him, craved him so much she could hardly think. Could barely breathe.

They couldn't get their clothes off fast enough. Wanting, needing, nothing between them but skin. No words exchanged now. None necessary. Their straining bodies, the sensual caresses, the press of his hardness against her softness said it all.

He took her standing, backing her against the wall and shoving himself inside her hard and fast and deep. Raw possession, so damn hot. Gasping, she bucked against him, urging him on. She felt her climax building, just before it swept over her like a tidal wave. Crying out, her nails digging into his skin, her body clenched as he shuddered inside her, reaching his own release.

As their heartbeats slowed, they stood, arms locked around each other, with him still inside her, neither willing to move. Or speak. Right after that moment of pure bliss, she realized they hadn't used protection.

Her heart stuttered inside her chest. She wasn't sure what to say, how to think. Truth be told, she hadn't been thinking. Of all people, she should know better. After all, this was how she'd ended up pregnant with Lauren.

Aware of her disquiet, he raised his head and looked at her. Expression troubled, he spoke her thoughts out loud. "We didn't... I didn't..."

"I know." Swallowing, she held his gaze. "I just had my annual well-woman and I'm healthy. What about you?"

"I had a complete physical last month and everything checked out good." He kissed her throat, making her shiver. "I haven't been with anyone except you, so we're good there. I'm assuming you're on birth control?"

"I am." After her accidental pregnancy, she'd vowed never to be caught unprepared again. Though she hadn't dated much, she took the pill just in case. Even so, she'd never again let herself get carried away by the moment. Until now. Until him.

"Good." He kissed her once more. "I know we agreed not to let this happen again, but what we have between us is too damn good to let it go. That said, I'm sorry."

"Don't be." She kissed him back, letting her lips linger on his, loving the slightly salty taste of his mouth. "I wanted it just as much as you did."

Taking a deep breath, she trembled with the enormity of her next words. "We're adults. As long as we're not hurting anyone, I don't see a reason why we shouldn't have a little fun now and then. As long as we don't try to turn it into anything serious."

"Are you sure?" His eyes searched hers. "You were pretty adamant about not mixing business with pleasure."

She winced. "I am and we won't. I can't allow this… attraction to distract me from my job. And now that we know that wasn't Nicole, I have two. Finding Nicole and also learning who killed that other woman and when."

"A possible serial killer?" he asked.

"No. There would have to be more than one victim and links to tie them all together. We only have one body, so we're looking at a murderer, nothing more."

"And a missing woman," he pointed out. "Whose brother is dying. I've been calling him regularly and filling him in, though he isn't really aware that Nicole has disappeared." He paused, his brown eyes searching hers. "I think I told you, but just in case I didn't, as soon as Nicole is located, I intend to take her to see her brother in Dallas. I'm hoping John can stay alive until then."

"You mentioned that. I haven't forgotten," she said softly, her heart aching for him and for his friend. "Like I said, I want to keep things casual. Neither of us are in the right place for any kind of relationship."

He kissed her then, a slow kiss right in the hollow place where her shoulder and neck met. "Oh, but if we were…"

Even though words remained unsaid, he had her aching for something that could never be.

After using his bathroom to freshen up, she drove back to the sheriff's department, feeling as if Mary would take one look at her and immediately know what she'd been up to. She parked, freshened up her lipstick using the rearview mirror and strolled inside.

Mary looked up when she entered, her expression verging on panic. "I was just about to call you."

Instantly alert, Rayna froze. "What's going on?"

"There's another body," she blurted out. "Pretty damn close to where the first was buried. Old Man Malone found it while using his metal detector."

Chapter 7

Parker watched from his motel room window as Rayna drove away. He'd been about to ask her why she felt so averse to a relationship, but had decided not to. He figured he could do a little internet sleuthing and find out on his own.

Or he could ask Sam. Assuming his uncle would tell him. If he asked, Sam might start wondering why Parker wanted to know. And Parker felt quite confident Sam would not approve of his nephew and Rayna having casual, though consensual, sex.

Asking Sam was definitely out.

And he wasn't sure why he wondered about Rayna's reasons. He wasn't exactly in a position to start a relationship anyway. No matter how badly he wanted to.

Sitting down at the little motel desk, he powered up his laptop and began researching. Thirty minutes later, he had his answer.

Rayna had apparently fallen hard for a criminal. Whether or not she'd known about his activities seemed unclear. But when he'd been arrested, allegations surfaced that Rayna might have been involved, even using her position as a police officer to help this Jimmy Wayne Ellis protect his crime empire.

Internal Affairs had investigated and found no wrongdoing. But that hadn't stopped the rumors from swirling amid public outcry for her arrest or firing. Reading between the lines, he suspected she'd been convicted in the court of public opinion and ostracized. She'd damn near lost her job. In fact, she'd resigned and moved away.

Parker would bet his last dollar that would have been when Sam had called her and offered her a job in Getaway.

Closing his laptop, he leaned back in the chair and thought. Unless she'd done her own internet snooping, Rayna knew nothing about him other than the fact that he was Sam's nephew. His appearance certainly appeared to be the opposite of anyone working in law enforcement. Or in the military, where he'd spent so many years of his life. For all she knew, he could be a criminal, too, just like the man who'd almost brought her life crashing down.

Though he suspected she knew him better than that. Still, he couldn't blame her for wanting to keep their interactions as casual as possible. Or as casual as superhot, crazy, passionate sex could be.

As his body stirred, he shook his head. Down, boy. He shouldn't have to keep reminding himself about the real reason he'd returned to Getaway. Finding Nicole. No matter what, he couldn't allow himself to get too distracted by a green-eyed spitfire with bright red hair and a lush figure.

Maybe Rayna was right to keep things simple. After all, as soon as they found Nicole, he'd be headed off to Dallas. She had put down roots here, had a family and a job she loved. For all intents and purposes, he was still a drifter, working odd jobs when he wanted and mostly living off the money he'd saved while serving in Afghanistan. By trade, he was a damn good mechanic. He could fix anything. And he enjoyed the work.

His true love, though, was restoring old vehicles to their original glory plus some and then selling them. He and John had partnered on a few of these before John had gotten sick. The last one, a 1955 Chevy pickup, Parker had been sorely tempted to keep, but John had needed money for medical bills, so when they'd sold it, Parker had given his friend his half.

Parker shook his head. What mattered most right here, right now, was finding Nicole. If, as the town psychic claimed, Nicole was still alive, then where was she? Had someone grabbed her, taken her for human trafficking? He'd heard about things like that, where young women were snatched, drugged and sold to be sex slaves in another country. Christ, he hoped not. From everything he'd read, tracking down people who'd disappeared for that reason could be damn near impossible.

But the other alternative was just as bad, maybe even worse. By now, Parker figured Nicole hadn't simply gotten lost or had been in some sort of accident. Her family would have heard something by now. Her cell phone still went unanswered, her social media accounts unchanged. Her credit cards and bank accounts had not been touched. Which meant... No. He didn't want to go there.

Needing to take his mind off dark thoughts that threatened to go even darker, he decided to go out for a stroll around downtown and then have a solitary meal and maybe a beer.

Driving to Main Street, he parked his bike in front of the hardware and feed store. He figured he could do a little window-shopping, stretch his legs and kill some time.

Being a weekday, crowds didn't cover the downtown sidewalks. People went about their business, but men in Stetsons and boots dipped their chin in greeting and women smiled, some friendly, others openly flirtatious. The brick-and-wood storefronts, lovingly restored, windows gleaming in the bright sunshine made downtown Getaway looked like a Western movie set. He smiled, enjoying himself and remembering once again why he loved this town.

He went inside Jake's Hardware and Feed, not because he needed anything, but because he liked that kind of place. Sure enough, aisles full of bagged horse pellets and dog food took up part of the store. The other part had tools and lumber and lawn equipment. In between sat everything else. From bird feeders and birdseed to wind chimes and plastic pink flamingos.

Wandering up and down the aisles slowly, he took it all in.

"Can I help you?" A portly man with a bushy brown beard stepped in front of him. His bright green work apron had the name *Jake's* emblazoned across the front.

"I'm just looking," Parker replied, smiling. "Fantastic inventory you have here."

"Thanks." The guy eyed him a moment before smiling back. "Well, I'm Jake's son. Name is Ben. Let me know if you need help with anything."

"Will do," Parker said, eyeing a nice set of barbecue tools.

Once he'd checked out the entire store, Parker headed back outside. This time, he mostly window-shopped, admiring a pair of hiking boots on display at the shoe store, bypassing the coffee shop and following his nose to the Tumbleweed Café. The scent of steak and burgers drifted in the air, luring him in.

Diners packed the place, leading him to think a lot of folks liked either a late lunch or an early dinner around here. Loath to take up an entire table, he took a seat at the bar. Luckily, he found one left right in the middle.

Little snippets of conversation swirled around him. He listened, casually at first.

"Another body," someone said, voice breathless with hushed anticipation. "Female again."

Parker froze. What the…?

"Do you think we have a serial killer?" someone else asked, sounding both angry and excited at the same time.

All around him, the talk seemed to be the same, centering on that fact that another body had been found.

Damn. He checked his watch, undecided whether he should stay put or go. He pulled out his phone, checking for missed calls or text messages, but nothing.

A moment later, the waitress came to take his order. Since his stomach growled, Parker went ahead and asked for a burger and a beer. "What's going on?" he asked, keeping his question pitched low. "It sounds like they're saying another body has been found."

"That's right," she responded, her heavily mascaraed eyes going wide. "Again, a woman, buried in the same kind of shallow grave."

"Where?"

"Right close to the first one. The same field." She glanced around, leaning in close. "I heard they're going to start excavating sections of the whole pasture, looking for more bodies. I'll bring your beer first." With an exaggerated shudder, she moved off to put in his order.

Immediately, his first impulse was to call Rayna. But as he eyed his phone, he realized she was probably up to her neck in the investigation. Which would be why she hadn't yet called him.

Though he itched to hop back on his bike and drive out to the site, he forced himself to stay put. Since he had no idea what time the body had been found, he needed to stay out of the way. Rayna had bent a few rules for him once already by allowing him on site of an active investigation. In view of what he'd learned, he didn't want to take a chance at putting her at risk.

He knew she'd fill him in on the details when she could. For now he'd simply have to be patient. Not easy to do, but since his gut told him the new body also would not be Nicole, he'd eat his burger, drink his beer and then detour to the sheriff's on the way home.

One thing for sure, news traveled fast in the town of Getaway.

The burger arrived, thick and juicy, along with a full platter of crispy fries. He ate slowly, taking his time and enjoying the meal. When the check came, he left a generous tip.

Leaving the café, he drove to the sheriff's office, still debating whether or not to pay Rayna a visit. In the end, he swung his bike into the parking lot. He figured Rayna would have called him if she thought the body belonged to Nicole, but, just like the first body, perhaps she couldn't tell.

Inside, at the front desk, Mary looked up from a phone call, her eyes red and swollen. She shook her head, but didn't speak, so he chose to ignore her and pushed past. Now his heart thumped, erratic in his chest.

He found Rayna in her office, talking on the phone. She waved him to a chair, listening intently. "Thanks, Sam," she finally said, and hung up the phone.

She met his gaze with sad green eyes. "We've found another body."

"I heard." Forcing himself to remain calm, he waited for her to say more. "That's all anyone was talking about at the café."

"I'm not surprised. News gets around fast in Getaway," she said. "But I can tell you definitively this time that it's not Nicole. We don't even have to wait on the medical examiner."

Surprised, he leaned forward. "She had ID?"

"Yes. Her name was Talinthia Dowling. She wasn't from anywhere around here. In fact, she had a New Mexico driver's license. She had to be just passing through on her way to somewhere else. We're trying to locate her next of kin right now."

Just passing through. *Like Nicole.* He suppressed a shudder. "Do you know how she was killed?"

"From all appearances, she was strangled." Her matter-of-fact tone warred with the empathy in her eyes. "Of course, I can't say for sure that's what killed her. The ME will have to do that."

He swore softly. "It's looking more and more like you might have some kind of serial killer on your hands."

"I know. And as soon as the press gets word of this, they'll descend on Getaway like flies on cow dung. I'd prefer to keep a lid on this, especially since we're going to be involving the FBI. But with the gossip already making the rounds, I suspect that's not even going to be remotely possible."

"You're probably right. Do you have someone on staff to handle all the public relations?"

She stared as if he'd been speaking another language. "Nope. We're a small town with an even smaller law enforcement department. The sheriff handles the PR. It's the one part of my job that I'm not entirely happy with."

"I can't imagine," he said. "That's got to be rough."

Looking away, she nodded. "I'll be honest. When I got the call about the newest victim, as I drove there, I kept worrying about how the hell I would find the right words to tell you if it turned out to be Nicole."

He winced. "Do you really think she's dead?"

Rayna met his gaze. "The first forty-eight hours are the most critical in any missing-person case, especially an abduction. We're way past that now. As the days turn into weeks, the likelihood of finding her alive grows slimmer."

As he started to speak, she held up her hand. "Wait. I'm not saying all this to try and take away your hope. You hang on to that with all you've got. If you're a praying man, I suggest you pray. But I want you to be prepared, just in case. Do you follow me?"

Slowly, he nodded. "I do." He decided to change the subject. "Listen, I was thinking. Since you were kind enough to have me over to the house for dinner, how about I take you out for a meal? You name the place. I'm thinking something different, maybe a steakhouse or an Italian place."

Rayna frowned. "You mean like a date?"

"If you want it to be, sure. If not, then how about just two friends going out for a meal?"

"In town?"

Too late, he remembered how touchy she was about her reputation. And now that he knew why, he could definitely understand. "We could drive to Abilene, if you don't want to be seen with me here in Getaway."

"Yeah, going out here in town isn't a good idea," she responded immediately. "If we're seen out on what appears to be a date... Well, I don't want to make this seem like more than what it is."

He managed to hide his surprising flash of anger. "I'm well aware of what this is. Friends with benefits, right? Since when don't friends go out to eat?"

Their gazes locked. She looked away first. "Point taken," she said quietly. "I would like to have a meal with you. Just not here in Getaway, if you don't mind. I like your idea of going to Abilene. When are you thinking?"

Before he could answer, the phone started ringing. Three of the lines lit up at once. With a muffled groan, Rayna glanced toward the front, making sure Mary was there to handle them.

"Tonight?" Parker smiled. "It seems to me like you need to get far away from this place for a few hours."

She surprised him by actually laughing, the husky sound tugging at her chest. "You're right about that. How about we go right now?"

"Now?" He glanced out at the squad room. "Are you sure you can leave?"

Getting up, she came around her desk. "I'm sure. The press has been blowing up our phones all day. I'm eventually going to have to hold a press conference, but right now I just need a break. Let me tell Mary I'm going. They all know how to reach me if anything happens."

Rayna endured Mary's quizzical look without offering an explanation. As soon as she and Parker stepped outside, she exhaled. She eyed his gleaming black motorcycle as they passed it, almost wishing she could just climb on back and let him take her away.

"If you can find a spare helmet, we can take the bike," he said, almost as if he'd read her mind.

"That's okay—we'll use my cruiser." She didn't bother to keep the regret from her voice. "Maybe someday, before you leave."

"Definitely."

Once they were inside the car, she pulled out of the parking lot. "Steak or Italian?" she asked. "I'm good with either one. Abilene has several great restaurants."

"Steak," he replied. "I could really go for a juicy T-bone."

"Perfect. And it's early enough that we should be able to get in without making reservations."

While she drove, she told him about asking the FBI to help out. "They've got a profiler working on the case. Though two bodies aren't solid proof of a serial killer, it could be. We'll know better what we're dealing with once we have a profile."

"That stuff really works?" he asked.

"What do you mean? If you're asking if the profilers

are accurate, they are. Once they figure out a profile for this potential serial killer, we'll have a much clearer idea of who we're looking for."

He nodded. "Back to what you said earlier. You really believe Nicole is dead, don't you? I know you want me to be prepared, but I'm guessing beyond the statistics you quoted, you must have your own gut reaction. I'm thinking that you've been a cop for a while, so what do your instincts tell you?"

One thing she never wanted to do was lie to him. "I can't rule it out. Honestly, Parker. She disappeared and has been gone way too long. On top of that, the MO is the same as the other two. Her age, the fact that she, like the others, is an out-of-towner, and her cell phone and car disappeared also."

"Put like that, I don't understand how I can possibly see another outcome, but I do." He shrugged. "It looks bad, I agree. And yes, I'll try to be as prepared as anyone could be in this situation. But for whatever reason, I feel Nicole is still alive."

Though she'd seen it before, she had to admire his determination to continue to believe in a positive outcome. Maybe she was too jaded, or she'd seen the worst side of humanity in her years as a law enforcement officer, but she couldn't see how this could possibly end well.

She took a deep breath and then doggedly continued. "Don't give up all hope. I want you to understand, though, that we've turned this town inside out looking for her. My officers viewed security camera footage of downtown businesses, interviewed waitstaff and gas station attendants, as many townspeople as we could, and have nothing to show she even visited Getaway. If not for that social media post she made with our city-limits sign, I'd be inclined to believe she never even stopped here."

The bleak look on his face tore at her heart. "I can't give up hope. I just can't."

Feeling awful, she touched his arm. "I understand. And if she's alive and in Getaway, we will find her. I promise."

Normally, the drive into Abilene relaxed her. Today, though, she couldn't seem to let go of some sort of supercharged tension. Glancing at the big man sitting silently in her passenger seat, she swallowed hard. She knew of one way to dissipate that tension, but it sure as hell didn't involve food or leaving town.

Maybe later. If she had anything to say about it, definitely later.

As predicted, the only people in the restaurant were the happy-hour crowd taking up half the bar. A few older patrons occupied the dining room, but there were plenty of tables and they were seated immediately.

Drinks were ordered—beer for him and a glass of Shiraz for her while they studied the menu. He ordered a T-bone steak, medium rare, with baked potato and the house salad. Once the waitress left, Parker leaned forward. Something in his expression, a glint in his eye, made her catch her breath.

"I'd like to tell you about myself," he said quietly, leaning back in his chair and regarding her with a serious expression. "You've never asked, and I always wondered if you performed a background check or something."

This made her wince. "I didn't. Everything happened too fast. And since we're keeping things casual, I didn't think I needed to. Not only are you ex-military, but Sam would have said something if you were a criminal."

"I met John, Nicole's brother in Afghanistan," he continued. "We served together and became good friends."

She nodded. "I remember you telling me that. I don't think I ever said thank you for your service, so I'll say that now."

Now it was his turn to wince. "Since I got out, I've picked up a few odd jobs here and there, but mostly I've been living on my savings. I saved quite a bit while in the Marines."

"What do you do for a trade?"

"I'm a damn good auto mechanic. And I'm even better at restoring cars. Someday, I plan to open my own shop."

Their salads arrived, giving her a minute or two to collect her thoughts. Heaven help her if she hadn't been on the verge of suggesting he return to Getaway and open his business here. Luckily, she'd caught herself in time.

"What about motorcycles?" she asked instead. "Do you customize them, too?"

"I have." He shrugged. "While I love my Harley, my passion is restoring cars."

His passion. Hearing the thread of excitement in his voice made her entire body tingle. To distract herself, she focused on her salad, eating with single-minded determination.

"What about you?" he asked, when she didn't speak again. "Have you always wanted to be a cop?"

"Pretty much." Looking up, she smiled. "Actually, I wanted to be like one of those detectives in the television shows. Where lab test results come back in a day and people work around the clock, scouring camera footage until a perp is located. I learned really quickly how unrealistic those were."

"Where did you go to police academy?" he asked.

His question made her tense up, searching his face to see if he knew. When he only continued to eat his salad, occasionally glancing up at her, she relaxed slightly. "Houston. It was tough but enjoyable. I got a job offer from Houston PD, but I ended up going to work in one of the suburbs."

"Sounds like that would be less dangerous," he said.

"It was." Bracing herself in case he decided to ask for specifics, she considered what she might say. Sam knew, of course. He'd been fully aware of the circumstances of her internal-affairs investigation when he'd called to offer her a job as patrol officer in Getaway. For all she knew, he might have mentioned it to his nephew, though unlikely. Sam had never been one to break confidences or gossip.

Should she come clean with Parker? After all, she hadn't done anything wrong except be too trusting and naive. She hated to imagine what he'd think of her, the normally competent and efficient law enforcement officer making such a terrible mistake.

Did Parker even have a right to know? After all, they'd made it clear they weren't embarking on any kind of relationship.

She couldn't decide. To her relief, the steaks arrived.

"This looks perfect." Parker smiled at the waitress, making her blush.

Trying not to roll her eyes, Rayna shook her head instead, smiling. She couldn't blame the waitress.

With his rugged masculinity, and bad-boy good looks, Parker tended to have that effect on women. At least, she amended silently, he had that effect on her.

Though the steak had been perfectly cooked and melted in her mouth, Rayna had to force herself to eat. This angst over her past wasn't like her. The only people who knew of her mistake were her mother and Sam. She really didn't intend on widening that circle.

"You don't like yours?" Parker looked up from his half-eaten meal. "Isn't it cooked right? Let me call the waitress."

"No need." She waved his concerns away. "It's fine. I'm just stressing a bit, that's all. Ignore me and eat your delicious steak."

Instead, he put his fork down. "What's stressing you?"

Wishing she'd never brought it up, she shook her head. "I don't want to discuss it. Enjoy your dinner. Maybe we'll talk about it on the way home."

Chapter 8

As they left the restaurant, Parker took a chance and reached for her hand. She glanced at him, clearly surprised, but kept her fingers laced with his until they reached her car.

The simple gesture made warmth blossom inside him that stayed with him long after she pulled her hand free and they got in the cruiser.

He suspected what had been bothering her in the restaurant. He'd pried a little too much, made her uncomfortable, and figured she questioned her decision to go to dinner with him. She had no idea that he'd done a little digging and already knew the details of her past relationship. Well, maybe not all of them. This guy must have been something, to pull one over on a woman as sharp as Rayna. No wonder she had trouble letting down her guard.

He tried not to mind.

"Did y'all ever have any luck locating Talinthia Dowling's family?" he asked.

"No." She shot him a quick, curious glance. "I'm surprised you remembered her name."

"How could anyone forget a name like that? It's pretty uncommon."

"It is. We even located her social media accounts." Rayna drummed her fingers on the steering wheel as she drove. "None of them have been touched since the day she disappeared. I've got people talking to people she had listed as friends, but as far as anyone knew, she had no immediate family. No parents or siblings, at least that she knew of. She recently aged out of the foster care system. She worked part-time to help put herself through college."

"She sounds like she was driven," Parker commented. "Someone determined to make a future for herself."

"I agree. And then to have it end like this." Rayna shook her head. "I'm still waiting to learn the identity of the first victim."

She drove like she did everything else, with quiet competence. Parker allowed himself to admire her profile, hoping he wasn't being too obvious about it.

When they arrived back in Getaway, she drove straight to his motel and parked. "I enjoyed it," she said, smiling with ease. "Now I've got to get home to my family."

He nodded, about to get out before he reconsidered. Leaning over, he kissed her. One quick, firm press of his mouth on hers. "See you around," he said before exiting the car.

After that, he forced himself to go to his room without looking back, even though she remained parked until he opened the door and stepped inside. Then and only then did she drive away.

Time to call John. He'd put it off long enough, aware he couldn't lie to his best friend, but afraid of what knowing the truth might do to him.

Taking a deep breath, he dialed the number for John's cell phone. The call went straight to voice mail. This in itself wasn't unusual, as John might be having a medical test, a shower or meeting with a physician.

Parker left a message and then tried the number for the hospital room. Someone answered on the second ring.

"Room 802." A feminine voice, sounding professional and slightly detached. "How may I help you?"

Damn. His heart stuttered in his chest. "I'm trying to reach John Wilson. Is he available?" All the while bracing himself, hoping John hadn't died.

"He's undergoing some tests right now," she said. "You might try again in an hour."

The relief that flooded through him left him weak in the knees. "Thank you. I'll do that."

After ending the call, he dropped onto his bed. They had to find Nicole. Had to. He wasn't sure how much longer John had left.

To be on the safe side, he waited two hours before trying John again. This time, his friend answered, his voice weak. His tone lightened when he realized it was Parker and he spent a couple minutes detailing the results of the last round of tests.

"The tumor has shrunk," he said. "Enough that they're going ahead and sending me home."

"Home?" Privately, Parker wondered if John would be strong enough to go home.

"Yep. There's nothing more they can do for me here. Actually, the only reason they didn't kick me out sooner is because I started having seizures."

Damn. Parker momentarily closed his eyes. "Did they figure out what was causing them?"

"Yep. The cancer has metastasized to my brain." John sounded so cheerful that it took a minute for his words to register.

Parker swallowed back a curse. This was bad. Very bad. For far too long it seemed he'd been watching his best friend slowly die. Now, things had accelerated.

"I'm sorry, man," Parker managed to say. "Really sorry."

"You ought to be. Where's my sister?" John asked jokingly. "It's taking way too much time for you to find her. Has she been in some kind of trouble?"

Though Parker hated to lie to his friend, he also didn't want to add to John's worries. Part of him thought the time had arrived to come clean, fill John in on Nicole's disappearance. The other part, the side that still held out hope that Nicole would be found safe, preferred to simply show up in Dallas with her by his side.

In the end, Parker went with what he'd have wanted John to do if their situations had been reversed. He told the truth. Or at least some of it.

"I don't know, John. I can't find her."

Silence. Then, predictably, John thought Parker might be joking. "Come on, man. I'm serious. What's taking so long?"

"I'm telling you the truth. Nicole disappeared. The last time anything was posted on any of her social media accounts was two weeks ago, at a welcome sign on the city limits of a small town near Abilene. The sheriff's office has looked, but can't find anything." He kept talking, filling the stunned silence with words, as if that could somehow make things better.

"I'm here now," he continued, when John still didn't speak. "I'm looking for her, too. Making sure the sheriff's office stays on top of things."

"Nicole…disappeared?" The hollowness in John's tone was a knife in Parker's heart. "I wondered what was going on, but…how is that possible? Did you find her car, her phone, anything that might show you where she went?"

"No. There hasn't been any sign of her."

"That's why she hasn't been returning my calls. I've probably left her three or four messages a day over the last week." John made a sound, a cross between a curse and a sob. "Find her, Parker. Please, I thought I had more time."

"I'm trying my best," Parker replied, well aware that wasn't enough. "If it helps any, the local psychic says Nicole is still alive." The instant he heard himself, he inwardly cringed.

"A psychic?" John asked. "Now I know you're truly desperate."

Since Parker still hadn't revealed that two shallow graves with female remains had been discovered and the very real possibility that Nicole had been grabbed by this same person, he understood John's disbelief. They had always been skeptics when it came to things like psychics and paranormal activities.

"It can't hurt, right?" Parker said. "I'm going to let you go. I promise I'll call you the instant I have news."

"It's been two weeks." Not only did John sound exhausted, but defeated, too. "Where the hell could she have gone?"

"I don't know." No way in hell did Parker plan to mention the suspected serial killer. He managed to get off the phone but then sat with his head in his hands, trying not to despair.

That night, his dreams were a strange mixture of happiness and sorrow. Rayna danced in and out of them, sometimes remote and professional and other times, sensual and beguiling. He hated himself for wanting her, for allowing that desire to distract him from what he needed to do most of all—find Nicole.

He went out for breakfast, needing to be around other people, though he couldn't really pour his heart out to a total stranger. Three times he reached for his phone to call Rayna, knowing she'd understand, but didn't go through with it. After his conversation with John, he knew taking a step back from this undefined thing with Rayna would be wise. After all, his best friend was dying, Nicole was still missing and yet he was spending time with a beautiful woman.

After breakfast, he took his bike for a spin, riding out to the field where the two women's remains had been found. He pulled up and parked, staring at the yellow crime scene tape fluttering in the breeze. Though the sheriff's office and the coroner had finished, the area still remained blocked off, as if in warning to any casual passerby.

Walking to the edge of the area, he stood and looked out over the field. Were there other bodies buried there? He'd read somewhere that serial killers generally stuck to the same area. No doubt Rayna or the FBI would begin searching. He wondered what they'd find. He couldn't help but hope Nicole wasn't buried there.

Jamming his hands into his jean pockets, he sighed. Despite all his skepticism in the past, he couldn't help but hope Serenity's prediction would turn out to be correct. Nicole was alive. She had to be. He just needed to locate her and get her to her brother's bedside before John passed away.

Once the ME had provided identification of the first victim—another stranger named Marilyn Gull, also from out of town and who had gone missing two months ago—Rayna performed the painful and unpleasant task of notifying her next of kin. Marilyn had been young, twenty-six, and had lived in Odessa. She'd been reported missing three months ago by her parents, who'd become alarmed when she didn't show up for church one Sunday morning. No trace of her had been found, not even her vehicle or cell phone. Rayna found the similarities between her and Nicole Wilson alarming, to say the least. Still, she took care not to mention anything of her concern to Parker.

Making these kind of awful phone calls made Rayna queasy. Still, she dialed the number, took a deep breath and got ready to break a total stranger's heart.

Once it was over—the anguished sobs, the anger and, finally, the acceptance—she hung up the phone and cradled her head in her hands, on the verge of tears herself.

She took a deep breath, trying to steady her shaken nerves. It didn't help. Finally, she got up, grabbed her car keys and decided to go for a drive. Sometimes driving around on back roads with her windows down and country music blasting helped her feel better.

"I'm going out," she said to Mary as she rushed past. Mary, who'd known what kind of phone call Rayna had made, simply nodded.

Pulling out of the parking lot, Rayna took every shortcut she knew to put town behind her. She didn't want to go anywhere near where the two bodies had been found, so she headed north and east, aiming her car for the least-populated area in the county.

When she passed the last farmhouse on the left, she knew there'd be nothing but open fields for miles. She rolled down the windows, cranked up the radio, singing along to Brooks & Dunn's classic song "My Maria."

She felt better almost immediately. Nothing could take away what had happened to poor Talinthia Dowling. But Rayna was in the unique position of being able to do one thing to help give the family closure. She would find the killer and bring him or her to justice.

This resolution brought a calmness to her. With her purpose once again clear, she returned her focus to where it belonged.

Before she reached the county line, she turned the car around and headed back toward Getaway, turning the music down and rolling up her windows.

Before she reached downtown, she spotted Old Man Malone's rickety pickup truck, pulled over onto the soft shoulder. She parked behind it, getting out and trying to spot the elderly man. There he was, in the middle of the pasture, ignoring the cattle and working his metal detector as if his life depended on it.

Carefully crossing under the barbed wire fence, she approached him.

"Afternoon, Sheriff," he greeted her, barely pausing in his quest to find treasure.

"Good afternoon," she replied. "I hope you got permission to conduct a search in this field."

"Didn't need it." The upward twitch of his mouth warred with his grouchy tone. "This is my land. I lease it out to the Millers, but I still own it. And according to the contract, I can pay a visit anytime I want."

"Okay." She nodded, glancing around. "What are you looking for?"

"Same things I always do." He squinted into the midafternoon sun. "Coins, jewelry, anything valuable that someone might have lost."

"But why here in this field? Isn't this land just used for grazing?"

He shrugged, now avoiding her gaze. "You never know where you might find something buried. Though this is on the opposite side of town from where you found those two girls…" He let his words trail off, knowing she'd catch his meaning.

"I see." Rayna didn't even try to explain how serial killers worked. They didn't go around scattering bodies in various fields. As a general rule, they kept their victims together, often revisiting the burial spots, where they took some kind of vicarious thrill from remembering. Mr. Malone didn't need to know any of that. Instead, she inclined her head respectfully. "Please let me know if you find anything significant, all right?"

"Will do, Sheriff Coombs."

Walking back to her car, she couldn't help but wonder if Getaway would ever return to normal. Probably not until the killer—and Nicole Wilson—was found.

She saw the news vans three blocks away from the station. Though she'd been expecting this, she'd still hoped for just a little more time.

Instead of pulling back into the parking lot, she circled the block, staying away from the station for now. She called Mary, who answered on the second ring and wasn't bothering to hide her annoyance.

"Getaway Sheriff's Office. How can I direct your call?"

Rayna laughed. "You only say that when you're about at wits' end."

Clearly recognizing her boss's voice, Mary snorted. "We've got reporters camped out front and in the reception area. They all want to talk to you. When are you coming back?"

"I'm down the street. I haven't had time to come up with an official statement."

"Neither has the mayor. He's been calling here every twenty minutes. I'm surprised he hasn't been calling your cell."

"He probably has." Rayna grimaced. "I had the music turned up, so if he did, I didn't hear it. I can't check it now, since I'm driving."

"I'm betting you have several voice messages," Mary said. "What would you like me to do?"

"Call the mayor back, please. Ask him if four o'clock will be convenient for him to hold a joint press conference with me. If so, tell him I'll meet him at his office at three thirty." She took a deep breath. "Then go out front and let the media know. News conference at city hall at 4:00 p.m. Got it?"

"Got it," Mary said, clearly jotting everything down. "Are you coming here?"

Rayna considered and then reached a sudden decision. "Not yet. I've got one more stop I'd like to make.

I'd prefer to arrive once everything has been handled. That way I won't be mobbed by reporters."

"Understood. I'll call you back as soon as I'm done."

Rayna swung the car around and headed back toward downtown. She needed to talk to Serenity. Though she knew many people might scoff at such a notion, the self-proclaimed psychic had been right more often than not. Maybe, just maybe, Serenity might be able to help.

With the afternoon heat making waves ripple up from the pavement, downtown Getaway appeared sleepy and deserted. Anyone with a lick of sense knew to stay inside the air conditioning, under a large ceiling fan. After the sun set, temperatures would drop somewhat, and the outdoor patios would fill up.

Serenity's store sat empty, though several completed floral arrangements had been lined up on the front counter for delivery. Serenity employed a high school boy to make the deliveries, and they were only done once he got out of school for the day.

A series of little bells made a tinkling sound as Rayna pushed the door open all the way. "Hello?" Rayna called. Serenity was nowhere in sight. Not in the floral area, or the rock section, where startlingly beautiful groupings of crystals and polished stones shimmered.

Turning right, Rayna entered the bookstore. Here, books were crammed together in groupings with titles such as Animal Totems, and Reincarnation. Often, Serenity could be found here, sitting on the floor with her back against the wall, engrossed in a book.

But this time, the bookstore, too, was empty.

Slightly alarmed, Rayna called out again. "Serenity? It's Rayna. Is everything all right?"

A moment later, Serenity appeared from the back of the store, where she kept inventory and supplies. She greeted Rayna warmly, not appearing at all surprised. "I'm sensing you're not here to shop."

"No, not this time." Taking a deep breath, Rayna decided to launch right into it. "We've found a second body. Another young woman, and apparently she was killed the same way as the first."

Serenity's calm gaze searched Rayna's face. "But neither of them was Nicole, correct?"

"Right. I'm worried. It would appear we have a serial killer operating right here under our noses in Getaway. I can't help but wonder how many more bodies there might be."

Serenity nodded. "I'm assuming you've been checking the missing-person database."

"I have. There are a lot. I had no idea how many young women disappear each year. Since the FBI is now involved, we've been able to eliminate several. Both of the victims were young—late teens or early twenties— and neither were from Getaway."

"Like Nicole."

Slowly, Rayna nodded. "That's my fear. I haven't mentioned it to Parker, but then again, I probably don't have to."

"She's still alive." Serenity spoke with quiet confidence. "Though I don't know how much longer that will be."

"If there is any way you can see where she is or who has her, or…anything, that would be so helpful." Aware she sounded desperate, Rayna didn't care. "Whatever it takes to catch the sick SOB."

Serenity grimaced. "I get it, believe me. Often, I

can't peer into the darkness, but only get glimmers of insight. I'll meditate on it and if I see anything, I promise to let you know."

"Thank you." Feeling only the tiniest bit foolish, Rayna turned to go. "The sooner the better," she said. "Because I agree with what you said. If Nicole Wilson is somehow still alive, she won't be for much longer."

As Rayna left Serenity's shop, her cell rang. Caller ID showed the sheriff's office, which meant Mary.

"Talk to me," she answered.

"You're all set for four, though it might be closer to four thirty," Mary said. "The mayor is on board, though he told me to make sure to forward him a copy of your statement. Evidently, he's not going to make one of his own."

"That's fine." Rayna checked her watch. "Though that means I've only got forty-five minutes to come up with something."

"Are you on your way in?"

Considering, Rayna finally answered in the affirmative. "But I'm going straight to my office, and I don't want to be disturbed under any circumstances. Otherwise, I won't have a cohesive statement to make to the press."

"Ten-four. See you in a few." Mary ended the call.

Rayna made it to the station undetected. Once inside, she sat down and wrote the most general, reassuring summary of the events she could think of. She called her FBI contact to see if the Bureau wanted to add anything. Since they stayed out of the limelight for now on this case, nothing needed to be added.

Finally, feeling as prepared as possible, Rayna

checked her makeup in the bathroom mirror, put on some fresh lipstick and headed over to city hall.

Even before she pulled into the parking garage, she saw the huge gathering in the courtyard area near the steps. Not only media, but apparently a lot of townspeople had learned about the press conference and gathered to hear the scoop firsthand. Though she didn't blame them, she was once again amazed at the speed at which gossip could spread in a small west Texas town.

Though she tried to take a back entrance into the courthouse, a few of the locals spotted her and alerted the media by calling out her name. Ignoring everyone, she hurried inside and went straight to the mayor's office. His frazzled secretary greeted her, rushing off to tell the mayor she'd arrived.

The speech went well, she thought. She stuck to a strict account of the facts, refusing to allow any speculation. The mayor spoke also, reassuring the public that they were working very hard to find whoever had done this.

Then a reporter from one of the big national news channels asked a question, unrelated to the case, that made her blood run cold.

"Sheriff Coombs, would you care to comment on your previous position on the Conroe Police Department?"

Even the mayor turned to stare at her when he heard that.

"No comment," she replied, her heart pounding. "This news conference is over."

Though she should have taken a dignified exit, going back inside city hall with the mayor, Rayna took off for her cruiser. Striding away without looking back, she

knew they filmed her and would use the video in whatever story they created. Hopefully, her past wouldn't
somehow become their focus.

All the way home, her hands shook. She gripped the
steering wheel, white-knuckled, and told herself to get
calm before she reached her house.

Deep breaths helped somewhat. By the time she
pulled into her driveway, she had herself a little more
under control.

Wanda met her at the door, not bothering to hide
her alarm.

"Is everything all right?" Rayna asked. "Is Lauren—?"

"Lauren's fine. But you'd better sit down," Wanda
replied, taking her arm with a no-nonsense grip and
steering her toward a chair. "I recorded the five-o'clock
news and there's a story on there you ought to see."

"Already? I just left the news conference." Suddenly
weary, Rayna shook off her mother's hand. "I'll watch
in a minute. Let me go put up my service weapon and
change first." Starting toward her room, she caught
sight of the answering machine blinking red. "Looks
like there's a message," she said, reaching toward it to
push Play.

"Wait," Wanda ordered. "Don't play those. Not yet."

"'Those'? As in multiple messages?"

Expression verging on panicked, her mom nodded.
"I finally turned the phone and the machine off."

"Mom, what's going on? Why are you acting so
weird?" As she spoke, she pulled her cell out of her
pocket, relieved when she saw no missed calls or messages. "I know this can't be about the serial killer case,
or my office would have been blowing up my phone."

Finally, Wanda's determined attempt at composure crumbled. "They know about Jimmy Wayne, Rayna. All the media attention on the case must have made some reporter start digging. All afternoon, they've been calling, wanting a statement from you on what happened in Conroe."

It took a heartbeat or two for her mother's words to sink in. "They *know*?" She couldn't keep the horror out of her voice. "I mean, someone asked about it at the news conference a few minutes ago, but how could they have dug out the facts so fast?"

"I don't know, but they did." Expression miserable, Wanda sniffed. "You made the Midland-Odessa news. At least it will be too small a story to hit the national outlets."

"I don't know. They were the ones asking about it at the conference." Rayna took the few steps to her bedroom closet so she could put her weapon in her gun safe and lock it before managing to get back into the living room to a chair. She sat before her legs gave out from under her. She'd change later. "Which means it won't be long before the national people pick up the story. They've already done pieces on a possible serial killer in a small west Texas town."

"Are you ready?" Wanda held up the remote. When Rayna nodded, she pressed the button to take the program off Pause.

Numb, Rayna listened in mounting horror as the news anchor rehashed her past, ending the story with both Jimmy Wayne's conviction for drug trafficking and her subsequent resignation from the Conroe Police Department. "From there, Rayna Coombs relocated to Getaway, Texas, where she worked as a patrol officer for several years before being elected to the position of sheriff."

A commercial came on and Wanda clicked the television off. Rayna sat there in stunned silence. To her chagrin, she found herself blinking back tears. "I really liked it here," she whispered, unable to look at her mother. "I don't want to have to give all this up."

"Then don't." There was a sharp edge to Wanda's voice. "Fight for yourself this time. You did nothing wrong."

Rayna started to shake her head, but then stopped. "I know you feel I ran away, but it was the best thing I could have done for this family."

"True. And staying here would be the best thing right now." Wanda came over and put her hand on Rayna's shoulder. "Have a little faith in the people of this town. They not only like you, but they respect you, too."

Or they did, Rayna thought glumly. She'd thought her coworkers had liked and respected her at Conroe PD. Instead, they'd turned their backs on her, believing her guilty without a single shred of proof. Unable to bear the way her formerly close team ostracized her, aware that soon her pregnancy would show, she'd latched on to Sam's offer of a job like a lifeline.

Now, all that was about to change. People would figure out whose child Lauren had to be. It was one thing for Rayna to be ostracized. She couldn't allow that to happen to her daughter.

"It's going to be all right," Wanda reassured her. "Just you wait and see."

With all her heart, Rayna wished she could believe her.

Chapter 9

The instant Parker watched the news story, he reached for his phone to call Rayna. Yet before he punched in her number, he thought better of it. She didn't know he'd already known. No doubt half of Getaway was blowing up her phone with calls.

She'd need him. In person. Or, he amended, she'd need a friend. He grabbed his keys and his helmet and hopped on his bike.

When he got to her street, the news vans were parked at the curb, her house under siege as they waited for her to step outside. He noticed they were careful not to venture onto her private property.

Pulling up, he rolled into the driveway and killed the bike's engine. Immediately, three reporters, two men and one woman, stepped out of the vans with microphones in hand, cameramen right behind them.

He ignored them and walked to the front door. As he knocked, he wondered if Rayna would assume he was a reporter and refuse to answer. Just in case, he shot her a quick text message to let her know.

It must have worked, because a moment later, she opened the door. Staying behind it so she remained shielded from the street, she motioned him inside.

"Did you see the news?" she asked, her anxious expression at odds with her calm tone.

Instead of answering, he pulled her close and hugged her. After the first moment of shock, she relaxed and hugged him back. They stood like that, locked in each other's embrace for a minute or two, until Wanda clearing her throat interrupted them.

Reluctantly, Parker let Rayna go.

"Would you like anything to drink?" Wanda asked brightly.

"Mom." Rayna shook her head. "Could you give us a moment?"

"Sure." Wanda disappeared. A moment later, they could hear her talking to Lauren.

"Parker." Rayna touched his arm, drawing his attention back to her. "What are you doing here?"

Aware he had to try to keep it casual, he shrugged. "I saw the news story and thought you might need some support. Judging from the reporters camped out in front of your house, I was right."

"Yeah." Her shoulders sagged. "I need to call the station and ask a couple of my officers to come here and get them to disperse. But I haven't, because I'm not really sure how my own people are going to react to me now."

"They'll support you."

"Do you think?" Still, she didn't raise her head. "My old team down south sure didn't. Honestly, I don't know what's going to happen."

"Look at me, Rayna," he ordered. He waited until she raised her gaze to meet his before continuing. "You've proved yourself to be competent and fair. From what I've seen, you're a damn fine sheriff. They know that. They have to know that."

"Oh, I hope so." But her expression didn't appear hopeful.

Parker's phone rang. He glanced at it, surprised to see it was Sam. He held up a finger at Rayna and answered it.

"What the hell is going on down there?" Sam demanded. "I've been getting phone calls from reporters for the last couple of hours, all wanting information about Rayna. I've been trying to call her, but she isn't answering her phone."

"Hold on," Parker said. "She's right here."

He handed the phone to Rayna. "It's Sam."

Clearly nonplussed, she accepted it. "Hey." Listening, she went out to the back patio to talk in privacy.

Once she'd gone, Parker wandered into the kitchen to look for Wanda. He found her and Lauren, sitting at the table, working on a child's puzzle.

"Is Mommy okay?" the little girl asked, her little brow wrinkling.

"She'll be fine," Parker answered, aware that as far as Lauren was concerned, Rayna had to be. "What kind of puzzle is that?"

Lauren brightened immediately. "It's a puppy. I love puppies. I hope Mommy will get me one of my own someday."

"But we won't ask her right now," Wanda interjected. "Honey, why don't you keep working on this while I talk to Mr. Parker here."

"Okay." Lauren bent back to the task of figuring out which puzzle piece went where."

"Where's Rayna?" Wanda asked, keeping her voice low.

"Sam called," he replied. "She's outside on the patio, talking to him now."

"Good." Wanda glanced at her granddaughter, still intent on her puzzle. "Maybe he can talk some sense into her. She thinks the entire town is going to turn against her now."

Because that was what had happened last time. Of course, since Rayna hadn't told him anything about that, he wasn't supposed to know. So he kept silent about understanding why Rayna would think such a thing. Instead, he tried pointing out the positive. "I haven't been here long, but from what I've seen, the citizens of Getaway seem to like and respect Rayna. I can't imagine something so trivial changing that."

Wanda's expression cleared. "Thank you. Those are my thoughts, too."

"Hey, you three." Rayna appeared in the doorway, still holding her phone. "What's up?"

"Mama, Mama," Lauren squealed. "Come look at my puzzle. It's a puppy, just like the one I want."

Though clearly exhausted, Rayna made the effort to praise her five-year-old's puzzle.

"Can we get a puppy, Mama?"

"Not right now," Rayna replied. "Maybe someday." She patted Lauren's arm and urged her to keep working. "I'll take a picture of it when you've finished."

"What did Sam have to say?" Parker asked, once Rayna had rejoined them. She blinked, registering his question.

"I'm sure he was helpful," Wanda interjected. "He's such a good man."

"He is. Sam's on his way here." Rayna sounded numb. "He must really think it's going to be bad if he feels the need to support me in person."

She had a point. Parker and Wanda exchanged glances.

"I don't really understand why this is even news," Parker ventured. "You didn't do anything wrong. You weren't fired or even reprimanded. You chose to leave and take another job elsewhere."

"True." Rayna cast a worried look at Lauren, who'd gone back to being engrossed in the puzzle. She lowered her voice. "I just don't want anyone bothering her because of who her father happened to be. She doesn't know anything about him and I'd like to keep it that way, at least until she gets older."

"Agreed," Wanda murmured. "But honey, let's not worry about things that haven't happened yet. Just because your former coworkers were jerks doesn't mean everyone here will be."

As if right on cue, Rayna's phone rang. "It's Mary," she said, her expression warring between concern and hope. "I'll call her back later."

But as soon as the phone stopped ringing, it started up again.

"Mary again." Rayna frowned, clearly concerned. "It must be important."

She answered and after her initial hello, apparently

couldn't get a word in. Finally, she told Mary that she was on her way in.

Expression dazed, she swallowed and met Parker's gaze. "You're going to want to come with me. Old Man Malone found Nicole's cell phone. Larry charged it and says it's clearly hers. Thank goodness she didn't password-protect it or we wouldn't have been able to get in."

"Was there something on it?" Parker asked, hoping against hope. "Something that might tell us where to find her?"

Rayna grabbed his arm, steering him toward the door. "Mom, will you keep an eye on Lauren until I get back?"

"Of course," Wanda answered.

She hurried into her bedroom closet to retrieve her service weapon, nodding at Parker to indicate they needed to hurry.

They were out the door and in her cruiser before Rayna spoke again. "Larry says there's a video on it. It looks like Nicole might have taken it right before she was abducted."

Abducted. The word hit him like a punch in the stomach. Despite suspecting and worrying all along, having actual confirmation felt a thousand times worse.

He swallowed hard. "Does the video show who took her?"

"I don't think so." She glanced sideways at him. "Larry would have mentioned it."

Numb, he dragged his hand through his hair. "I see."

Starting the engine, she hesitated before putting the car in Drive. "Parker, are you okay?"

"Yes." From somewhere, he summoned a smile. "I'm fine."

They made it to the station in record time, though Rayna didn't turn on her lights or use her siren. After she parked, they jumped out of the patrol car, practically running inside.

Glad she'd allowed him to accompany her, Parker braced himself for what he'd see on the video.

Mary waved but didn't speak as they rushed past. They found Larry at his desk, still studying the phone.

"There you are," he said, finally looking up. His gaze drifted past Rayna to Parker. He frowned. "Are you sure he should be here?" he asked.

"It's fine." Rayna gave a reassuring nod to both men. "Fill me in and then I'd like to view the video myself."

"Sure thing, boss. I cleaned the phone up good and after I got it charged, it works fine. The screen isn't even cracked." Larry's expression softened. "By the way, I saw the news story. That was wrong, just wrong, what they did to you. Both in Conroe and on the television news tonight." He took a deep breath. "I just wanted to let you know that I'm behind you one hundred percent."

"Me, too," Mary hollered, from across the room. "Love ya, Sheriff Coombs."

For a brief moment, Parker could have sworn he saw the sheen of tears in Rayna's beautiful green eyes. She blinked rapidly and they were gone. "Thanks, guys."

"Here you go." Larry held up the phone.

"Thanks." Taking it, she turned toward her office. "Come on, Parker. We'll review it there. Larry, I'll get with you if I have any questions."

Once inside her office, she closed the door and dropped into her chair. Parker grabbed one of her guest chairs and pulled it around the desk so he could sit beside her.

She placed the phone in front of them. "Let's take a look."

First, she went to photos and began scrolling through them, stopping when she reached the one showing Nicole at the Getaway city-limits sign. There was only a video after that. Rayna clicked on it, hesitating a moment before pressing Play.

They leaned forward, intent on the screen. Judging from the jerky movement of the video, Nicole had been running. Though short of breath and clearly panicked, she tried to talk while she ran.

"Nowhere to hide," she gasped. The phone panned to show fields similar to the one where the bodies had been found. "I'm not gonna make it..."

Then she must have tossed the phone, or dropped it. She screamed, and a man's voice snarled obscenities at her. Unfortunately, due to the angle the phone had landed, nothing but dark dirt and bits of plants showed.

The recording ended a moment later.

"Why'd it stop?" Parker wondered out loud. "Since it didn't end when the phone hit the ground, I would have thought it would have kept going until the battery ran out."

"Me, too." Rayna shrugged. "Though that's not much to go on, at least it proves Nicole was grabbed somewhere around here." She reached out and squeezed his shoulder. "Now we've just got to hope she's still alive."

"Right." Oddly enough, Parker felt less certain now than he had before. "I wonder if I should tell her brother what's going on. I mean, he knows she's missing, but that's it."

"Would you like me to call him?" Rayna asked, her voice gentle. "As sheriff, I sometimes have to make those kinds of calls."

"No." He didn't even hesitate. "I'll do it. I owe him that much. Thanks for offering."

She nodded.

"What now?" he asked.

"We're going to contact the cell phone provider and have them do some GPS tracking for us." She checked the phone, frowning. "No recent calls, either, at least outgoing. She's had a bunch of incoming, and there are numerous voice messages. I'm going to have Larry check them out."

"Her family and friends have been very worried."

"Understandably. We'll also look into her life at Texas Tech. See whether or not she had any boyfriends, or former lovers. Just in case someone might have been mad enough at her to follow her and grab her."

"What? You don't think this is related to the other two girls?"

"What I think doesn't matter. We can't go on hunches or guesses. We have to check out all angles." She stood, weariness in her shoulders. "Let me drive you back to my house so you can pick up your motorcycle. Looks like I'm going to be working late tonight. She sighed. "At least the reporters should be gone since we had the news conference, so we won't draw any attention."

After dropping Parker off, on the drive back to the station, Rayna reviewed all the things she should have said to Parker. Expressions of sympathy, concern, support probably. Instead, she'd had to force herself to keep her attention on the road and driving. All she wanted to do was get lost in the case.

It wasn't every day that they had a video from an abducted—or probably abducted—victim. Part of her wanted to leak it to the press, though she knew she wouldn't. As soon as Sam got her, she wanted him to take a look at it.

In the meantime, they'd keep this under wraps. She needed to talk to Mr. Malone and not only thank him for his find, but ask him not to say anything about it. Knowing Getaway, that might already be a lost hope. It depended on where he'd gone after bringing the phone to the sheriff's department. If he'd gone home, they were most likely good. If not...

Since she didn't have his phone number, she hopped in her car and drove out to Mr. Malone's place. He answered the door on the second knock.

"Saw you on television earlier," he said, stepping aside so she could enter. "If I were you, I'd sue for slander."

"Thanks." Stunned, she realized with all the furor over finding Nicole's phone, she'd managed to forget about the news story digging up her past. "Listen, until we do a bit more investigating, would you mind keeping quiet about finding the phone?"

He scratched his chin. "Why? It seems to me like exactly the sort of thing folks should know. Might give them hope."

"We don't want the killer to know we have it."

Her words made him blanch. "You think she's dead?"

"Honestly, we don't know. But it's extremely likely. She's been missing over two weeks."

"Gosh, I hope not. That feller—Parker something or

other—seems like he's good people. He's really been hoping for a good outcome."

She nodded. "We all are, Mr. Malone. And while I understand it's difficult to keep quiet about something as big as finding the missing girl's phone, I'm just asking for a few days. The FBI is involved now and they might be able to extract something that could tell us who took her." A long shot, but still possible.

"Okay." Mr. Malone finally agreed. "You'll let me know when it's safe to tell my friends, right?"

"Of course. And if you want to keep looking, that would be helpful, too. Who knows what other evidence you might find."

He brightened at that. "I will," he said, his voice much more enthusiastic. "You'll be the first to know if anything else turns up."

"Thank you."

As she turned to go, he reached out and touched her on the shoulder. "About the other thing, keep your chin up. I'm sure everyone in this town will stand behind you."

She almost asked him if he truly believed that, but decided it best to simply thank him again and leave.

Driving home, she pondered his words. Could Old Man Malone be right? Would the people she'd served for so long as a deputy and now the sheriff truly continue to support her? They'd elected her to this position after all. She was almost afraid to hope.

Back at the house, she learned Lauren had finished the puzzle and Wanda had gotten her ready for bed. "You're just in time to read to me!" Lauren exclaimed. "I already picked out the book I want."

Rayna's heart swelled. What had happened with

Jimmy Wayne had been awful, true. But she'd gotten a beautiful little girl out of the whole mess, which made it all worth it.

After the story, she tucked Lauren in, kissed her cheek and turned out the light. Wanda sat in the living room, knitting, the television uncharacteristically silent. She looked up when Rayna approached.

"Are you all right?" Wanda asked, studying her daughter's face intently.

"Yes. What about you? Why aren't you watching your TV shows?"

"Because I wanted to talk to you first without any distractions." Wanda even put her knitting aside.

Not sure if she should be worried, Rayna sat on the couch next to her mother. "Okay. What's going on? Is it about the news story?"

"Yes, sort of. My phone hasn't stopped ringing since you left. I finally turned it off. Same with the house line—it's off the hook. Everyone in town wanted to talk to me about what they heard on the news."

Dread coiled low in Rayna's stomach. "What exactly did they have to say?" She braced herself, twisting her hands together in her lap.

"Every single person called me to voice their support for you." Wanda beamed. "In fact, I'm thinking you'll probably have a lot of messages left for you at the station when you go in tomorrow."

Rayna stared, hardly able to believe her ears. "Are you sure?" she asked. "I mean…"

"Rayna, every single person in this town knows how hard you work for them. You're not only an amazing sheriff, but a good person. They love you, honey. They really do."

At a loss for words, Rayna felt her eyes fill. "I...I don't know what to say."

"Stop worrying, for one thing." Wanda moved over and wrapped her daughter in a tight hug. "Those people at your former job were awful. The people of our little west Texas town are nothing like them."

Not quite certain she believed it, Rayna still nodded. "I hope that's true."

Wanda hugged her once more before settling down on the couch to watch television.

Just as Rayna was about to turn in for the night, the doorbell rang. Instantly alert—because who came visiting at ten o'clock at night?—she looked out the peephole first.

She'd have recognized that white-haired, stocky man in the black cowboy hat anywhere. Grinning from ear to ear, she yanked open the door. "Sam!"

They hugged, she a bit too tightly. When she finally let go, she ushered him into the house, pointing at Wanda, who'd fallen asleep on the couch watching TV. "Let's go into the kitchen so we don't disturb her rest," she said.

She could have sworn Sam looked disappointed. "I was hoping to visit with Ms. Wanda," he said, following Rayna to the kitchen. "Maybe next time. I'm sorry it's so late, but that's a bear of a drive here from Corpus. I thought I might actually have to stop partway and get some sleep."

"I'm glad you didn't." She went to the refrigerator, turning to smile at him. "Would you like something to drink? Tea, water, beer, Dr. Pepper?"

"Do you have any bourbon?" he asked, rubbing his hand across his chin. "It's been a mighty long trip."

"I sure do." She went to one of the cabinets, pulling out a half-empty bottle. "On the rocks?"

"Yes please. You still remember." He accepted the glass from her, clearly pleased.

"I do." She poured herself a glass of wine. "I really appreciate you coming all this way. That means a lot to me."

After taking a sip, he shrugged. "You probably won't need my support, but I'm here just in case you do. Getaway is full of good people. They'll recognize the truth when they see it."

"So far, they've been wonderful. Wanda's gotten tons of supportive calls. And I checked with my night shift crew and over a hundred people have already called and left messages of encouragement." Again, she found herself blinking back tears. "It's amazing, Sam. Just amazing."

"They're good people." He took another sip. "I'm going to have a lot of visiting to do while I'm here, but I appreciate if you could fill me in on what's going on with the Nicole Wilson case."

By the time she gave him all the details, they'd both finished their drinks.

"I'd better get going," Sam said. "I called ahead and got a room at the Landshark. I'm really tired. I'd better turn in."

"You're welcome to bunk on my couch," she offered. "It makes out into a bed."

He dipped his chin. "I appreciate the offer, but I'm too old for that kind of nonsense. The Landshark will do fine."

"That's where Parker is staying," she said. "I know he'll be glad to see you."

Sam checked his watch, barely stifling a yawn. "Well, it'll have to wait until morning. He and I are meeting for coffee and some eggs. I'll stop by the station after breakfast."

"Perfect." She hugged him again, the familiar woodsy scent of his aftershave making her smile. "Thanks so much for coming, Sam. Your support means the world to me."

"Tell Wanda and that sweet daughter of yours that I said hello."

"I will."

On the way out the door, Sam stopped and gazed down at the still sleeping Wanda. When he realized Rayna saw, he grinned. "She's a good-looking woman," he whispered. "Can't help but stare."

Though he'd been quiet, something made Wanda stir. Slowly, she opened her eyes. When she caught sight of Sam, she bolted upright. "Sam?"

"Hey, Wanda." His answering smile seemed sad. "How are you?"

Not looking away from him, Wanda took a step closer. "I'm good. You?"

"Great, great." Sam glanced at Rayna. "Would you mind giving us a moment here so we can talk in private?"

"Of course." Stunned, Rayna backed out of the room. Unsure where to go, she ended up heading into her bedroom. She stayed there until about five minutes later, when she heard the front door close. Still, she waited until she heard a car start up before making a beeline for the living room.

"Mom? What was that all about?" Catching sight of

Wanda, Rayna stopped short. "What's going on? Mom, are you crying?"

Wanda waved her away, making a strangled sound halfway between a sob and a snort. Tears continued to stream down her face, though she mopped at them with a paper napkin she'd been using under her water glass.

Concerned, Rayna tried to hug her. But Wanda pushed her away, clearly not wanting or needing comfort. "I'm fine," Wanda insisted, even though she obviously wasn't.

Since Rayna had no idea what to do, she dropped down onto the couch and waited Wanda out. She knew once her mother regained control of her emotions, she'd sit down and tell Rayna what was wrong.

Except this time, she did not. Still sniffling, Wanda turned and left the room. A moment later, she closed her bedroom door, shutting Rayna out.

"What the…?" Sam must have said something to upset Wanda. But what? She'd only left them alone for a few minutes.

Grabbing her phone, Rayna called Sam. Instead of him answering, the call went to voice mail. She left a message, even though she knew he wouldn't call her back tonight.

She decided to go bed also. Maybe Wanda would feel more like sharing in the morning. If not, Rayna planned to badger Sam until he told her what he'd done.

Chapter 10

Though Parker hadn't seen his uncle Sam since graduation from basic training, he would have recognized the older man anywhere. With his shock of wavy white hair, well-trimmed matching beard and mustache, Sam Norton looked like he should have been either a racehorse owner or the founder of a whiskey maker. He walked with a bit of a swagger, a quick smile and firm handshake always at the ready.

Though when he saw Parker waiting for him outside the Tumbleweed Café, he wrapped him up tight in a huge bear hug. "Good to see you, boy." His booming voice turned more than a few heads. When people realized who the commanding voice belonged to, they surrounded him and Parker, glad to see their former sheriff.

And in the numerous conversations that followed, more than one person expressed support for Rayna Coombs.

Finally, Sam managed to break free and grab Parker's arm so they could get inside the restaurant. "Can't keep a hungry man from his food," he joked as a parting shot.

In the main dining area, people began recognizing him and again, it appeared they would have no peace. Patient and kind, Sam greeted each and every single person, remembering not only their names, but those of their kin and even their pets.

Despite himself, Parker was impressed. Finally, Sam grabbed the hostess and asked, in his usual loud voice, for a private booth so he and his nephew could talk uninterrupted.

A few people laughed, one apologized, and several others promised to catch up with him later. The hostess led Sam and Parker to a secluded booth in the back near the kitchen, and people left them alone.

"You have a gift," Parker marveled as he sat.

This made Sam grin. "I do—that's a fact." He sat back while the waitress brought them water and menus. Stopping her, Sam asked for coffee. She immediately brought two steaming cups.

"Thank you, darlin'," Sam drawled.

She grinned. "I'll be back in a few to take your orders."

"Sounds good." Sam grinned back. His smile faded when she left and he eyed Parker with an intent gaze. "Now tell me what's been going on."

"Have you been to see Rayna yet?" Parker asked first. He didn't want to step on any toes, especially hers.

"Yes. But I want to hear your perspective on things."

Parker decided to stick with the missing-person case instead of touching on anything personal. After all, Nicole was the real reason he was here in Getaway.

Quickly, he outlined the information they had so far.

"Wow." Expression serious, Sam sipped his coffee while he considered. "I assumed Rayna turned the phone over to the FBI?"

"I think so." Parker found himself wishing they'd asked her to join them. "Though watching that video was awful, at least we now know she was abducted near Getaway."

Sam nodded, but his grim look told Parker his thoughts. "You know with a serial killer, time is of the essence."

"So Rayna has said."

Sam took another sip of his coffee. "I don't want you to get your hopes up."

"I hear you. Rayna says the same thing." Now Parker drank his coffee, carefully considering his next words. "Okay, I know this is going to sound weird, but Serenity told me she believes Nicole is still alive."

Instead of ridicule or derision, Sam took a moment to think about what Parker had said. "Serenity is often right," he finally said. "Though I have also known her to be wrong. I can promise you this. Rayna and the deputies working for her will do their best to find Nicole and bring her out alive."

Parker sat back. "I know. Rayna seems very competent. And I've met Larry, even looked through some of his files. I have complete faith in their abilities."

Sam's bright blue eyes narrowed. "I assume you've seen the news stories on Rayna."

"I have." Though it still pained Parker that Rayna hadn't trusted him enough to talk to him about her past, he could also understand her reluctance. After all, it wasn't as if they were building something permanent.

"What's up with you and Rayna?" Sam asked. Luckily, the waitress arrived just then to take their order, saving Parker from answering.

They ordered eggs, bacon, toast and hash browns. She refilled their coffee cups.

"I'm pretty hungry," Parker said once she left, hoping Sam would forget about his earlier question.

"Me, too. Now you and Rayna. Are you dating or what?"

"I'm only here until Nicole is found," Parker protested. "I don't have time to date anybody."

"That's not answering the question," Sam chided. "Every time I spoke with you on the phone, all you talked about was her."

Sam had a point. But Rayna wasn't something Parker wanted to analyze, never mind discuss. "She's a great cop," he said. "I have the utmost confidence in her ability to find Nicole, but... I think I'm going to go ahead and organize my own search."

Judging from Sam's frown, this wasn't the answer he'd been expecting. Luckily, their food arrived, giving Parker a brief reprieve.

Both men tucked into the breakfast, eating with a similar sort of single-minded intent. They finished roughly at the same time, pushing back their plates. Sam gave a satisfied sigh.

Parker took a sip of his coffee and waited. He had a pretty good idea what was coming next.

"Does Rayna know about this?" Sam finally asked.

"Not yet. I don't know if she'll approve or disapprove, but I figure as long as I stay out of her way—"

"I have a better idea," Sam interjected. "Why don't you ask her if you can ride along while she's working the investigation? Whether with her or one of her people. As long as you don't interfere, I think that would be a lot more helpful than you stirring up trouble on your own."

"I've already ridden along with Rayna." Parker's mouth twisted. "I wouldn't stir up anything."

"You may not think so, but if someone from Dallas, an outsider—that would be you—starts going around questioning townspeople, there's bound to be some bruised egos and hurt feelings. Hell, you might even get shot."

Certain his uncle had to be kidding, Parker waited for Sam to laugh. Instead, Sam leaned forward, clearly serious. "You don't understand these people. I do. I've lived in this town almost all of my life. I can ask Rayna if you can do a ride-along if you'd like."

Privately, Parker thought Sam might be making a big deal out of nothing, but there was the possibility the older man had a valid point. "Sure," he finally said, downing the last of his coffee. "But if she says no, I'm going to start on my own."

"Fair enough," Sam agreed. "I'm going to see her this morning. I'll let you know what she says."

Using the department text and email system Mary had developed a few years ago, Rayna sent a message to her entire staff scheduling a meeting first thing that morning. Sam must have still been on it because he'd called and asked to sit in. Of course she said yes.

He showed up before she did, waiting in the parking lot for her to arrive. Once inside, they walked together back to the conference room. She allowed the first ten minutes of the meeting for people to express their delight at seeing him.

Finally, she marched to the front of the conference room and cleared her throat. "Everyone, please take a seat."

Everyone seated and silent, she listed the known facts in the serial killer case. She talked about Nicole, showed them clips of the video and began outlining a plan of action.

"While the FBI is analyzing the phone, we're going out and questioning the citizens. I don't want you to make anyone feel like a suspect, though internally I expect you to consider them one until proved otherwise. I've made everyone a list of people I'd like you to talk to, along with geographical areas where you're going to be knocking on doors."

One of the newer officers protested. "But won't this type of thing offend our citizens? They're not going to like knowing we consider everyone a potential suspect."

Larry and Sam exchanged a look that clearly said *Rookies*. By a herculean effort, Rayna managed to keep her own face professional and expressionless.

"Your job is to take measures to make sure no one feels like a suspect," she reiterated. "Routine questioning, doing our job, dotting our *i*'s and crossing our *t*'s." She let her gaze drift over her small group of officers. "Keep this in mind, folks. Though it's difficult to consider, we most likely have a murderer living among us—worse than that, a serial killer. He—or she, though they're hardly ever female—will kill again. Our job is to stop him before he does. And if by some miracle, our missing person Nicole Wilson is still alive, we need to rescue her before she is killed. Questions?"

The usual flurry of questions started. Most of them made sense. One or two of the newer officers appeared to resent the FBI for being involved in the case. Rayna quickly nipped that notion in the bud.

"The FBI is our *partner* in this investigation," she reminded them.

"And they have access to a lot of technology we don't," Sam interjected.

"Are you coming out of retirement to work this case?" Larry asked. Rayna couldn't tell if he sounded hopeful or worried.

Sam shook his head and looked at Rayna, as if asking her thoughts.

"I'm actually glad Larry asked that question," Rayna said. "You're certainly welcome to assist us if you'd like."

Her statement made Sam guffaw. "I think I'll hang around town for a bit," he allowed. "I can be a consultant if you need me. But no, my days of actively working cases are over."

She eyed him. "I'm about to go out and talk to a few people." Holding up a sheet of paper, she tilted her head. "I have my own list."

The gleam in Sam's blue eyes told her he was intrigued. "I think I'll ride along with you," he said. "For old times' sake."

Knowing better than to laugh out loud, she nodded instead. "Let's go."

"Wait." He grabbed her arm. "I need to ask you something. What do you think of letting Parker ride along with you instead of me?"

"Parker? Why?"

"Because he's thinking about doing his own investigating. Even though I warned him riling up the townspeople wasn't a good idea. It'd be better—and less destructive—to allow him to be a small part of the official investigation. Even if all he does is observe."

Heaven help her, but her entire body flushed. She had enough difficulty keeping her thoughts straight on their chance encounters. Deliberately spending hours with Parker would be a challenge, to say the least.

But Sam did have a point. The good citizens of Getaway were friendly, but didn't take well to outsiders getting in their business. She'd learned that the hard way when she'd first arrived in town.

"I don't have a problem with that," she finally allowed. "As long as you promise to keep him from doing anything disruptive."

Now Sam did chuckle. "Rayna, I'm afraid you're on your own with that one. I'm only riding along with you today. I don't get back to town often enough. The rest of my time here I plan to spend visiting." He winked. "I'm hoping I can get your mother to join me."

Though she'd just reached for the door to push it open, she swung around. "Wanda?"

"Do you have more than one mother?" He shouldered past her without waiting for an answer.

Dumbfounded, she followed. He unerringly went to her squad car, waiting impatiently for her to unlock it. It once had been his, so he knew it well.

Inside the car, she contemplated starting the ignition and trying to pretend she hadn't heard his comments, but couldn't do it. "What did you say to make my mother cry last night when you were at the house?"

He shook his head. "That's none of your business."

"Fair enough." She took a deep breath. "Then tell me this. Do you have the hots for my mother?"

He didn't even crack a smile. "What if I did? She and I are of similar ages and she's a beautiful woman."

"Mom doesn't really date," she protested, even though she'd been after her mother for months to get out there and meet some men.

"Maybe she just hasn't met the right person," Sam suggested. "Would you really mind so terribly?"

She had to think about that. "I don't want her to be hurt, Sam. I think you're an amazing guy and all that, but you're not going to be here long. What if you two start seeing each other and then your leaving breaks her heart?"

"I think your mother is old enough to make that choice for herself," Sam chided gently. "Why don't we leave it up to her?"

"You're right." Pushing the button to start the engine, she shifted into Reverse and backed out of her parking spot. "But so help me, Sam. If you hurt her…"

"I won't." He touched her arm. "If you want to worry about someone getting their heart broken, worry about me."

His cell phone rang. Sam answered, listened for a moment, and then said they were leaving. "That was Parker," he explained. "We might as well pick him up on the way."

Her heart skipped a few beats, though she managed to give a casual shrug. "Roger that."

Sam waited until they were away from the station before he spoke again. "What's going on between you and my nephew?"

Rayna frowned. She saw no reason to lie, since Sam knew her well enough to see right through her. "That's kind of personal, don't you think?" she asked instead.

Her response made Sam chuckle. "So there *is* something going on. Parker dodged my question, too."

"Sam, you remember what happened to me in Conroe," she warned.

"*That's* what you're worried about?" His incredulous tone had her glancing sideways at him. "Parker isn't a criminal. You can't even compare the two."

"I didn't know what Jimmy Wayne was doing the entire time I dated him. Not only did I feel used, but I felt stupid and naive. It's difficult for me to trust anyone after that."

"Again, Parker isn't anyone." He smiled. "Granted, I'm prejudiced. That boy has been through hell. Two tours in Afghanistan and to this day he doesn't like to talk about that."

Not sure what he wanted her to say, she settled for a nod.

"He's got some skills, too. Ever since he was a teenager, he's loved working on cars. He has the touch. I told him if he were ever to set up shop, he'd have people lining up from all over the country."

"Sam, why are you telling me all this?" she asked. "I get that you're proud of Parker, but it feels almost like you're trying to sell me on him."

His unabashed grin was pure Sam. "Maybe I am. Just in case there might actually be something going on between you."

Because she knew how Sam could be like a bulldog once he got something in his head, she figured she might as well answer.

"If there is, it's just two adults having a little fun when they can." She shrugged. "No harm in that. I'm able to keep both parts of my life completely separate."

Rayna pulled up to the Landshark Motel, with its kitschy lighted sign featuring a blue shark with legs carrying a suitcase. Coasting to a stop near Parker's room, she saw him come outside.

She caught her breath at the sight of him, with the sun glinting off his dark hair. He wore shades, which made him look sexy as hell. A shiver snaked up her spine and her mouth went dry, just looking at him.

Sam shot her an amused look, as if he knew. He opened the passenger door and got out. "You can ride shotgun," he told Parker. "I've changed my mind about going."

"What?" Both Rayna and Parker spoke at the same time.

Sam shrugged. "I'm tired. I'm going to go take a nap. I'd only be a major distraction anyway." He winked at Rayna, though Parker probably saw. "You two have fun without me." He took off, shooting a jaunty grin at Parker as he sailed past him.

A moment later, Parker got in the front seat of her car. "What was that all about?" he asked, eyeing Sam's back as the older man all but fled toward the back of the motel.

"I'm not sure," Rayna replied grimly. "Though I suspect he thinks he's matchmaking. All the way over here, he sang your praises."

Parker groaned. "Sorry about that. He's got a good heart, but you already know that."

"New sunglasses?" she asked, shifting into Drive and easing out from the parking lot.

"Yeah." His grin made him look even sexier. How that was possible, she didn't know. "I dropped my other pair when I got off the bike this morning. So I got these."

Since all she could think about was how badly she wanted to kiss him, of course she had to get herself back on track. "Here's what I plan to do today," she said, her tone brisk and businesslike. "I've got a list of people I want to question. The important thing is not to make them feel as if they are suspects."

"I've heard. Sam mentioned that at breakfast."

"Right." She cleared her throat. "Anyway, I'd really prefer that you don't participate in the questioning. I'm allowing you to accompany me as a ride-along, but you're a civilian. If I were to allow you to ask questions, we could have a real problem making any charges stick later. Okay?"

"Yes, ma'am," he drawled. "Sam already briefed me."

"Then I guess I need to be grateful to Sam."

Leaving town, they traveled down the two-lane road, turning left onto a gravel lane marked with a sign that read FM3343. They turned into a long driveway and drove through a set of rusted wrought-iron gates, pulling up in front of a well-kept older house with overgrown hedges.

"This," she said, turning to face Parker after she killed the engine, "is where the most famous resident of Getaway lives. Myrna Maple, the advice columnist."

He gaped. "We're going to meet her? I remember always trying to run into her around town as a kid, but it seemed like no one ever saw her. When I got older, I tried to find out where she lived, but she must have taken great care to stay hidden. Nicole wanted to meet her more than anything."

"She likes her privacy." Getting out of the car, she

waited for him to catch up. "I've only met her a couple of times myself, and both of those were before I became sheriff."

"And why are we questioning her?"

"We're questioning just about everyone," she said. "Or at least as many people as we can get to this time. I decided to take everyone who lived on ranches, farms or large properties outside of downtown."

As they stepped up onto the front porch, a stocky middle-aged man in denim overalls came outside to meet them. "Can I help you?" he asked, his expression curious.

"Phillip Maple?" Rayna held out her hand. "I believe we've met once or twice."

"Yes." He shook, his grip light, as if he was afraid of hurting her. She liked a firm handshake herself, but she understood how some men thought.

"Is your mother home?" she asked.

"She is, but has taken to her bed." He stepped closer, invading Rayna's personal space. It took all her willpower not to step back. "My mother is quite elderly," he continued. "As I'm sure you know. She's been feeling poorly, and is spending a lot of time sleeping. I'm afraid she's not up to any visitors today."

"I understand." Rayna crossed her arms, mentally urging him to back away. "Do you mind if I ask you a few questions instead?"

Apparently, this so startled him that he took an involuntary step back. "About what?"

She pulled the photograph of Nicole from her shirt pocket. "This young woman disappeared. We haven't found her vehicle or anything, but we're going around asking everyone if they'd seen her."

Barely glancing at the picture, he shook his head. "Sorry. I rarely go into town, and when I do it's just to pick up supplies. I don't do much socializing."

She moved the photo closer to him. "Maybe you might have seen her broken down on one of the back roads around here?"

Finally, he accepted the pic, holding it gingerly in between his thick fingers. "She's very pretty," he mused. "I think I'd remember if I saw a woman who looked like that. I'm sorry. I wish I could help you." He handed the photo back. "Tell you what—if I do see her, I'll be sure to call."

"Thank you." Eyeing Parker, she turned to go. Halfway down the front porch steps, she turned back. "How long has it been since your mother was in town?"

He shrugged. "Months. She's elderly and can barely walk. It's easier for her to stay home."

"Is she still writing her column?"

For the first time since they arrived, Phillip appeared abashed. "Actually, no. Not entirely. I write it and then she edits before we send it in. It's a collaboration. I can't let her stop yet. That column pays the bills."

"You don't work?" she asked, inwardly wincing at the rudeness of her question. "I mean, I know this isn't a working farm or ranch. I thought maybe you might have a side hustle, too."

"A side *hustle*?" Pursing his lips, he mouthed the word as if he found it distasteful. "No, that I definitely do not have. I take care of Mother. I wouldn't be able to leave her for long. She is my full-time job."

"Understood." Rayna dipped her chin. "It was nice meeting you. Thank you for your time."

Phillip remained standing on his front porch, watching as she and Parker got in the car. She backed up and turned around, all the while silently considering the interaction as she drove them back down the rutted gravel road.

"He's a strange one, isn't he?" Parker finally asked.

"Yes." She pinched the bridge of her nose. "Not very friendly, but most likely harmless. He keeps busy taking care of his mother, which is admirable."

"Especially since Myrna Maple is a national treasure. Her advice columns have been syndicated for as long as I can remember."

They hit up five more farms before they drove to the Sanders place, which would be their last one of the day. Ted Sanders seemed honestly happy to see them, though his twin teenage daughters frowned and disappeared into their rooms.

"They're unhappy because I've been super strict on them ever since those two bodies were found," Ted explained. "It's rough, but I can't take a chance of some sicko getting ahold of either of them. They seem to think carrying their phone with them at all times keeps them safe, but you and I both know that's not the case."

Something about the way he worded that last statement had her wondering if Old Man Malone had spilled the beans about finding Nicole's phone.

"I'm wondering if either of the girls might have heard anything," Rayna explained. "Teens gossip as much as adults. Would you mind asking them to come out here for a moment to talk to me?"

Ted scratched his head. "Sure. No problem." Putting two fingers in his mouth, he blew an ear-piercing whistle.

Rayna exchanged an amused glance with Parker, who appeared startled.

The girls appeared instantly. Judging from their sullen expressions, they weren't happy about being summoned.

"Girls, the sheriff here wants to ask you a few questions," Ted said. Instantly, the twins froze.

"Come on, Yvonne and Yolanda," Rayna said. "I've known the two of you since you were little girls. Why are you acting like you think I'm about to arrest you? Have you done something wrong that I don't know about?"

Still silent, they both shook their heads, cutting their eyes back to their father. Both wore heavy mascara and eyeliner, along with a dark purple lipstick that was not the right shade for their fair complexions.

Right then, Rayna decided she'd have better results if she talked to them privately. "Ted, would you mind if me and the girls went for a quick walk? You and Parker here could talk about sports or whatever."

This last comment made the girls giggle. "The only sports dad likes are bull riding and NASCAR," Yvonne said. She glanced shyly at Parker, almost as if she might be beginning a crush.

Clearly oblivious, Parker brightened. "I love NASCAR."

"You do?" Yvonne sounded disappointed.

"I do," Parker answered firmly. Through all this, Yolanda kept her eyes studiously averted from Parker, which struck Rayna as odd.

"You girls go walk. The two of us will be fine." Ted waved them away. "We'll be right here waiting for y'all to get back." He turned to Parker. "How about a beer while we talk drivers?"

"Sounds good."

The two men headed into the kitchen.

"Let's go." Rayna led the girls outside. "Would you rather sit out here on the front porch or take a stroll down the road?"

Again, the twins looked at each other before answering, making Rayna wonder if they had some kind of silent code.

"We're good either way," Yolanda finally answered. Yvonne nodded, still silent.

Though the porch swing looked inviting, Rayna suspected they might open up more if they were away from their house. "Let's take a walk. Maybe you two can show me around your farm."

Yvonne made a face. "There's nothing to see. Pigs and cows, mud and poop. Even the chickens stink. You wouldn't like it, I promise."

"I'll take you at your word." Rayna made a quick about-face. "Then we'll go this way. Walk down the drive until we reach the road and then come back."

The identical expressions on both girl's faces told her they thought that idea would be pointless.

"Humor me," Rayna said. "Come on. Let's go." She took off, trusting they'd follow. After a moment, they shuffled along after her.

She walked until she stood in the shade of a massive cedar tree. "This is pretty," she said, looking out over the pastures from the slight rise in the land.

When they caught up with her, they both looked around, disinterest plain on their young faces.

"What did you want to talk to us about?" Yolanda finally asked, jamming her hands into her jean pockets.

"I'm sure by now you've heard of the two murdered bodies we found, right?"

"Of course." Yvonne shuffled her feet. "That's all anyone talks about at school. It made my dad so worried, he changed our curfew and now he monitors all our activities. Thanks to this, we're literally prisoners."

"Literally," Yolanda agreed. "It's awful."

"No, what's awful is getting strangled and then buried in a shallow grave," Rayna said. "I need to know if any of the kids are talking about something that might be related to this. Like a new guy Snapchatting them, wanting to meet. Someone no one knows, but who might paint himself as hot."

Yvonne frowned. "An older guy?"

"Maybe. Or even the same age."

"We haven't seen anything like that," Yolanda interjected, her color high. This of course made Rayna suspicious.

"Are you sure?" Rayna asked, staring directly at Yolanda.

"Positive," Yvonne insisted, clearly covering for her sister. "But we promise to tell you if we do."

Short of badgering the teens, that was all she could hope for. "Thanks, girls." They turned to make their way back to the house.

Right before they reached the front porch, Rayna lightly touched Yolanda's shoulder, which startled her. "Sweetie," Rayna said, keeping her voice soft. "Here's my card. If you think of anything you want to tell me, anything you might have forgotten, just give me a call."

Turning to Yvonne, she also handed her a card. "Ditto for you."

Both girls mumbled their thanks. They stepped inside the house and took off for their bedroom.

Rayna found Parker and Ted in the kitchen, sitting at the table, laughing and drinking beer.

"Want one, Rayna?" Ted asked, smiling broadly.

She shook her head. "Sorry, I can't. I'm still on duty."

Parker stood, draining the last of his can. "Are you ready to go?"

"Yes." She looked at Ted. "Thank you for letting me talk to your girls."

"No problem. And Parker, come back whenever you want. It's been a while since I had someone to watch NASCAR with."

"I just might take you up on that," Parker said.

Once they were inside the car, he glanced back at the farmhouse. "Hell of a nice guy. It's got to be hard, raising two teenage daughters on his own."

"I agree. I've always respected that about him."

Her cell phone rang just as she turned on to the highway. "It's the FBI," she told Parker, right before she answered. "Sheriff Coombs."

"Sheriff Coombs, it's Special Agent in Charge Prado. Our profiler has finished working up a composite of what you're looking for. I've emailed it to you."

"Great. I'm not in the office right now, so can you tell me over the phone?"

"To be honest, it's a profile similar to those of ninety percent of serial killers. Middle-aged white male, likely a social misfit, can be charming and sociable when he wants to be, though he tends to keep to himself. Might be slightly overweight or underweight, etc. You know the drill."

She did. She'd done extensive reading on serial killers when she first became a law enforcement officer. "Thanks, Prado. I'll be in touch if we learn anything new."

"You do that. Keep in mind, since you've located two of his bodies—which most likely aren't the only ones— he's either going to do one of two things. Lay low for a while, or ramp up the killing." Prado gave a humorless laugh. "Which tells us exactly nothing."

Rayna relayed the information to Parker, her voice grim.

He cursed, his frustration evident. "Sometimes it feels like we're just going in circles."

They reached the Landshark and she pulled up without parking. "I'm going to leave you here," she said. "I need to stop back at the office and do some paperwork."

"Okay." He leaned over and gave her a quick, casual kiss on the lips. Every instinct she had made her long to deepen it, but she resisted. Still, she sat in the car, mouth burning, and watched until Parker disappeared inside his room.

Her phone rang just after she dropped Parker off. To her surprise, it was Ted Sanders. "Listen, Rayna," he began, concern deepening his voice. "Yolanda has something she'd wants to say to you."

Intrigued, Rayna waited while he passed the phone to his daughter. "You asked if there'd been a new guy contacting any of the girls in my class," she began. "That man you brought with you today…my dad says his name is Parker Norton."

"That's right. Why?"

"Because he's been trying to Snapchat and Viber with several of my friends." She swallowed, the sound audible. "He's hot, though I'm sure you already know that. And he and I have been getting really close, which is why I was surprised to see him today." She sounded as if she was about to cry. "But I wanted to tell you, in case he's the serial killer."

Feeling queasy, Rayna thanked her. A moment later, Ted came on. "What are you going to do about this?" he demanded. "Even if that Parker guy isn't the murderer, he's way too old to be contacting teenage girls. I can't believe I sat and had a beer with him. Sicko."

"Agreed." Rayna took a deep breath, her heart pounding, trying to think rationally. "There's always a chance someone is using a photo of him as their profile picture. He might not even be aware."

"True. But then again, he might be guilty as hell." Anger simmered in Ted's voice. "Promise me you'll take care of this."

"Believe me, I will," Rayna said grimly. "I'm on my way back to his motel to have a talk with him right now."

Chapter 11

Parker had just turned on the television when a series of furious, sharp knocks sounded on his door. He checked through the peephole, surprised to see Rayna outside.

"What did you forget?" he asked, opening the door. As usual, just the sight of her hit him like a punch to the gut. All swirling red hair, flashing green eyes and the most kissable lips he'd ever seen, even if they were pursed in a tight line at the moment.

"Rayna? What's going on?"

She stormed into his room, expression furious. "I just got a phone call from one of the Sanders twins."

"Okay." Crossing his arms, he waited for her to say more.

Instead, she held up her hand. "I need a moment." Turning her back to him, she took several deep breaths. When she turned back around, her expression had gone deadly calm, though a combination of hurt and anger blazed from her beautiful green eyes.

Stunned, he reached for her. She twisted away, clearly avoiding him. "Rayna, what is it? What's wrong?"

She lifted her chin and met his gaze straight on. "Yolanda Sanders told me you've been contacting high school girls, trying to befriend them. Is this true?"

It took a moment for her words to sink in. Clearly, she was serious. "Of course not," he answered, still not entirely certain this wasn't a joke. "Why would she say such a thing?"

"I'm going to need your cell phone," Rayna said. "You can hand it over willingly, or I'll get a warrant. Believe me, it will go better for you if you cooperate."

"Better for me..." Digging his phone out of his pocket, he handed it over. "Rayna, you know me. Why would you think I'd do something like this?"

Careful not to look at him, she pulled an evidence bag from her bag and dropped the phone in it. "Why would anyone do something like that? In fact—" she rounded on him, her mouth a hard, tight line "—why would someone kill young women and bury them in shallow graves? Are you sure you're looking for Nicole? Or have you already found her?"

With that, she exited the room, back ramrod straight, face expressionless, though clearly working at not crying.

Stunned and shocked, he let her go, no longer certain of anything except that she had the wrong person. He could almost swear he felt his heart break.

How could Rayna, *his* Rayna, the woman he'd shared so much of himself with, believe he was capable of such a thing? Did she even truly know him?

The other thing he didn't understand was if someone else had used his photograph, why target him? Could it be because he refused to give up in his search for Nicole?

Not knowing what else to do, he went looking for Sam. He found his uncle sitting by the pool, sipping on a drink in a red plastic cup.

"Why do you look like someone punched you in the gut?" Sam drawled. Then, eyes widening in alarm, the older man sat bolt upright. "Damn. Please tell me they didn't find Nicole's body."

"No, not that." Parker pulled out a chair and sat down. He outlined Rayna's accusations and the fact that she'd confiscated his phone. "I'm not sure which bothers me worse," he concluded. "The fact that someone is pretending to be me or the way Rayna obviously believes it."

Sam swore. "I hate technology," he griped. "That's one of the reasons I retired. All those social media apps. I've heard too many times about some creep using one of them to stalk a young, trusting girl."

"At least once they check out my phone, they'll see it wasn't me," Parker said. "I'm also guessing they'll contact the application to verify the IP address. Why on earth someone would do this to me, I'll never understand. I'm way too old to begin with."

Sam studied him. "They're not only messing with you, they're trying to shake Rayna. Whoever is doing this must not only know her past, but is aware the two of you are...close."

"Were," Parker put in sharply. "She's made it clear what she really thinks of me. Lowlife scum, apparently."

"Give her a break." Sam touched Parker's arm. "She

trusted and loved a guy who not only used her, but made a complete fool of her. It cost her the respect of her colleagues. She almost lost her job. The smallest sign that such a thing is happening again would definitely set her off."

"No." Parker shook his head. "She didn't even give me a chance to speak. Just showed up like judge, jury and executioner. She didn't ask any questions or even ask for a plausible explanation. It's clear what she thinks of me."

"And what the entire town is going to think of you," Sam added, "once this gets out. Maybe it'd be wise for you to skedaddle back up to Dallas and let the investigation go on without you."

"Why would I want to do that?" Frustration and rage simmered over. "I haven't done anything wrong. I can't show up at John's bedside without his little sister. Plus, if I did that, it would look like I'm guilty and running away. Since I'm not, I'm staying put until Nicole is found. This is a mess."

"Right now, it is. But it all will work out once Rayna and her crew realize you have nothing to do with this. It's called catfishing, I believe."

Parker snorted. "I know what it's called. I think everyone alive on the face of this earth does. So why didn't that possibility even occur to Rayna?"

Sam stared. "You really care about her, don't you?"

This stopped Parker in his tracks. "Maybe," he finally admitted. "Or I thought I did. Obviously, I made a mistake."

"No, you didn't. Let Rayna do her job. Right now that's got to be her first priority, even over you."

Though intellectually, Parker could understand, he

still smarted from the way she'd instantly believed the accusations against him. Even once he was cleared—which he would be—he knew he'd have a lot of trouble getting past that. It felt like betrayal.

Parker stood. "I'm going back to my room," he said, his head aching. "I need to think."

"I understand." Sam heaved a sigh, his face expressionless. "For the record, I know damn good and well you could never do what you're being accused of. And that sort of thing is pretty easy to disprove. Eventually, Rayna's going to realize she accused the wrong person."

"Maybe so," Parker replied. "But by then, it's going to be too damn late."

All the way back to his room, he replayed the conversation with Rayna. What he could have said, should have said, and what she hadn't. In the end, the what-ifs irritated him enough that he dialed her number.

"Your call has been forwarded to an automatic voice mail system." Of course she wasn't taking his calls. He considered going to see her in person, but decided it might be better to wait until they both had cooled off. After all, like Sam said, if disproving the accusations against him turned out to be easy, he imagined he'd be hearing from Rayna as soon as that happened.

A knock came on his door. Parker opened it, surprised to see the owner of the Landshark standing outside. "Can I help you?"

"Yeah." David McMartin shifted his weight from foot to foot. "I'm afraid I'm going to have to ask you to leave."

"What?" Certain he hadn't heard correctly, Parker stepped outside. To his surprise, McMartin moved back.

"You've got to go," the motel owner repeated, his voice firm. "As in, now."

"I've prepaid for the rest of the week," Parker pointed out. "What's going on? I haven't broken any rules or damaged anything."

The hard look on the older man's face should have warned him. "I can't have someone who tries to pick up teenage girls staying in my motel. In fact, most of Getaway would prefer you to leave town."

Though he shouldn't have been, Parker was shocked at how quickly gossip traveled in this town. "First off, I didn't do what I've been accused of. And second, no arrest warrant has been issued, so you have no legal grounds to toss me out."

"I don't care." McMartin set his chin in a hard line. "My motel, my rules. Pack your stuff up and get the hell out. If you're not gone within thirty minutes, I'm calling the sheriff's office."

Parker crossed his arms. "Go ahead and call them. Because I'm not going anywhere." He closed the door in the other man's face.

Too agitated to sit, he paced the small room. This entire thing had gotten ridiculous. First he'd been accused of something he hadn't done and next it seemed he'd been convicted without a trial.

While he waited to see what would happen, he used the hotel room phone and called Sam. When he told his uncle what McMartin had said, Sam swore.

"Let me call Rayna," Sam said, ending the call before Parker could protest. Staring at the bulky old-fashioned phone, he realized he'd still have to deal with her, no matter how much doing so would hurt. She'd instantly thought the worst of him, even after having gone through something similar herself. He still couldn't get over how much that hurt.

He'd come to care for her. Far more than he should have. With that acknowledged, he realized it had been in the back of his mind to return to Getaway and put down roots. All because he'd fallen for a woman who didn't reciprocate the feelings.

Some noises from outside the parking lot had him going to the window and peering outside. His first concern—his bike—proved to be false. Instead, there appeared to be a group of men pulling their pickup trucks in a circle and gathering in the parking lot.

For him? Surely not. Though when he considered what he'd been accused of and how he might have reacted had it been his daughter who'd been approached, he could understand.

Should he call Rayna? Or, he amended, aware he needed to think more impersonally, the Getaway Sheriff's Office?

Deciding to wait for now, he walked away from the window and turned on the television.

Sam called a few minutes later. "Have you seen what's going on outside?"

"I did. What do you think they're doing?"

"Not sure," Sam admitted. "But I'm about to go out there and find out."

"Did you talk to Rayna?" Despite everything, Parker's heart rate accelerated just saying her name. Proving, he thought wryly, that he really was a fool.

"Not yet. I'll call her after I get a handle on what's actually going on. For all we know, they could be getting together to go bowling or something."

This supposition made Parker laugh. "Right. Would you mind filling me in on what you find out?"

"No problem." As was his way, Sam ended the call without saying goodbye.

Parker found himself pacing the small room, unable to concentrate on the television, so he turned it off. Frustrated, he grabbed his laptop and pulled up one of the larger social media sites, even though it seemed he remembered hearing that teens didn't use it as much.

He went straight to his own profile, a place he rarely visited except to post photos of cars he'd restored. Nothing new there.

Next, he typed his name into a search bar. A moment later, he saw another profile with the same name and picture. Clicking on it, he reported it as false. While he wasn't sure what social media site the teenagers had been contacted on, he knew he didn't want to go there. He reached for his phone, intending to take a screen shot of both his profile page and the false one, since he knew it would soon be taken down, but realized Rayna still had it.

Again, he itched to talk to her about this, even if he had to use the motel room phone.

Beyond that, he didn't know what else to do to prove his innocence. He knew his cell phone wouldn't show any record of calls or texts or whatever with teenage girls because he hadn't made them. Would that be enough? What was enough in a situation like this?

He cursed, feeling trapped. Should he get an attorney? Telling himself to calm down, he reminded himself that formal charges hadn't been made. There actually was good reason why not. Not enough evidence.

The room phone rang, startling him. Sam again,

sounding grim and pissed off. "They're here for you," he said. "Ted Sanders and some of his buddies put the word out. Most of these guys out there are fathers of teenage daughters."

"What do they want?" Parker asked, wary.

"Your blood." Sam snorted. "McMartin is about to blow a gasket. He's afraid they might try to burn your motel room down to get to you. I'm sure he's called the sheriff by now."

"Burn my..." Parker shook his head, disbelieving. "Are you serious?"

"Sort of. Listen, these guys are just talking right now. They want to beat the tar out of you. But give 'em a few beers and that might escalate. That's why Rayna and her people need to get out here and break this up before it gets any worse. I'm going to call her now."

"Sam..." But Sam had already gone.

Parker wanted to slam his fist into the wall.

It didn't take long to get a judge to issue a warrant, which Rayna passed along electronically to Parker's cell phone carrier. Detailed phone records were sent to her immediately. While she felt oddly guilty perusing Parker's personal call history, fury and regret still made her mouth taste like ash. She reviewed every call with single-minded intent, looking for anything to prove or disprove his guilt or innocence.

She hated the thought that she'd been played again, taken in by a man who'd pretended to be something he was not. This had driven her to act impulsively, unprofessionally, which she regretted. However, if Parker was guilty, she'd make sure he was brought to a swift and ruthless justice.

Except… In her mind, there wasn't a single possible scenario where she could imagine Parker doing what Yolanda Sanders had accused him of. She truly didn't believe Parker had done anything wrong. If that turned out to be the case, then she had treated him terribly, the same way people had once treated her without any proof that she'd done something wrong.

Thinking back to that time, she considered the difference between Parker and Jimmy Wayne. With Jimmy Wayne, it had been different. The instant he'd been arrested and charged, she'd suddenly understood the reasons for many of his actions. Blinders had been pulled away from her eyes.

Not so with Parker. He seemed like the most upfront, straightforward guy she'd ever met. And she'd just begun to trust her gut instincts, certain she'd finally developed that true cop second sense. Hah. Look where believing that had gotten her. According to Sam, the entire town knew she and Parker had a *thing*. Hearing that made her feel ill.

But what if Yolanda had been mistaken? While Rayna had to admit that was unlikely, she considered the possibility that someone had used Parker's picture. After all, neither Yolanda nor any of her friends had claimed to have met Parker in person.

So all they had was a couple of social media accounts with Parker's photograph on them. And some text messages sent from a prepaid cell phone that appeared to be a burner. In short, no proof that Parker was guilty.

Sam called, clearly irate and furious that idle gossip had gotten Parker kicked out of Getaway's only motel. "He's refusing to leave," Sam added. "I have a feeling

David McMartin might be calling you to ask for law enforcement assistance in forcibly evicting him."

"There are no grounds," she said, even though she knew Sam would already be aware. "As long as he's paying his bill on time and hasn't been engaging in any criminal activity, McMartin can't—"

"I know that, you know that, but I doubt McMartin does. In fact, I wouldn't put it past him to get on the horn to some of his cronies and try to handle this themselves. They're camped outside in the motel parking lot."

Which could become dangerously ugly, to say the least. She understood exactly how Parker must feel. After all, she'd been there herself. People had rushed to judgment and proclaimed him guilty without all the facts. Truthfully, now that she'd gotten over her earlier shocked anger, she realized she might have been a bit hasty in that area herself.

"I'll swing by and check out the situation in a few," she told Sam. "I need to talk to Parker again anyway."

"Good," Sam replied, ending the call. Since she didn't get a sense of urgency, she resumed combing through the information Parker's cell carrier had sent.

Once she looked over Parker's phone records, she began to realize she probably owed him an apology. Even more so as phone calls began to pour into the office, all from irate citizens demanding that she arrest him.

The rush to judgment without facts made her see more clearly how her own actions must have affected him.

Sam called again, less than an hour later, explaining

that Parker was now receiving death threats. "They're still gathering in the parking lot and the group is growing larger as we speak. I don't like this at all."

Neither did she. "Where is Parker now?" Rayna asked, a headache beginning to throb behind her eyes.

"Still in his room. I think he's probably afraid to leave because he knows McMartin will deactivate his key card. Hell, he's probably already done that. Otherwise, I think Parker would have packed up his things and took off on his motorcycle."

"No, he wouldn't," Rayna answered, certain. "Because if he did that, it would make him look guilty."

"You need to take steps to protect him." For the first time since she'd taken over as sheriff, Sam made a demand. "I'm really worried this situation is going to erupt in violence. Tensions are really boiling over."

"How do you know?" she asked, genuinely perplexed. "Haven't you been hanging out at the motel? Did you go out and talk to them? Or did you go into town?"

"I'm still here, trying to keep an eye on things. Not only did I go out and talk to Ted Sanders and his friends, but people have been calling me," he told her. "All damn afternoon."

"Calling *you*?" she asked, stung. "Why you instead of me? You're retired."

"I think they know that. They haven't called you because they know you and Parker have a thing going on."

"A *thing*?" Though she knew what he meant, her shock and outrage left her unable to say more.

"Semantics." Impatience deepened his voice. "Looks like that group of irate fathers gathering in the Landshark parking lot is doubling in size. Maybe tripling. I have a feeling if Parker comes out of his room, there'll be hell to pay."

"Seriously?" Heart racing, she realized once again, the speed gossip spread—like wildfire—managed to catch her off guard. "How many people?"

"I don't know. Several pickup trucks. And it's growing by the minute. It's time to put on your law-enforcement-officer hat," Sam barked. "You owe Parker some protection. Send Larry or someone, but get him out of here before trouble starts. Even if he refuses to leave."

Before she could respond, Sam hung up.

Stunned, she got up and went to get Larry. Halfway to his desk, she made the decision to deal with this herself, and have Larry stand by as backup. Her first task would be to disband the vigilantes in the parking lot. Her second, pay Parker a visit and have a face-to-face conversation. Even if Parker didn't want to talk to her, *especially* if Parker didn't want to talk to her. Because Sam was right. She owed Parker more than just protection. She owed him an apology. The more she considered the situation, the less likely it seemed he'd done anything wrong. Someone had probably used his photograph, easily obtained off the internet.

Speaking quietly, she filled Larry in on what was going on. Of course, he pushed to go with her. But she told him she wanted to handle this herself and that she'd call if his help was needed. With no choice, he nodded, his frown remaining.

When she pulled up at the Landshark, she realized Sam had been right about the tensions. Groups of middle-aged men gathered in the parking lot. Right now, it appeared they were simply having a tailgate-type get-together, but combine tempers with alcohol and things could escalate. Especially if Parker walked outside.

Parking, she got out of her cruiser and walked over to join them. She located Ted Sanders and approached him. "Hey there," she said, keeping her voice pleasant. "What's going on here?"

Ted narrowed his gaze, frowning. "We don't want trouble with you, Sheriff Coombs. But we intend to run this SOB out of town. Getaway ain't got room for people like him."

"I understand," she began.

"Do you?" Ted cut her off. "This is my daughter we're talking about here." He pointed toward the group of men, all watching them. "Their daughters, too. I know you're friends with him, but you can't tell me it'd be any different if he'd been messaging your little girl."

"We don't know for sure it actually was him." And then she explained about catfishing and cell phone records, touching lightly—very lightly—on the serial killer. "It's actually looking like it was someone else using his photograph."

Ted studied her for a moment, the indecision in his gaze telling her to be quiet and let him digest what she'd said.

"Are you sure?" he finally asked. "Because if it isn't him, then I want to know who the hell is doing this. If, as you mentioned, this guy is trolling for his next murder victim, you'd better get busy catching him."

She nodded. "That's my plan."

Shaking his head, Ted walked away and went to talk with the others. Rayna watched as several got on their phones while others climbed back into their pickup trucks and drove away.

After fifteen minutes passed, most of them were gone.

Rayna didn't dare let out a sigh of relief until the last man left. Then and only then did she straighten her spine and walk to the motel office, so she could let David McMartin know, too.

Though the motel owner started off indignant, after hearing everything she had to say, he allowed he might have been hasty to rush to judgment. "I'll go and apologize to Mr. Norton right now."

"Please wait a minute," she replied. "I need to apologize first."

Chapter 12

The next knock on his door made Parker tense up. A series of three staccato knocks. "What now?" he wondered out loud. Had Ted Sanders and his gang of pals finally gathered up enough courage and come to confront him? Good. He was tired of staying here in this little room like he had something to hide. Time to get all this nonsense out in the open.

Turning the dead bolt, he yanked the door open. "What do—?" He stopped, the words dying on his lips. Rayna, the slight breeze lifting her wavy red hair. She wore aviator sunglasses, which definitely made her look like a cop, but were also sexy as hell.

As usual, his heart stuttered in his chest at the sight of her. Until he remembered and steeled himself to be emotionless despite her charm. He glared at her, seeing his own scowl reflected in her mirrored sunglasses.

"I didn't expect to see you again so soon," he said, his voice sounding surly, even to himself.

"May I come in?" she asked, her voice soft, perhaps even contrite. Or maybe he heard what he wanted.

"Suit yourself." But he stepped back, making room for her to enter. Once she'd moved past him, bringing with her that vanilla scent, he let the door close.

"You're angry with me," she said flatly.

He crossed his arms. Since there was no point in denying the truth, he didn't bother to answer.

"I don't blame you." Digging in her pocket, she retrieved a sealed plastic baggie and handed it to him. "Your phone."

After accepting it, he took it out of the baggie and checked the charge before setting it down on the table. "Is there anything else?" he asked, managing to be excruciatingly polite while clenching his teeth. How he could simultaneously want to kiss her and yell at her, he wasn't sure.

"Yes." She lifted her chin, removed her sunglasses and met his gaze. "I'm sorry. I should have known better, especially as sheriff. That's one of the first things they teach us in the police academy. Stick with the facts and leave emotion and hunches out of it."

Gaze still locked on his, she swallowed, the motion of her throat drawing his attention. "And I should have known better as your friend."

Friend. He noted the word, but held back from commenting. He'd actually been foolish enough to think that what they'd begun to build together was much more than mere friendship.

Mistake number one.

Even now, watching as she tried to find the words to

explain away her actions, he still wanted her. Wanted her with an intensity that had him curling his hands into fists to keep from touching her. Mistake number two.

"Are you going to say anything?" she finally asked.

"What is there to say?" He kept his voice neutral, revealing none of the emotions battling inside his heart.

"Accept my apology?"

"Sure." He shrugged. "After all, I have to work with you in the continuing effort to find Nicole."

Slowly, she nodded. "Look, Parker…" The anguish in her voice had him taking a step toward her before he caught himself.

"I felt betrayed," she finally said softly. "After I ended that call with the Sanderses, I let what happened in the past guide my reactions today. I should never had done that. I know better. And I know you."

"Regardless of your job, you assumed I was guilty without even having all the facts," he pointed out, finally revealing some of the hurt he felt. "You didn't even question me. Just marched on in here, hurled accusations, demanded my phone and told me it's better if I cooperate. As if I was a stranger you'd arrested on the street. As if you didn't know me at all."

"I did." Nodding, she continued to hold his gaze. "And I'm admitting I was wrong. I've already talked to Mr. McMartin, as well as Ted Sanders and his friends. They've all been made aware that you weren't the one contacting the teenagers at the high school. Clearly, someone wanted to make it look like you were." She took a deep breath. "We will get to the bottom of this, I promise you."

"I'd rather you find Nicole," he said. "As far as I'm concerned, that's my top priority."

"Agreed." She put her sunglasses back on, hiding her eyes. "But I have a feeling the two might be intertwined. Whoever is contacting these young girls might be looking for his next victim."

Horrified, he stared. "That occurred to me, but since so far every woman he's murdered is from out of town, I figured whoever was doing this might be trying to throw you off his tracks. Because it seems he tends to grab women just passing through, women who won't be instantly missed. Why would he risk exposure by changing his method of operation?"

"That's a good point. We thought the same thing. Right now, I don't have an answer to that." She finally turned away, hand on the doorknob, about to go.

"Wait." He hated the desperation that clawed at him. "Admittedly, I'm an outsider, but what exactly are you doing to find this guy?"

"We're already working around the clock trying to locate Nicole." An evasive answer. "We're hoping to use this new information to get a lead on who's behind this."

He wanted specifics. "Like what, set up a sting operation? Have someone acting like a teenager contact this person pretending to be me?"

She grimaced, her mirrored glasses firmly in place. "That's one possibility. Like I said, we're working on it. I promise I'll keep you updated as much as I can."

"Thanks." An awkward silence fell. He wasn't sure what else to say. He moved to go past her, so he could open the door and show her out.

At the same moment, she turned to go, nearly colliding with him in her haste. Instinctively, he reached out to steady her, his hand grazing over the soft skin on her arm. That small touch nearly undid him.

"Parker…" She looked up at him, lips trembling. Heaven help him, but desire for her nearly broke his resolve, despite everything.

Something of his longing must have shown in his face. She lowered her sunglasses and took a step toward him, eyes huge. He saw his own raw need reflected back in her eyes.

"No." He dredged up strength from somewhere and twisted away. "We can't. Keep in touch if you hear anything new on the case."

The finality in his tone had the desired effect. She nodded, professional Sheriff Rayna back in place. "Will do," she said, letting herself out the door.

The lavender-vanilla scent of her lingered long after she'd left and made his mouth go dry.

That night instead of sleeping, he thought about calling her at least twenty times. He resisted, knowing they couldn't go back to the way things had been and simply pretend nothing had happened. Part of him wanted to—oh, how he wanted to—but he knew he couldn't take that awful sense of betrayal if it happened again. Once had nearly destroyed him.

To his surprise, Rayna called him right before he'd decided to give up, turn off the lights and go to bed.

"Are you busy?" she asked, the tremor in her husky voice making her sound slightly nervous.

"I'm glad to hear your voice," he blurted out, wincing after. "I was just about to go to bed."

"I should, but I don't think I'm going to be able to sleep," she said. "I decided to go for a walk but instead I got in my car and went for a drive. And well… I ended up at your motel."

His damn stupid heart skipped a beat or two. "Are you—?"

"In my car in the parking lot. I didn't want to just show up uninvited and unannounced." Her self-conscious chuckle, still low and throaty, had his body stirring.

Right then and there, all his resolutions went up in a blaze of pure lust.

"Come on in." He didn't even hesitate. "Another hour of sitting here alone and I'm going to go crazy." Craving her. He didn't say that out loud, but he figured she knew anyway.

"On my way."

Ending the call, he stared at his phone in disbelief. By the time she tapped lightly on his door, he was already hard. One deep breath, two. Steady. He opened the door and she stepped into the room, her wild, fiery hair matching her eyes. He met her halfway, claiming her mouth with his. The taste of her, sweet and sultry, filled his mouth, her scent swirled around them.

No words were needed. Kisses, caresses, these were enough.

Somehow, they shed their clothes. Apparently, she needed to feel his skin against hers as badly as he did, because the instant they were naked, she pushed him down on the bed and climbed on top of him. She stopped short, hovering close but not close enough. More than anything, he yearned to pull her up and over, so he could drive himself into her wet softness.

Instead, she gave him a sexy smile. "Wait," she said. So he did.

With eyes half-closed, he watched her take his

arousal in her small hands. She peered up at him, grinning, and then lowered her mouth over him.

Groaning, he tried like hell to keep himself still. But as she moved her impossibly perfect mouth, stroking him with her tongue, his body moved of its own accord and pushed into her. He wanted more, needed more, but not like this. This had him on the verge of losing control too quickly, too soon.

With a growl, he arched up, grabbed her arms and flipped her so she lay under him. Covering her with his body, nearly mad with need, he pressed himself against her, teeth clenched, hoping for enough self-control to take it slow.

"Oh, no, you don't," she said, smiling sweetly as she arched her body up into his. "I want it hard and fast and deep. Now."

Damn if he didn't oblige her.

She met him stroke for stroke, her wildness feeding his frenzied desire. They came together, he following her the instant she began shuddering, her body clenching his. After, they held on to each other, reluctant to let go.

"Will you ever forgive me?" she asked, mouth pressed against his chest, her soft voice a combination of both forlorn and satisfied.

"I'm working on it." He gave her an honest answer, while he breathed in the scent of her hair, helpless to resist the lure of her.

"Thank you." She moved her mouth over his skin, featherlight presses of her lips. "I know I should have stayed away, given you time, but—"

"Rayna." Raising her chin, he kissed her, cutting off her words. "I'm glad you didn't. I don't know what it is, this thing between us, but it's strong. More than physical, I think. Or at least that's how it seems to me," he amended. For all he knew, she could feel completely different.

"Same here," she told him, pulling him close for another lingering kiss. "Logically, I should totally stay away. But I couldn't stop thinking about you. I know how badly I hurt you and I'd do anything to make up for it."

Horrified, he recoiled, looking askance at her. "Is that what this is? Your way of making reparations?"

She frowned. "Is that really what you think? After the crazy passion we manage to generate between us? Seriously, Parker. I'm not here as some sort of repayment of a debt. I came because I wanted you. Needed you. As you can see."

This made him relax. Somewhat. He hated being vulnerable, yet that was how he felt around her. His emotions raw, open and exposed.

"Don't ever doubt me again," he ordered, tightening his arms around her. "Because I honestly don't know if I would survive it."

She nodded. "Me, neither. I know better than to jump to hasty conclusions. You deserve better." She bit her lip and looked down.

"I do." At her startled look, he laughed. "Seriously, though. If I'd been in your shoes, I might have taken that same leap of rapid logic."

Unsmiling, she shook her head. "You're not the sheriff. I am. That's not the kind of mistake I should be making, whether with you or with some stranger I don't even know. As a law enforcement professional, I've been taught to look at evidence. Instead, I let emotion over-rule my training. I assure you it won't happen again."

"It better not." He kissed her. Neither of them spoke for a while after that.

Leaving Parker sprawled out on the motel bed was harder than she'd thought. More than anything, she'd wanted to curl up next to him for the remainder of the night. But she had her home and her family to get back to, so she'd said a reluctant goodbye and slipped out the door.

Driving back to her house, she sank into a weird combination of self-doubt and contentment. Despite experiencing pure joy with Parker, she still questioned her own judgment. Should she be spending time with him? Rationalizing, she knew doing so on her own time was her right. What the two of them did after hours was their own business and hurt no one.

Except she'd managed to cause a great deal of hurt. She knew Parker well enough by now to understand how badly her distrust had cut him. All she had to do was to imagine the tables turned and her betrayal punched her in the gut.

Where did they go from here? Had they ever had any kind of future together? If so, did they still? She wasn't sure. Hell, she didn't even know what she wanted, except never to hurt him that way again.

At least she'd tried to make it better. After a disastrous day, she'd sucked it up and gone and apologized for her horrendous mistake. She hadn't been sure how he'd react—she wouldn't have blamed him if he'd thrown her out. Instead, Parker had seemed to actually accept her apology.

Or had he? The passion that blazed between them at the slightest provocation did tend to muddy the waters a bit.

Head aching, she pushed away all self-doubt and over analysis. Now she had work to do. In addition to attempting to locate Nicole and find out who'd murdered two women, she also needed to learn the true identity of whoever was stalking high school students, before something awful happened. Instinct told her all three were linked.

Ever conscious of a ticking clock, she called Sam. He picked up on the second ring. "I see you worked things out with Parker," he drawled. "I couldn't help but notice you leaving his room a few minutes ago."

"Couldn't help it, huh?"

"I was still sitting outside at the pool," he pointed out. "What's up?"

"I need your help," she said. "I know you're retired and all, but this thing just keeps growing by leaps and bounds. First, we're looking for a missing woman. Next, we're finding bodies and asking for the FBI's help in finding a serial killer. And now we've got someone messaging teenage girls. I can't help but think not only is this all tied together, but if we don't catch this perp, everything is about to get worse really fast."

"I agree. And I'll be happy to help, but Rayna, it'd be best if I stay in the background. If folks around here think they see me showing up and taking over, they're going to lose all confidence in you. Understand?"

"It makes sense," she agreed. "And that's completely up to you. However you want to work it. I just have a feeling I'm going to need all the help I can get."

As soon as she got home, she left a message for the

FBI agent, SAC Prado, who'd been her point of contact, filling him in via voice mail on the latest development. When she'd finished, she asked for a call back with any pointers he might have.

Inside the house, she found Wanda and Lauren engrossed in a movie. Even though it was way past her daughter's bedtime, Rayna went around and perched on the edge of the couch next to Lauren, pulling her close for a hug. She smelled like baby shampoo and sweetness, her beautiful daughter.

"Mom…" her daughter protested, squirming away. "I'm trying to watch the movie."

"Okay, okay." Rayna got to her feet and held up her hands. "I just wanted you to know I love you."

"I know," Lauren said, her attention already back on the television.

"She knows," Wanda chimed in softly. "We've already eaten and she's had her bath. I left a plate in the refrigerator for you to heat up. Go ahead and change and eat. We're fine here."

"Thanks, Mom." Reaching out, Rayna squeezed Wanda's shoulder. "It's been a really rough day."

After changing, she ate and joined her family in time to catch the ending of the movie. After putting Lauren to bed, reading her favorite bedtime story and kissing her before she turned out the lights, Rayna contemplated turning in herself.

"So early?" Wanda protested. "I was hoping we'd have a few minutes to talk. How about I pour us each a glass of wine and we do that?"

Rayna eyed her mother. Did Wanda seem slightly nervous? "Sure. But just one glass. I'm totally wiped out."

Nodding, Wanda actually checked her watch. "That'll be just about perfect. I'm expecting company in half an hour."

"Company?" Rayna eyed her mom. "This late?"

Instead of responding, Wanda grabbed the electric corkscrew and opened a bottle of Shiraz. After pouring them each a glass, she carried them over to the kitchen island. "Do you want to talk here or go sit outside on the patio?"

"You're making me nervous," Rayna said. "This sounds serious." And after the kind of day she'd had, the last thing she needed was more heavy news.

But this was her mother and she owed it to Wanda to listen.

"Might be," Wanda drawled, taking a long sip of her wine. "Sam and I are seeing each other."

"Sam?" Whatever Rayna might have expected, it certainly hadn't been this. "You and Sam are dating?"

Wanda blushed and took another sip of wine. "Yes." Looking down, she played with the bottom of the glass. "We actually started seeing each other before he moved down to the coast."

Shocked, Rayna nearly choked on her wine. "You were? How is it that I didn't know?"

"We didn't see the point of making anything public since we both knew it wasn't going anywhere."

"I get that, but I'm not just anyone. I'm your daughter. Why'd you feel the need to keep it a secret from me?"

With a shrug, Wanda downed the rest of her glass and refilled it. "I don't know. I mean, you were working for him at the time and it seemed…odd. And then you got elected to sheriff and neither of us wanted to give people any reason to gossip. You know how it is here in Getaway."

Slowly, Rayna nodded. "Wow," she said. "Just… wow."

"It's not a big deal," Wanda insisted. "We're just having a little fun before he heads back to the coast. Neither of us are looking for anything serious. You know, kind of like you and Parker."

"Point taken." Rayna leaned over and kissed her mother's cheek. "As long as you're happy, that's what matters."

"I am." Wanda's phone chimed. She glanced at it and smiled. "Sam is here. He doesn't know I decided to tell you."

Rayna jumped up and grabbed her wineglass. "I guess that's my cue to make myself scarce. Have a good night, Mom."

Once she reached her room, she closed her door. After scrubbing off her makeup and changing into her pajamas, she finished off her wine. She brushed her teeth, briefly considered watching TV, but decided to go to bed early instead. It had been a long day and tomorrow would most likely be the same.

The next morning, she woke early, feeling slightly refreshed. Since Lauren and Wanda still slept, she slipped out of the house with only a cup of coffee, figuring she'd grab breakfast at a drive-through along the way.

Barely after sunrise, she decided to stop at the café and enjoy a leisurely breakfast with a few farmers and truck drivers as company. By the time she paid her check and left, she felt restored and much more confident of her ability to face the day.

The minute she set foot inside the sheriff's office, her

phone rang. Special Agent in Charge Prado. Answering, she waved at Mary and went straight to her office, just in case she needed to take notes.

"What about setting up a sting operation?" Prado suggested. "Have someone pose as a high school girl and interact with this guy. She can agree to meet up with him. Of course, you and your officers will be there waiting so you can take him down."

"I love that idea," she replied, remembering how she and Parker had discussed it. "But this is a small town. Everyone knows everyone else. That, combined with the tiny size of my law enforcement force, means I don't have anyone who can pretend to be a teenager."

Prado laughed. "We do. Let me do some checking and I'll get back to you. Once I select an agent for the task, I ought to be able to send her down this afternoon or tomorrow. I'll try to make sure she meets the same physical criteria as the others. We'll need the full cooperation of the school, as well as their agreement to secrecy. She'll enroll there and pretend to be a student."

"Which means this could take some time."

"It might," SAC Prado agreed. "Then again, it might not. Whoever this unsub is, he might see someone new as ripe for the bait. I'm thinking he'll probably jump right on it."

"Let's hope so. Please give me a call when your agent is on the way."

"Will do."

Rayna felt much better once she finished the call. At least they had a plan of action. She couldn't wait to tell Sam.

Buoyed, she went and poured herself a cup of coffee and carried it back to her desk. Until she heard back from SAC Prado, she'd need to see what else she could dig up on the case.

In between that and lunch, she dealt with five phone calls, all from parents who had daughters at the high school. They'd heard about the person using Parker's picture making contact with their kids. At least this time they had their facts right. Instead of demanding Parker's head on a stake, they wanted to know what she planned to do about keeping their daughters safe.

She'd just finished answering the last parent's questions and hung up the phone when Larry tapped lightly on her office door. Rayna looked at him standing in the doorway, his expression warring between sympathy and resolve. "Sorry to bother you, Rayna," he said. "But I just got off the phone with Bertha Abernathy. Seems Donella didn't come home from school today. She isn't answering her phone and none of her friends have seen her." He checked his watch. "I know it's only been a few hours, but Bertha's worried. Says this isn't like her daughter."

A chill snaked up Rayna's spine. Ignoring it, she remained calm. "She's a senior, right?"

"Yep. Bertha said she just turned eighteen."

"Okay. This in itself doesn't seem too alarming," Rayna said. "You know as well as I do that teenagers are apt to disappear sometimes, especially if there is a member of the opposite sex involved."

"True." Larry scratched his head. "But considering what's been going on around here, I figured this time it might be something more serious."

Worse, Rayna corrected mentally. *Worse than serious.* Donella could be the serial killer's next victim.

"Since she's eighteen, even if we can find some sort

of evidence that could prove she'd been abducted," Larry continued, "Donella technically would be considered an adult, so we couldn't send out an Amber Alert."

"Correct." A dull headache began.

"I told Bertha we'd do some checking around, even if Donella can't be considered a missing person until twenty-four hours has passed." Larry scratched his neck. "Hopefully, she'll turn up and all this worrying will be for nothing."

"Hopefully so. So far, whoever has been killing those young women has stuck to grabbing nonlocals."

"I heard about Parker," Larry added, plopping down into one of the chairs across from her desk. "To be honest, I never really believed it was him. Call it a cop's instinct or whatever. But Parker didn't seem the type."

She nodded, and then winced as pain shot through her head. "I agree." And then she repeated her conversation with SAC Prado.

"Great idea!" Larry bounced up out of the chair, expression animated. "And it just might work." His expression darkened. "I just hope it's not too late."

"Let's hope so. I can only pray Donella simply took a joy ride to Lubbock or something. Since the other vics were all outsiders, I'm keeping my fingers crossed this mystery person didn't let things escalate so quickly." Though privately, she considered this highly possible, given that he'd been contacting high school students while posing as Parker.

"You and me both." Larry sighed. "It'll just about kill Bertha if anything happened to her baby."

"That's what's driving me crazy about the other victims," Rayna admitted. "How awful it must be for their families." She thought of Parker, refusing to give up on Nicole. "Nicole Wilson's older brother is dying of cancer. She was heading to Dallas to visit him when she vanished. I can only pray we're able to pull out a miracle in her case."

Larry nodded. "Since Parker's not here, I've been meaning to ask you what you think. Considering how long she's been missing, Nicole Wilson is probably dead, isn't she?"

Now it was Rayna's turn to squirm. "I hope not, but it seems highly likely. Both of these women were in their early twenties. Nicole had just turned twenty." She swallowed. "I'd prefer if you didn't mention that to Parker Norton, though. Not until we have some sort of lead."

"Understood." Larry grimaced. "I sure as hell hope this serial killer hasn't grabbed Donella. I've known that girl since she was four years old. Her parents are friends of ours, have been for years."

"I'm sorry." Rayna stood and approached Larry. She squeezed his shoulder. "If it helps any, I honestly don't feel like the serial killer took her. That would mean not only would this killer be deviating from his or her usual pattern—women in their early twenties who were not from around here—by taking someone whose family would immediately report her missing, running a much higher risk of being caught. You know that'd definitely turn up the heat."

"Which it has," Larry said. He'd straightened, a purposeful gleam in his eyes. "If she's around here, I'll find her. I'm going out to start looking now."

"You do that." Rayna shook her head. "I'm spending my afternoon fielding calls from the press. They've been sniffing around ever since we found the second body. I shudder to think of what will happen when they get wind of this."

"When it rains, it pours. Right, boss?"

"Right." Rayna shooed him out of her office. "You'd better get busy looking for Donella. Please give a call when you find her."

"Will do."

Once Larry left, Rayna went back to work editing her written statement for the press conference she planned to call for the next morning. Now that too would be on hold until they hopefully located the missing teen. If they didn't... She didn't even want to think about that possibility.

Sam pulled in right before Mary was about to go home for the day. He came directly to Rayna's office. "I heard about Donella. Hell, the entire town is up in arms. Bertha and a bunch of the other parents are organizing a search party. They wanted me to ask you if Parker Norton has an alibi. Despite everyone knowing it was someone else using Parker's picture, they still are suspicious of him."

"An alibi for when?" she asked, resisting the urge to rub her aching temples. "Does anyone know the exact time Donella went missing?"

"Bertha said she got up and got ready to go to school, just like always. She walked to the bus stop, but they checked with the bus driver and she never got on the bus. Bertha didn't know she was absent until she didn't show up at home after school. That means the time frame would be yesterday between seven and seven fifteen, when the school bus got to the stop."

"Have you asked him?" Rayna wanted to know. "I imagine he was either asleep in his room or having breakfast at the café. Either way, he's not really a suspect." She outlined what they'd learned from his phone.

"Rayna, you've got to find this missing kid and quickly. If this person is growing more determined and grabbing locals, he or she is going to kill her much more quickly."

The dull ache started again. "I know, Sam," she said quietly. "The only problem is that we don't have a single credible suspect. Even the FBI is stumped. They've given us a profile, so all we need to do is find someone who fits it."

"Yeah." The grimness in Sam's voice matched her mood. "Thanks for sharing that with me. I've started a list."

"Thank you," Rayna said. "Larry's doing the same. When you're done, why don't you and he compare notes?"

"No problem. I'd best get back to working on it." Sam crammed his Stetson back on his head and left.

Alone again, Rayna took a look at the notes she'd made for the press conference.

"Rayna?" Mary stuck her head in the office, her eyes wide. Seeing the normally composed dispatcher so rattled had Rayna jumping to her feet.

"What's wrong?" Rayna asked. "I thought you were headed out the door. Are you okay?"

"I was. But Serenity is here." Mary swallowed hard. "She says she has some important information for you about the missing-girl case."

A chill traveled up her spine. "Bad news?" she asked, figuring she might as well brace herself.

Mary frowned. "She didn't say."

"Send her back."

"Will do."

A moment later, Serenity appeared. Today, she wore some kind of ceremonial robe, made of pale yellow silk, embroidered and edged in tiny white beads.

"What a beautiful dress," Rayna said, standing. "How are you today, Serenity?"

"Exhausted," the older woman said with a sigh. "So many visions and visits from spirits. They wouldn't leave me alone until I came to give you the information."

"Have a seat." Indicating a chair, Rayna asked if she'd like anything to drink. "We have water and coffee. There's even a soft drink machine if you'd rather have something from that."

"I'm fine." Serenity lifted a flask. "I have ginger tea." She settled into one of the chairs, arranging her elaborate robe around her carefully.

"You've heard about the missing teenager?"

Serenity nodded. "Donella. She's alive and with Nicole."

"You're sure?"

"Positive. I've *seen* them, huddling together on a mattress on a concrete floor."

Rayna took a deep breath. "Did you happen to see where?"

"No. My visions don't work like that. I wish they did. I tried to push for more information, like seeing their captor's face or the outside of the building. Instead, the vision just faded away." Serenity shrugged. "The lesson is that I should be grateful for what I'm allowed to see. I'm just given information in flashes."

"I understand," Rayna said, struggling not to show

her disappointment. "If you see anything else, please let me know."

Standing, Serenity moved gracefully toward the door, her regal robe flowing as if a queen wore it. She turned, studying Rayna with sobering intensity. "I have one more message," Serenity said. "And this is for you personally. A certain kind of love only comes once in a lifetime. It's an amazing gift when you find it."

Not sure how to respond, Rayna nodded.

"Don't pretend you don't know what I'm talking about," Serenity continued. "If you're not careful, you will lose the greatest love you'll ever have." With that, she sailed away.

Watching her go, Rayna let herself drop back into her chair. Parker. Serenity had delivered a message about Parker. Time to be brutally honest with herself. She really cared about the man. Loved him even. But was that enough to risk everything?

Because thinking about that in the middle of all this other craziness made her head hurt even more and her stomach ache, she focused on the rest of what Getaway's local psychic had said. Because Serenity had been right more than she'd been wrong, Rayna made a conscious choice to believe her. Donella had been taken by the same individual who'd grabbed Nicole. And both were still alive. Hope—a rarity in the kind of work Rayna did.

A joyful thought, but also an unsettling one. She didn't know how long they had, but knew if they didn't find the girls soon, the odds were they wouldn't both stay that way.

Chapter 13

Parker couldn't help but notice the way people looked at him now. Like he'd already been tried and convicted. Venturing downtown, he'd straightened his shoulders and kept his head held high. He'd made sure to meet the gazes of everyone he spoke with, almost wishing someone would actually say something so he could respond.

He'd done nothing wrong. And he refused to hide in his motel room like a guilty man. He and Sam had gone to breakfast together. Parker supposed that helped, since if people wanted to acknowledge Sam, they had no choice but to do the same to him. Sam took care of that, refusing to let any of the people he knew try and get away with pretending not to see Parker.

At the Tumbleweed Café, all anyone wanted to talk about was the missing teenager, Donella Abernathy. They stopped by the table to chat with Sam, asking his opinion of the case and what exactly Rayna might be doing to bring the girl home.

When the third group of men left, Parker shook his head. "I'm going to see if I can organize a search," he said. "Get people together and fan out, looking for any clue where Donella might have gone."

Sam looked up from his eggs and bacon and studied him. "That'd be a bold move."

"Would it?" With a shrug, Parker turned his attention to the last of his pancakes. "I'm tired of having people eye me like they'd like to string me up."

"By the balls," Sam finished for him, a gleam of humor in his eyes. "I'm not sure what kind of reaction you'd get, saying you want to go searching."

"I don't care." Though Parker did. "What's more important is finding that girl. And who knows, if I do something proactive, it's possible people might stop looking at me that way."

Sam considered him over the rim of his coffee cup. "Go for it," he finally said. "I don't see how it could hurt. And who knows, you might help."

Though Parker hadn't been asking for permission, he always appreciated his uncle's insight. "Would you like to participate?"

"Now you're thinking." Sam grinned. "With both me and Rayna vouching for you, people can't really doubt you."

"Maybe not," Parker allowed. "But that wasn't why I asked. You know people. I don't. I could really use your help. I'd like to start the search this afternoon, around two."

"In the heat of the day? Why not wait until morning, when it's cooler?"

"Because I'm not sure how much time Donella has," Parker said. "From what Rayna has said, the first twenty-four hours are crucial."

"True. Point taken." Sam pushed to his feet, tapping on his water glass with his fork. "Everyone, listen up," he drawled.

The restaurant went silent. Even the sound of the cutlery clattering on plates stopped.

"My nephew here, Parker Norton, and I are putting together a search for Donella Abernathy. I'll have a map drawn up, sectioned into coordinates. Anyone who wants to participate, meet up at the steps of city hall at two today. We'll be assigned areas to groups of four or five, depending on how many people show up to help. Tell your friends, your neighbors. Let's get this girl back home where she belongs."

At first, no one spoke. Looking out over the group of diners, Parker saw some thoughtful looks and a few frowns, but as people started talking again, he swore an undercurrent of excitement rippled through the crowd.

"You just might have got yourself a search party," Sam said. "I'll help you get that map and get it marked off in sections. We need to pick up some air horns, too—maybe we can borrow some from Jason at the Army Navy Supply Store."

"Air horns?" Wondering if Sam was teasing, Parker eyed the older man.

"Yeah. That way, if anyone finds her, they blow the horn to alert the rest of us."

The waitress came by and dropped off their check. Parker grabbed it, shaking his head as Sam reached for his wallet. "It's on me," he said. "You drove."

Sam thanked him. "We're going to stop by the office supply store. I'll need to make some copies once I make a map of Getaway and divide it into sections."

After they finished running errands, they stopped back by the motel so Sam could take a nap. When Parker teased him about that, Sam winked. "My lady friend keeps me up all night," he said. "I've got to get my beauty sleep one way or another. I'll pick you up at one thirty or so."

Once Sam had disappeared inside his room, Parker hopped on his bike and went for a ride. He left Getaway behind and took the interstate, cruising past sunbaked fields and flat farmland that stretched for miles.

By the time he turned around to head back to Getaway, he felt ready to tackle anything. Including finding a missing girl while she was still alive.

Grabbing a couple of tacos at the drive-through for lunch, he ordered extra for Sam. Once back at the Landshark, he spotted Sam dozing in a lounge chair by the pool. At least his uncle had pulled the chair under one of the large umbrellas so he wasn't melting in the hot sun.

He opened his eyes when Parker walked up. "You smell like Mexican food."

"That's because I stopped for tacos. I got you a couple, if you're hungry."

Sam sat up. "I could eat."

They ended up sharing a shaded picnic table and having their lunch outside in the heat. Sam barely even seemed to perspire, while Parker started wishing for air-conditioning ten minutes after sitting down.

Evidently, Sam noticed. "We're going to head out in half an hour, if you want to go back to your room and get ready. I'll meet you in the parking lot."

"Sounds good." Not bothering to hide his relief, Parker went straight to his room.

A few minutes in the ice-cool air-conditioning helped tremendously. He changed, going for plain T-shirt and jeans, along with his most comfortable boots, since he knew he'd be doing a lot of walking. He crammed a Dallas Cowboys cap on his head. By the time he had to meet Sam, he felt a hundred percent restored, ready to face the baking Texas heat again. He filled his water jug, grabbed a small bag of almonds and stuffed them in his pocket, and headed out the door. He put on his Ray-bans as he went.

Sam waited, Stetson pulled down low, lounging against his car, once again oblivious to the hot sun. He looked up as Parker approached, and grinned. "Looks like you're ready to do some hiking, except for one thing."

Perplexed, Parker eyed his uncle. "What's that?"

"Your hat." Sam pointed. "It should be a Texans cap."

Parker laughed. "I guess we'll just agree to disagree."

Sam harrumphed and unlocked his car. "Let's go."

Parker eyed the older man's alligator boots. "Are those comfortable enough to do this kind of walking? I'd hate for you to ruin them."

Now it was Sam's turn to laugh. "Boy, I ain't searching on foot. I'm too old for that. I plan to wait at city hall—central base—and let people report their progress."

Shaking his head, Parker smiled. "Can't say I blame you. I just hope we get enough people to man a proper search. If we don't, we're just going to have to double up on quadrants."

"Oh, you'll have enough people," Sam said. "Even

if they just show up out of curiosity to see you. But people in this town care, and everyone wants to find that poor girl."

"I do, too," Parker replied. "And I sure hope you're right."

When he and Sam pulled up at city hall, Parker eyed the ten or so gathered people and sighed. "Well, I'm thinking you were wrong. But at least a few of them showed up."

"It's early yet." Ever the optimist, Sam held up his stack of notecards. "I need at least twenty-four, so I can have six groups of four. With you and I, we're half-way there."

Parker spotted a patrol car, parked discreetly over to the side. "Looks like Rayna sent some of her people out here."

"It's policy," Sam replied. "Just in case. You never know if things might go south."

"Go south how?"

Sam only shrugged. "No idea. Look." He pointed. "There's two more. See. I told you you'd have enough people."

"Should we go join them?" Parker eyed the assembled group, eager to get going.

"Not just yet." Sam glanced at his watch. "We're early. Let's keep an eye out and see how many more show up."

Eyeing the bright blue, cloudless sky, Parker wondered why Sam didn't want to stand around in the sun since he seemed to love it so much. Either way, Parker was good sitting in the air-conditioned car a few more minutes, especially since the outside thermometer showed 102. Typical Texas heat. Since he'd lived here almost his entire life, he'd gotten used to it, though he couldn't honestly say he enjoyed it.

A few more people walked up. Checking his watch, Parker touched Sam's shoulder. "I'm going to go meet up with them."

"Wait just one second." Sam pointed. "A bunch of pickup trucks just pulled up. Looks like the same group that got together in the motel parking lot. I sure hope they're not here to start any trouble."

Concerned, Parker said, "Me, too. But I'm going to act like everyone is here for the right reason—finding Donella Abernathy. That's what really matters."

"Agreed." Sam pushed open his door and got out. "Are you coming or not?"

Nodding, Parker followed his uncle.

As they approached the assembled group, Parker saw more and more people arriving from the parking lot. Five minutes remained until the announced meeting time, and as he counted at least thirty people, he knew they'd have enough to split into the agreed-upon areas.

Sam wandered among the small crowd, shaking hands and exchanging pleasantries. Everyone appeared generally glad to see him; a testament to his popularity even after he'd retired and moved away.

Again, Parker eyed the parked patrol car, wondering who Rayna had chosen to send to keep an eye on the search. He couldn't help but wonder if she might have even come herself. He did a quick head count, surprised to realize there were close to fifty people.

At exactly two, Parker climbed up on the steps and used one of the air horns Sam had insisted they buy. The strident sound certainly got everyone's attention.

"Thank you so much for coming out to help search

for Donella Abernathy," Parker began. "We're going to split up into smaller groups and search assigned areas. Sam and I drew up some quadrants, so we're going to ask you to pair up in groups of eight people. There will be a couple of people left over. If you can't figure out where to go, come see me."

Obligingly, people started to move around, aligning themselves with friends or neighbors. Sam had taken a seat on a metal bench, watching it all with a benevolent smile.

Parker finally relaxed somewhat. He hadn't realized until now how tense he'd been with the uncertainty of how his attempt to help would be perceived.

Apparently, Rayna had gotten the message out that he'd been cleared.

"All right, everyone," Parker called out. "Looks like we're just about ready. I'm going to come around and hand out your area assignments."

"You." A woman's voice rang out, her tone strident and accusing. "I saw you with Donella the day she disappeared. And I heard you were contacting her and a bunch of other girls up at the high school."

Stopping in his tracks, Parker frowned. "I'm not sure who you think you saw, but it wasn't me. I've never met her. And as to the rest, someone else was using my picture on social media. I've been investigated and cleared. Now, let's get back to the map and the search quadrants, why don't we?"

"No." She crossed her muscular arms. "I don't think any of us should have to take orders from someone like you."

"Come on, now," Parker urged. When he'd anticipated any problems, he sure as hell hadn't foreseen this. Did people just make up stuff in order to fan the flames of gossip?

It definitely appeared that way.

The burly woman cocked her head, eyeing him like she might be considering whether or not to take a swing. "We need to force the sheriff to lock this man up. Who's with me?"

To Parker's disbelief, the crowd began to shift into two groups instead of eight. Clearly, there were those who sided with her, and those who did not.

Why wasn't Sam getting involved in this? A quick glance at the older man revealed his uncle still sitting, watching quietly, apparently completely unconcerned.

"Lock him up," someone murmured. A few others picked up on that and repeated it.

Fine. Parker straightened his shoulders and lifted his chin. "We're here to find a missing girl," he reminded them. "If you want to gossip and tell lies about me, do it some other time. Now please, sort yourselves out into groups of eight people or so. Once you've done that, I'll hand out the search areas and we can get this show on the road."

Rayna could tell, even from inside her squad car, the instant the mood changed in the small crowd gathered near the city hall steps. One moment, the slowly growing group had been milling around while Sam passed out assignments, and the next, they appeared to be taking sides.

Heart pounding, Rayna took a deep breath and got out of her car. Strolling nonchalantly up to the crowd, she kept her ears open for some sort of hint as to what was going on. Less than ten seconds later, she got it.

"That's why you're trying to organize a search," a man wearing an Astros cap shouted, his face red. "To distract us from the fact that you're the one who took her."

Whoa, Nelly. Rayna eyed Parker, who seemed torn between anger and explanation. He seemed to settle on the latter. "I didn't take her. I wanted to organize this search so we could find her and bring her home, before anything happened to her."

"Lies," a frizzy-haired older woman with no makeup shouted. "I saw you talking to her. I know you're the one who grabbed her. I know it."

"Elizabeth Green," Rayna called out the woman's name. "Mind telling me exactly what's going on here?"

Finally spotting Rayna, Parker froze.

Face red, Elizabeth stormed over. "I know he's your boyfriend, but you need to arrest him." She pointed to Parker, her finger trembling. "We can't allow a serial killer to be trying to organize us to search. That would leave poor Donella no better than dead."

The group that had begun gathering around them murmured agreement. Rayna shook her head and took a deep breath. "First off, Parker Norton is not a serial killer. I've already established the fact that he's not the one who tried to contact the high school girls. Were you not aware of this?"

Instead of backing down, Elizabeth only narrowed her eyes. "I wasn't, but that doesn't matter. I *saw* him talking to Donella the very day before she went missing. Now, explain that." Several of the onlookers muttered similar accusations.

Shocked, Rayna kept her face expressionless.

"Parker?" she asked, turning to face him. "Is there an explanation you'd like to offer?"

"I don't know Donella," he said. "As far as I'm aware, I've never met her." His crossed arms and closed-off expression told her he didn't expect to be believed.

Elizabeth glared at him, clearly fulfilling his expectations. "Liar," she snarled. A few other people shouted out other, even less complimentary names.

"Okay, people." Rayna kept her voice firm. "That's enough. Elizabeth, do you have any proof that it was actually Parker you saw with Donella?"

Slowly, the other woman shook her head. "Proof like what?" she asked sullenly.

"Any other witnesses?"

"Well, Donella. But clearly, she's not here." Elizabeth smirked, her blue eyes hard.

"What time?" Rayna asked. "What time did you see Donella having this conversation?"

"I don't know. After school. Maybe around three. Yesterday."

"Donella never got on the school bus to go to school that morning," Rayna said. "The school marked her absent. Now you're telling me you actually saw her *after* school?"

For the first time, Elizabeth wavered. "Um, I…"

The boisterous crowd went silent.

"Did you or did you not see her after school, Elizabeth?" Rayna pressed. "This could be very important information and we'd need to get it to the FBI as soon as possible."

Face red, Elizabeth looked down. "I didn't see her," she mumbled. "I just…"

Rayna waited, but the other woman didn't appear to want to finish. "You just what?"

"Wanted him arrested." Elizabeth pointed a trembling finger at Parker. "We all know he's your lover. But you shouldn't give him special privileges due to that."

With an effort, Rayna kept herself calm. "I don't give him any special treatment," she said. "Believe me when I tell you that he has been thoroughly investigated, both by my department and by the FBI. He's been cleared of all wrongdoing."

"Oh," Elizabeth responded, her voice very small. "May I go now?"

Though Rayna briefly considered giving the woman a lecture on the dangers of lying to the sheriff, she also knew Elizabeth had likely had enough public humiliation to last a lifetime. She nodded, unsmiling, and watched as Elizabeth hurried away to her car.

"As for the rest of you," she said, making sure her voice carried. "Don't you have a search to get to? Parker, I'll step back and let you continue what you were doing."

Something flickered in his eyes—relief or gratitude, she couldn't tell—and he nodded. "Thank you."

He turned and faced the crowd. "Since no one seemed interested in forming groups, I'm just going to count off and assign them." He pointed to one person at a time, stopping when he got to eight. "You're group number one. Here is your assigned search quadrant. And use this air horn to let everyone know if you locate her."

Rayna watched as he did the same thing with the next eight people, and the next. She finally retreated back to her squad car, gladly getting inside and turning the engine on so she could let the AC run. She eyed Sam, still sitting on the metal bench, clearly basking in the hot sunshine. As long as she'd known that man, he'd loved the summer heat.

Her cell rang, caller ID revealing SAC Prado with the FBI. She answered, ever hopeful for good news. "We've been going over the list your officer gave us of people who might match the profile we provided. So far, I haven't crossed any of them off, but I do have a question about someone who was not on the list."

Interesting. "Go ahead."

"What about the former sheriff?" SAC Prado asked. "The guy that hired you as a deputy. How well do you know him?"

"Sam?" Rayna smiled. "I trained under him years ago at the academy. And then worked for him before he retired and I ran for sheriff. Why do you ask?"

Instead of answering, Prado asked another question. "During your association with him, did he ever make any advances toward you, touch you inappropriately, anything like that?"

Horrified, Rayna shook her head. "Of course not. Sam's not like that. He's a completely honorable man." Then, as she realized why the FBI agent was asking, she shook her head again. "Surely you're not considering Sam as a suspect?"

"We can't rule anyone out yet. And it might be totally coincidental, but Sam arrived in town and then the teenager went missing."

"True, but the other missing young woman, Nicole Wilson, disappeared long before Sam came back."

"Good point. Sam doesn't really fit our profile anyway. But I'm a big believer that you can't be too thorough. For now, I'll move his name to the not-likely list."

"I agree." Rayna couldn't believe how relieved she felt.

"Any other potential suspects you want to mention?" Prado asked. "We honestly feel like we're spinning our wheels while we wait for this unsub to screw up and make a mistake. Which he will. We've just got to make sure we catch him."

"Not yet," she admitted. "We've got an organized search going on right now for the teenager who disappeared. We're hoping we can bring her home soon."

"Better do it quickly," Prado said. "You know as well as I do that the first twenty-four to forty-eight hours are the best chance you have of finding her alive."

Chapter 14

As luck would have it, Parker ended up with the search area that included Old Man Malone's place. Since the older gentleman had shown up to take part in the search, Parker had included him in the final group, which he planned to lead.

"Way to go back there," Mr. Malone muttered, elbowing him. "You showed that woman. People like that, making up lies to suit their own purposes, need to be arrested. As a matter of fact, I'm going to suggest that to Rayna next time I see her."

Though privately, Parker agreed, he refrained from commenting. Since his group had been comprised of the ones who were left, he had ten people total. He handed everyone a copy of their search quadrant. "Let's go," he said. Some of the other groups had piled into cars and driven to their assigned areas, but this one was close enough that they could walk to it.

"My street is on here," Mr. Malone said, hurrying to keep up. "I think you should let me be the one to knock on my neighbor's doors."

"Fine with me." Parker shrugged. "But not all of them. There's just too many. I figure we'll split off into groups of two or three and handle it that way."

"Mind if I join you?" a feminine voice asked from behind them. His heart jumped. Rayna.

"Hey there, sheriff." Old Man Malone grinned from ear to ear. "Way to go not letting those idiots back there shame you into not having a life."

A dusky hue spread over her pale face, but she smiled and nodded. "Thanks. I still can't believe that woman lied about Parker for no valid reason."

"Lock her up." Mr. Malone chortled. "Stupid is as stupid does."

Her lush mouth twitched as she tried not to smile. "I'll keep that in mind," she said, her gaze meeting Parker's. "Are you okay with me coming along?"

"Why wouldn't I be?" he asked, conscious of several others watching. "It's great to have law enforcement with us, just in case we get some pushback. Our area is mostly residential, with only a few houses that are on the outskirts of town."

"Sounds good." She fell into step next to Mr. Malone. "Where's your metal detector?" she asked.

"In the trunk of my car," he admitted. "I didn't think it would be helpful in this kind of a search. After all, we're looking for a person, not an object."

"True," Rayna said. "But last time you managed to find that cell phone. Something like that might help point us in the right direction."

The old man brightened. "I didn't think about that.

After this search is over, I might just go back out on my own."

"I might just go with you if you do," Parker interjected.

"Sounds good," Malone replied.

"Parker?" A man wearing a black cowboy hat walked up. Parker thought he recognized him as one of Ted Sanders's friends who'd gathered in the motel parking lot. "I just want to apologize to you for the way you've been treated," he continued. "You came here trying to find your friend's sister and instead, you've been accused of just about everything under the sun." He held out his hand. "I'm really sorry about that."

Parker shook his hand. "I appreciate that, man."

They'd reached the neighborhood they needed to search. "Fan out, two or three together," Parker ordered. "Knock on doors, talk to people, ask questions. If you see anything suspicious, don't confront the person, just come back here and talk to the sheriff."

"Exactly." Rayna nodded her agreement.

"Let's go, people," Mr. Malone chimed in. "Who wants to buddy up with me?"

As people paired off and walked away, Parker found himself alone with Rayna. "I guess we're a pair," she said, her smile a bit too bright. "Let's take the houses over there."

"Wait." He caught at her arm. "I need to thank you for stepping in back there. That situation had the potential of getting ugly fast."

"Just doing my job. Elizabeth is kind of a dramatic person and prone to exaggeration. Everyone knows that about her, but this is the first time I know of where she's been caught in an out-and-out lie."

"I mean for believing in me," he said quietly. "Several people apparently took her at her word when she lied about seeing me with the missing girl."

She gave him a sidelong glance and shrugged. "I told you I wouldn't make the same mistake again."

They'd reached the first house and trudged up the steps onto the large front porch. Parker pressed the doorbell and stepped back, waiting for the door to open. When it finally did, an elderly woman stood there beaming at them. "My neighbor Mr. Malone said people might be coming by. While I haven't seen anything strange, I made cookies and a pot of tea. Would you like to come inside and have some?"

"I wish we could," Parker replied, genuine regret in his voice. "But we're trying to find a missing teenager and can't stop looking right now."

Her face fell. "I understand." Then she brightened. "How about I give you some cookies to go." She turned around without waiting for an answer and disappeared inside her house.

Rayna and Parker exchanged amused looks.

"She's a really good baker," Rayna whispered. "Her cookies are amazing."

The older woman returned, carrying two baggies filled with cookies. "I wasn't sure what kind you liked, so I gave you one of each. There are chocolate chip, oatmeal raisin and peanut butter."

"Thank you so much." Accepting them both, Parker handed one of the baggies to Rayna. She also asked the woman if she was certain she hadn't seen any sign of Donella. When once again the answer was negative, Rayna thanked her and side by side, they walked to the next house.

"You have no idea how much I want to eat this," she commented, holding up the baggie. "I love oatmeal-raisin cookies."

Their gazes met and held. If she only knew how badly he wanted to kiss her. Time and place, he reminded himself, lifting up his own cookies. "I'm sure if you have one, it won't impede our search."

This made her laugh.

At the next house, no one answered, though he rang the doorbell several times. A dog barked somewhere inside, but clearly no one was home.

As they walked down the sidewalk, Rayna slipped her hand into his. For a second, his heart stuttered in his chest and he froze, but he managed to continue moving and acting as if this was an ordinary occurrence.

"This feels...right," she said, smiling up at him. "Since everyone keeps calling you my boyfriend, we might as well take this public, don't you think?"

He wanted to ask her what *this* was exactly, but her cell phone rang. Pulling her hand free from his, she gave a small self-conscious laugh and glanced at the screen. "I need to take this," she said. "It's Ted Sanders."

Though hearing the name made him tense, he nodded.

Rayna only stayed on the phone for a second, saying very little. When she ended the call, she turned to face him. "You're not going to believe this," she said incredulously. "Donella Abernathy showed up at Ted Sanders's ranch."

He spoke out loud his first thought. "Maybe it's time to consider Ted a suspect."

Though she gave him a sharp glance, Rayna didn't comment.

Instead, she gestured at the others still knocking on doors up and down the street. "You'll need to call off the search. Bring everyone in and tell them Donella has been found, but not where. I need to head out there."

"I want to go with you," Parker said. "Sam's still waiting at city hall. I'll let him get everything shut down."

"He'll enjoy that," Rayna finally said. "Though I'm not too sure how Ted Sanders will react to you showing up at his place."

Parker shrugged. "Excuse me for not really giving a—"

"We're done with this block," Old Man Malone interrupted. "Ready to move on to the next."

"No need," Rayna said. "Donella Abernathy has been located. She's alive and safe."

"Wahoo!" the older man shouted. He grabbed the air horn from Parker and used it. Not once, not twice, but three times.

Immediately, all the other searchers came running.

"They found the girl!" Mr. Malone told them, his cracked voice now jubilant. "She's alive and safe."

Everyone started talking at once. Shaking her head, Rayna touched the old man's arm. "We're going to ask Sam to make sure all the other searchers know. Would you mind helping him with that?"

"I'd be honored." His rheumy eyes sparkled. "Let's head back now, y'all," he told the others, practically shouting over all their voices.

Back at city hall, Parker stood back while Rayna spoke with Sam. His uncle nodded, expression still serious, and then eyed Parker. "Are you sure taking him along is a good idea?" he asked. "You know as well as

I do that we don't usually allow citizens to ride along on things with this sensitive of a nature."

"It's fine," Rayna insisted. "Ted Sanders is there, too. And Parker's been involved in this since the beginning, sometimes involuntarily, so I think him coming along is vital."

"Your call." Sam shrugged. "I'll take care of getting everyone back here and pass along the good news. Now, skedaddle."

Rayna spun around without another word and marched over to her patrol car. Halfway there, she looked back over her shoulder at Parker, and lowered her aviator sunglasses. "Are you coming?"

On the drive out of town, Rayna fiddled with the radio, made a few calls to let Larry and the others know the situation and finally turned to Parker. "I just want you to know that I'm going to have to ask Donella if she can ID you. I'm telling you now, so you won't be shocked or upset."

"Fine by me." Parker understood and appreciated the heads-up.

"And for the time being, I'm going to have to ask you to stay in the background. No questions, no comments, just quiet observation. This is really important and unless you agree, I can't allow you inside."

"You know, this is probably the first time in my life I've ever wished I was a cop," Parker groused. "I don't like it, but I get it. So yes, I agree to remain a silent observer."

Her smile almost had him smiling back. Almost. But all he could think of was the possibility that Donella had escaped the same man who had Nicole. And if that turned out to be the case, would she be able to lead them to him?

When they arrived at the ranch, Ted himself let them in. He glared at Parker, but said nothing, leading them into his kitchen.

Donella sat in one of the chairs, her hair stringy and tangled, wrapped in a thick blanket despite the summer heat. She looked up when they walked in and even attempted a smile, though she failed miserably at that.

"Are you prepared to make an arrest?" Ted asked Rayna, keeping his voice low, though Parker could hear. "If she points out your friend here, will you be able to cuff him and lock him up."

Without taking her eyes off the teenager, Rayna nodded. "I doubt it will come to that, but yes."

"Donella, have you ever seen this man before?" Ted asked, pointing at Parker. His closed-off expression showed what kind of answer he expected to hear.

Eyes red and swollen from crying, Donella squinted up at him. "No, sir. I mean, several of the girls at school were Snapchatting with a guy who looks like him. But I never did."

"What about in person?" Ted pushed. "Ever seen him in person before today?"

Slowly, Donella shook her head, wincing as if the slight movement hurt her. "No. Should I have?"

Rayna moved to intercede, shooting Ted a furious look. "To put this as clearly as possible, is this man the one who kidnapped you?"

Donella's swollen eyes widened. "No. He's too tall and not fat enough, for one thing."

"Thank you." Rayna smiled gently. "Can you tell us where you were? Any idea at all?"

"I have no idea." Again, the young girl shook her head. "It was always so dark." Her large brown eyes welled up and she began to weep again. "I just want my mama."

"She's on her way," Ted promised. "I called her as soon as I realized it was you."

"Thank you." Visibly struggling for control, Donella took a deep breath. "I can't believe I really escaped. The basement… I think we were in a house—the basement window got unlocked. I saw it and tried to jump up and reach it, but it was too high."

As she peered up at Rayna, Donella's mouth moved, but nothing came out except a sob. "Please, Miss Rayna. You've got to find him. I'm afraid he's going to kill Nicky. She let me stand on her hands so I could reach the window. She helped me escape, but couldn't get out herself." She hung her head, crying again. "I ran away and left her there. Please, please find Nicky and get her away from him."

Nicky? Parker took a step forward, barely managing to refrain from asking. A sharp glance from Rayna stopped him in his tracks, helping him remember his promise.

"Who?" Rayna asked, her voice tender. "Was there someone else there with you?"

"Yes." Donella's head bobbed up and down. "Her name is Nicky. She said only her older brother calls her that. She's been there a few weeks. For whatever reason, he kept her longer than any of the others. She's gotten really skinny and is sick. She coughs so much I'm worried she might die. Either way, I think he's fixin' to kill her. He was going to make me take her place."

Parker clenched his jaw and sucked in air. It took

every ounce of self-control he had not to speak. Every frickin' ounce.

"Who's *he*?" Rayna prodded. "Did he happen to give you a name?"

"No." Donella shook her head, sending her stringy hair moving. "We had to call him Boss."

"Boss," Rayna repeated. "Can you tell me what he looked like?"

"He's older—at least thirty," Donella said. "Kind of round." She cast a quick glance toward Ted Sanders. "I think he wears glasses, but I'm not positive. He kept the room so dark, it was hard to see."

"Were you on a farm or somewhere in town, do you think?" Rayna continued her line of questioning.

"I... I don't know." Donella started to cry again, this time silent, fat tears streaming down her dirty cheeks. "When I got out of the basement, I ran. There were fields, lots of fields. I didn't know where I was, so I kept going. I was so afraid he might find me."

Aware he'd be breaking his promise, Parker stepped forward anyway, kneeling next to her. He had to know for sure. He got out his phone and showed her a photo on the screen. "Is this Nicky?" he asked, his voice gentle.

Still muffling sobs with one hand over her mouth, she bobbed her head up and down.

"It's going to be okay," Parker said, squeezing her shoulder lightly.

Just then the front door burst open and Bertha Abernathy rushed into the room, her husband, Elmer, trailing close behind.

She took in Donella, still bawling, and Parker's ineffective attempt to comfort her. "Get your hands off my daughter," she demanded, spinning around to glare at Rayna. "Why isn't this man in handcuffs?"

Before Rayna could answer, Donella looked up at her mother and began sobbing even louder. "Mama," she called. "Mama."

Bertha turned back to her daughter. "My baby girl!" she shouted. "Alive!" She ran to Donella, throwing her arms around her daughter in a tight hug. The two of them began sobbing so hard their words were unintelligible. Elmer tried to fit himself in, and finally Bertha allowed him. The three Abernathy family members rocked and cried, leaving Ted and Parker and Rayna to stand around awkwardly.

"Once they all calm down, I'll tell Bertha she has nothing to worry about with you," Ted finally said. "Man, I'm sorry about thinking the worst of you. When it comes to my girls, I can be pretty fierce."

Parker nodded, though he didn't say anything in the way of absolution. Not yet, at least. He wasn't quite ready.

"All's well that ends well," Ted finally said, jamming his hands into his jean pockets.

"It's not over, not by a long shot," Parker replied, his tone as firm as his resolve. "Donella mentioned my friend's sister Nicole. Nicole is the entire reason I came to Getaway in the first place. We've got to find her, and whoever grabbed her, before he decides to kill her."

Rayna insisted on driving Donella to the ER, waiting in the hall outside the examination room with her parents. Again, Parker remained silent, even going so far as to take a seat in the main waiting room rather than the smaller one behind the double doors. Part of Rayna—

the woman, not the law enforcement professional—wanted to go to him and take him in her arms.

Of course she couldn't. She had to be the sheriff right now. There was no other choice.

"I still don't understand why we're even here," Bertha grumbled, her arms crossed. "Donella already told everyone that he never touched her."

"I know. But this is just a precaution," Rayna told Bertha for the third time. Behind her, Elmer nodded his agreement. "We need to make sure he didn't hurt her in any way."

"She said he didn't touch her." Bertha's shrill voice contained both anger and angst. "I believe her."

"I do, too," Rayna soothed. "We just need to check her out, then she can go home."

Elmer spoke up. "Let the doctors look her over, Bertha. I'd rather know beyond a shadow of any doubt that our baby girl's okay."

Slowly, the tension in Bertha's firm jaw relaxed and she nodded.

The door opened and the doctor, a young female with large glasses and dark hair in a neat bun, asked Bertha and Elmer to come inside so they could speak in private. A few minutes later, Elmer emerged, beaming.

"She's fine," he said, clearly relieved. "We're going to take her on home. Bertha's helping her get dressed." He shook Rayna's hand. "I'm going to go fetch the truck." And he rushed off to do exactly that.

While she waited, Rayna called Larry on his direct line and asked him to make sure and have the entire crew assembled at the station. "I'll be there in thirty minutes," she said, checking her watch.

"Uh, yeah." Larry's normally calm voice was agi-

tated. "Mary needs to talk to you, right now." Without waiting, he put her on hold. A second later, Mary
picked up.

"Rayna," Mary said, alarm in her voice, "I've got
someone on the phone claiming to be Myrna Maple.
She says she's being held prisoner by her own son.
She sounded really weak, too, and hung up before I could
ask for more details."

Rayna froze. "I visited with Phillip Maple the other
day when I was out trying to drum up potential witnesses. He acted like everything was normal." She
cursed. "Mary, call Special Agent in Charge Prado
and let him know what's going on. Tell him I'd like the
FBI's help. I'll be there as quickly as I can. I'm leaving
now." She ended the call.

"What's going on?" Parker asked. While she'd been
talking, he'd crossed the room to her side. "I heard you
mention Myrna Maple's son."

Quickly, she filled him in. "There's the chance—and
keep in mind that this is a *chance* only—that Phillip
could be the serial killer."

His expression went hard. "Are you serious?"

"Well, we don't have much to go on," she admitted.
"It could be that he just snapped and did something to
his mother." While she spoke, she frantically did an
internet search on her phone, certain she could find a
photograph of him somewhere. Finally, she did. He'd
attended the Fourth of July parade, riding along in the
Cadillac convertible with his mother.

"I need to show this to Donella," she said. "Wait
here."

Before she could push through the double doors,
Bertha and Donella emerged, arms around each other.

"Donella, I have a really quick question," Rayna said. "Take a look at my phone. Have you ever seen this man before?"

Glancing at the screen, Donella started shaking. "That's him," she whispered, her mouth working. "I can't believe it. That's the man who kept me and Nicky in his basement."

"Thank you." Ignoring Bertha's glare, Rayna patted the teenager's shoulder. She pivoted, hurrying toward her car, while calling Mary and asking her to get a rush search warrant for Phillip Maple's home. "I don't care if you have to get Judge Waters out of the bath, do it. We don't really need one, since Myrna called asking for help, but I prefer to cover all the bases."

She busted outside, running. When she reached her cruiser, she realized Parker was right by her side. Shaking her head at him, she didn't argue when he climbed in the passenger side.

When they screeched in front of the station and parked, she rushed inside, gratified to see her entire force had assembled.

"I filled them in," Mary supplied. "And Judge Waters has issued an emergency search warrant."

"Good." Her officers were already suited up, just awaiting her orders. "I'll need two of you to stay here with Mary, in case something else happens in town that has to be handled. Any volunteers?"

No one raised their hands. She couldn't blame them. "Fine. I can't take the entire sheriff's department. Sid, you and Angel will remain here. Larry, Tom and Russell, I want you to go out there with me."

"I'm going, too." Parker stepped forward, his jaw firm.

The room went silent. All the deputies watched to see what Rayna would do.

"I can't allow you to come this time," Rayna said regretfully. "We have protocols for this type of thing. Bringing a civilian is against all the rules. We can't allow you to put yourself in that much danger."

"Then deputize me, or whatever you have to do. I will be an asset, I promise you. I have military training," Parker insisted, the hardness of his expression telling her this time, he wasn't backing down. "I did a lot of recon missions. Let me help." He took a deep breath. "As a bonus, I have my CHL, so I'm already armed."

"Mary already called the FBI," she began, looking for another excuse. Mary nodded.

"And they'll have to drive in from Lubbock or Midland or wherever," Parker said. "I figure they won't be able to be here for at least an hour, maybe more. You know as well as I do that time is of the essence."

"Agreed."

"But Parker," Larry interjected, clearly trying to be helpful, "we don't even know if Nicole is in there. It's entirely possible Phillip Maple just has a seriously unhealthy relationship with his mother."

"Donella Abernathy IDed him as the guy who held her captive. Didn't Mary tell you?"

Mary grimaced. "I tried. But there was so much information and I was trying to deal with the FBI, that I might have left something out."

The room erupted as everyone began talking at once. Just like that, several officers understood the stakes had been raised.

"We don't know if Nicole is alive," Rayna said softly. "I hope she is, but..."

"She is." Parker tapped his chest. "Gut reaction, Rayna. Serenity was right. She said Donella and Nicole were still alive. We need to get out there now. Phillip Maple is our guy."

Larry nodded in agreement. "I think he's right," he said. "And Rayna, deputize him. We need all the help we can get."

Taking a deep breath, Rayna looked around at her officers. "What do the rest of you think?"

Overwhelmingly, everyone voted to let Parker join them. Even Mary, who hesitated a moment before muttering "What the hell" under her breath. "Sam would vote yes, too," Mary said, her nose twitching. "This is a small town and we've always done things our way here."

Though she supposed she could call Sam and ask his opinion, they didn't have time. Especially if the reason Myrna's call had been cut off was because Phillip had discovered her making it.

"Looks like you're in," Rayna said. "I don't know about deputizing you, but please don't shoot anyone unless your life is in danger."

Solemnly, he nodded. "You have my word."

Chapter 15

Even though he had extensive training in this type of operation due to his time in the military, Parker planned to do his best to keep out of Rayna and her team's way. He'd learned the hard way how a lack of teamwork could screw with an operation.

Though if the chance arose to get in and rescue Nicole, he knew he would take it.

Three squad cars pulled up onto the Maple property, the fourth remaining at the station with Getaway's two remaining officers.

Rayna got out, gesturing to everyone else to take up position using their vehicles as makeshift shields. Which meant she thought there was a very real possibility Phillip was armed and should be considered dangerous. Even though they blocked the only way to drive out of the place, fields were on the other side of the house. It might seem unlikely their quarry would try to escape on foot, especially with a seriously weakened captive, but he knew enough to consider all and any possibilities.

"Phillip Maple." Rayna got on the bullhorn. "This is Sheriff Coombs. We have a search warrant and want you to come out with your hands raised."

The front door opened. Would this really go down so easily? But no, instead of Phillips, an elderly woman staggered out from the open door, which promptly slammed behind her. Attempting to walk toward them, she fell and went sprawling in the gravel.

Heedless of her own safety, Rayna went in at a crouching run and helped the woman to her feet. Half carrying, half urging her along, she brought her over toward the rest of them.

Once she was close, Parker kept the shock from showing on his face. Some of the other deputies weren't able to do the same. Myrna was filthy and stick thin, and her parchment skin displayed numerous bruises, some purple and red, others having already faded to pale yellow. Shaking, she could barely stand.

Rayna asked Larry to call for an ambulance. She got Myrna to sit in the passenger side of her vehicle. "Can you tell me what happened?" she asked, kneeling.

"Phillip's gone crazy," Myrna cried. "All this time, I thought he was being helpful, caring for me. I finally figured out he was putting pills in my tea. All I did was sleep. I took to my bed and he made sure I never got out of it."

She took a deep, shuddering breath. "When I stopped drinking the tea, he started beating me. I thought he was going to kill me."

Carefully, Rayna gave Myrna a soft hug. "Was there anyone else in there with you?"

Parker held his breath while he waited for her answer.

Myrna turned her rheumy eyes on Rayna. "Honey, there were several. He was always bringing young women home. The thing is, I never saw any of them leave." She began to go weak in earnest, wheezing as she tried to breathe. "I don't know what kind of monster my boy has become."

"I'm sorry," Rayna said.

Myrna's Adam's apple bobbed in her too-thin, wrinkled throat. "Please don't hurt him," she begged. "I know he's sick, but he's still my son. Don't shoot him unless you absolutely have to."

Parker stepped forward. "Ma'am, we'll do our best," he said. "Do you know if he has any young women in there with him right now?"

Nothing but confusion filled the elderly woman's eyes as she looked at him. "I... I don't know. It's possible."

His heart sank, though he tried not to show it. He met Rayna's gaze, noticing that nothing but a kind of quiet competence filled her beautiful and determined face.

Rayna nodded once before turning her attention back to her team. "Are you ready to go in?" she asked.

"Wait." Myrna gripped her arm. "I'm supposed to give you a message. I almost forgot—all the drugs he gave me must have muddled my mind. Phillip told me to tell you to leave. He sent me out, and he wants you to go."

"I'm sorry, we can't do that."

"He said if you don't, he'll kill the girl."

Everyone froze. "What girl?" Rayna barked. "I

thought you said you didn't know if he had someone else in there or not."

Confusion once again settled over Myrna's face. "Well, there must be. Or else why would Phillip have said that?"

For the first time Parker realized the old lady might be deliberately trying to fool them. Clearly, Rayna thought the same thing, judging by the way she shook her head in disgust.

Rayna gestured toward Larry and Tom. "You two, go around to the back. You two, take the east side, you two, take the west. The rest of you, come with me. We're going to try to go in the front door."

The most dangerous possibility. Of course. Rayna wasn't the type of leader who would send her people into hell and hang back herself.

"I'm going with you," Parker said, as if there'd ever been any doubt.

Drawing her weapon, she eyed Parker, who'd also drawn his. "Stay close to me."

He stared at her for a heartbeat, and then jerked his head in a quick nod. While he'd learned to take orders in the military, every masculine instinct he had urged him to protect her, not the other way around. Still, he understood the basic concepts of teamwork, and how one person refusing to follow orders could put all the others in danger.

Yet, he could see the flaws in Rayna's plan. He opened his mouth to tell her, but she cut him off with a single sharp glance.

The house would be surrounded. By Rayna's way of thinking, Phillip would either realize he had no way of escaping, and he'd surrender, or he'd try to go out with guns blazing. Clearly, the third possibility had not yet occurred to her.

Phillip could decide to go scorched-earth and burn it all to the ground. Parker had seen enough hostage situations go south to believe it very well could be the latter.

"Don't kill my son!" Myrna wailed. "Please. Give him a chance to turn himself in." She crumpled to the ground, crying out in pain.

Rayna rushed over to her and helped her up, half carrying her to the front seat of her car. "Sit here until medical help arrives. Please, let us do our jobs. We're trying everything we can before we resort to violence."

Once she'd walked away from the elderly woman, she shook her head. "This just sucks."

Parker took her arm. "What about hostage negotiation?" he asked. "Don't you think you ought to try that first? Before we rush the place?"

She stopped so quickly that he nearly mowed her over and raised a questioning brow as she eyed him. "Are you trained in hostage negotiation?"

"No," he admitted. "Though I've sat in on my fair share of them. What about you?"

"No training." She sighed. "But my people won't move until I give them the order." Reversing direction, she jogged back to her car and grabbed the bullhorn. Handing it to him, she nodded. "Give it your best shot."

Gratified by her trust in him, he accepted the bullhorn. "Phillip Maple, this is Parker Norton. I'm not with the sheriff's office. I want to talk to you about letting this end peacefully."

Nothing but silence. But then he hadn't expected Phillip to simply pop out of the house with his hands up.

"Do you have Myrna Maple's landline phone number?" he asked Rayna. "Maybe he'll talk to me that way."

"I can get it." Pulling out her cell, Rayna called Mary and asked for the information.

Parker waited with his phone ready. As Rayna called out the numbers, he dialed. Listening, he counted one ring, two, three and four. Just as he'd begun to believe Phillip Maple wasn't going to answer, Phillip picked up the phone.

"What?" Phillip snarled.

"Thank you for answering," Parker said calmly. "My name is—"

"Parker Norton. I know who you are. Sam Norton's nephew. You probably don't remember me, but we met once when we were kids."

"Did we?" Keeping his voice calm and respectful, Parker figured the other man was giving him an easy way to try and establish trust.

"Yeah. You were with your uncle at the fair. All the other kids wanted to be your friend."

Was that a trace of bitterness he heard in Phillip's voice? Parker decided to pretend he didn't notice. "I always felt so out of place around the kids who lived here," he said. One thing he'd learned early on was in this type of situation, sticking to the truth as much as possible worked best.

"I don't believe you," Phillip snarled. "You were always so cool, so happy. And everyone said you were nice. Friendly." He laughed, the sound not only devoid of humor, but full of menace, causing Parker's neck to tingle in warning.

"But not to me," Phillip continued. "When I finally got up enough nerve to try and talk to you, you acted like I was beneath you. A chubby, awkward boy in glasses. I bet you never knew you made me cry."

Confusion filled Parker. He didn't have any memory of meeting Phillip, never mind dissing him. In fact, even as a kid, Parker had made it a practice to always be as kind as possible to everyone.

Now, however, he knew better than to say that to Phillip.

"I'm sorry," he said instead. "I wish we could have a do-over."

Silence. Perspiring slightly, Parker waited to see how the other man would respond.

Rayna's radio crackled. "Awaiting orders," Larry said. "We're all in place."

"Hold tight," she murmured, turning away from Parker in apparent hopes of keeping Phillip from hearing. "Parker's talking to him now."

"I heard that." Phillip's voice had gone expressionless, devoid of any emotion. "And you tell your friend the sheriff if they don't get off my property, I'll kill this young woman."

"But you won't…" Parker bit back the rest of what he'd been about to say and cursed. "He hung up."

Rayna shook her head. "I think it's best if we go in, then."

Reluctantly, Parker concurred. "But at this point, the chance of him not harming Nicole is next to nothing. Why don't you call and try to talk to him one more time? He apparently has a grudge against me for something that happened when we were kids."

For a long moment, she considered him, her eyes narrowed. Finally, she nodded. "It's worth a try."

A siren sounded in the distance, getting closer. "The

ambulance," Rayna said. She turned to Myrna, still huddled in the front seat of her cruiser. "We're going to get you some medical help. They should be here any moment."

Heart rate accelerating, he nodded and turned nonchalantly away. He knew exactly what he needed to do. For this plan to work, timing would be everything. "Call him from your phone. If he has caller ID, I doubt he'll pick up from my number."

"Good thinking," she replied. "Read it off to me, please."

He did, watching while she punched it in. The instant she finished and turned away, he took off, running behind Rayna's back toward the house by way of the storage shed. He used the trees for cover, keeping his burst of movement short and quick. If Rayna took her focus off the call, she'd see him. He hoped he'd have a few seconds of time, because then she wouldn't realize what he'd done until it was too late to stop him.

When Phillip Maple picked up after only one ring, Rayna resisted the urge to turn to Parker and give him a thumbs-up. Instead, she kept her head down, concentrating on the call.

"This is Rayna Coombs," she said in response to Phillip's snarled greeting. "We've got your place surrounded. Why don't you do this the easy way and come out with your hands up?"

He unleashed a string of profanities that would have made a lesser woman blush. Rayna, however, had heard them before, though not all at the same time. She simply waited until he'd finished before speaking again.

"Seriously, Phillip. I know you don't want to do this

the hard way. It's your choice. You can come out of there alive or in a body bag. Which will it be?"

"How about a trade?" he asked, a smirk in his voice. "You for the last girl. She's pretty sickly anyway. I really don't think she's going to make it."

She thought about telling him how little she trusted him to do anything fair. Instead, she tried once again to be the voice of reason. "Even if I did that, what good would it do? Sure, holding a sheriff's deputy hostage might buy you some time, but in the end, you're still surrounded by armed law enforcement personnel."

"So what?" he scoffed. "The Getaway sheriff's department is already small. If it comes to a gun battle, how many of your people do you think I could take out?"

"The FBI is here, as well, Phillip," she lied. The fact that they were actually on their way was a mere technicality. "They got involved when you became a serial killer. And you know as well as I do that the FBI doesn't play games."

"If that's the case," Phillip responded, his tone silky smooth, "then I might as well go out in a blaze of glory. After all, as you say, I've got nothing to lose."

"That's not what I—"

Instead of listening, Phillip slammed the phone down, ending the call.

"Well, that didn't go well," she began, turning to tell Parker. The instant she realized she was alone, she understood what he had done.

Cursing under her breath, she radioed her team. "Looks like Parker might have gone in alone. I'm going in after him. Hold your position until notified. And if you see movement, don't shoot. Repeat, don't shoot."

"Boss, are you sure that's a good idea?" Larry asked. "Maybe we should—"

"I'm going in. End of discussion." And she thumbed the radio off.

Eyeing the house, she decided to take the way she guessed Parker must have—using the trees and storage shed for hiding places. She knew Phillip would be amped up, probably armed and watching for the slightest movement.

Though she wasn't pleased that Parker had taken his own initiative despite promising to obey orders, now that he had, she could only hope he'd managed to get into the house while she had Phillip on the phone. If he had, then there might still be a chance that this could end without bloodshed.

Past the shed, she darted for the largest tree, keeping it between herself and the house. One heartbeat, two. No reaction from the house, no shots fired.

But that didn't mean she was out of the woods yet. Taking a deep breath, she headed for the next tree.

She made it all the way to the house undetected. Crouching low to stay under the windows, she headed for the front door. To her surprise, the handle turned easily. Unlocked.

Heart pounding, she pushed open the front door. Gun out, she jumped inside, into what appeared to be a sitting room. "Sheriff's Office," she shouted. "Phillip Maple, come out with your hands up."

Silence. Still trying to keep as small a profile as possible, she headed toward the back of the house. The kitchen—clear. A small bathroom—clear.

One more room. A TV room or a den. Peering around the corner, she found Phillip, holding his pistol to the temple of a clearly terrified young woman. Though she was emaciated and filthy, her clothes torn and her feet bare, Rayna recognized Nicole.

"Drop your weapon, or I'll shoot," Phillip ordered. "Do as I say or her blood will be on your hands."

Rayna bent over and carefully placed her gun on the floor in front of her before slowly raising her hands. "Let her go," she demanded.

Parker stepped out from behind the curtains, where apparently he'd been hiding. Unnoticed by Phillip, he moved forward, clearly intending to try and disarm the other man and free Nicole.

"Come on, Phillip. Let her go. If you want to walk out of here alive, use me as your hostage."

Phillip laughed. "You don't get it, do you? None of us are getting out of here alive."

At that, Parker leaped, slamming into Phillip hard enough to cause him to release his grip on Nicole. She stumbled forward and Rayna grabbed her, yanking her to safety while Parker wrestled with Phillip for his gun. Parker's sheer size and muscular body worked for him, and he managed to knock Parker's pistol from his hand. It hit the floor, by some miracle not discharging. Rayna leaped for it, snatching it up and clicking the safety on.

By now, Parker had pinned Phillip's arms behind him. Murmuring to Nicole to stay put, Rayna hurried over and slapped her handcuffs on Phillip.

Rayna thumbed her radio, calling for backup even as she moved Nicole toward the back door. Hopefully the ambulance from earlier would still be on scene—if not, she'd have to ask for another one.

Larry and Tom burst through the back door. "Sheriff's Office," Larry shouted. His eyes widened as he caught sight of Parker, still standing behind a cuffed and subdued Phillip.

"Looks like you have everything under control," Larry drawled.

"Read the prisoner his rights and take him downtown for booking," Rayna ordered. "Is the ambulance still here?"

"No, ma'am. Would you like me to call for another?" Tom asked.

"No." Rayna reached a snap decision. "Parker and I will take Nicole to the hospital ourselves."

Since Nicole was too weak to walk very far, Parker carried her outside, depositing her gently in the back seat of Rayna's cruiser. Through all of this, Nicole had remained very stoic, but she broke down in the back of the patrol car, sobbing incoherently all the way to the hospital.

Using lights and sirens, Rayna got them there in less than ten minutes. She'd called ahead, letting the ER know they were en route. As soon as they pulled up, an orderly hurried over with a wheelchair and they whisked Nicole back, leaving Rayna and Parker to fill out paperwork the best they could.

Once this task had been completed, they were directed to sit in the waiting area.

"She wouldn't even talk to me," Parker said, his expression agonized.

"She didn't talk to anyone," Rayna pointed out. "Most likely, she's in shock. Think about what an ordeal she's been through."

Parker nodded and pulled out his phone, staring at it for a moment before he shook his head and slid it back into his pocket. "I can't even call John and let him know

we found her. Not until I know more about her condition. I'm sure he'll have a lot of questions."

"Just wait a bit. Once she's been checked out, you
can call him. Maybe Nicole will even be able to talk to
him. No doubt he'd love to hear her voice." She touched
his shoulder. "How about I go get us some coffee or
something?"

"Sure. Coffee would be great."

Like many hospitals, this one had installed a small
Starbucks to the side of the main lobby. Rayna got two
coffees, doctored hers up the way she liked it and left his
black. When she returned to the waiting room, Parker
wasn't there.

"He got to go back," the charge nurse told her. "I
can buzz you back there, too, if you'd like. They're in
room 9."

After pushing through the double doors, Rayna located room 9 and headed that way.

She paused in the doorway for a moment.

Seated at Nicole's bedside, Parker looked exhausted.
No doubt he'd welcome the jolt of caffeine from the
coffee. Since his attention was fixed on the young girl
sleeping so peacefully, Rayna studied the man she now
knew she loved more than any other.

His cell phone rang, startling him and waking Nicole.

He answered and listened, going very pale. "Thank
you," he managed to say, clearly grappling with his
emotions. "That was the hospital," he told Nicole, who
watched him, wide-eyed. "Your brother has slipped into
a coma. They're calling in hospice care."

The young woman, who'd already been through so
much, shook her head in denial. "No. Not yet. He can't
leave yet." She began fussing with her IV, trying clum-

sily to remove it. "I need to get out of here. You've got to take me to see him."

"You're not going anywhere right now," a nurse said, coming through the doorway just in time to witness Nicole's feeble attempt at escape. "You're severely dehydrated and have several infected wounds. You need fluids, antibiotics and rest."

Nicole lifted her chin. Though clearly still weak, she strengthened her voice. "My brother is dying. I need to see him before he passes."

The nurse stared. She appeared torn between sympathizing and doing her job.

"The hospital just called," Parker explained. "He's slipped into a coma and they've transferred him to a hospice care center. We don't know how much longer he has, but his one request was to see his baby sister before he died."

Though the nurse looked down, she didn't respond.

Rayna took the nurse's arm and steered her into the hall. "I'm sure you're aware of the circumstances behind your patient's condition," she began. "She was held prisoner by a serial killer for several weeks. Is there any way we can get her discharged with medication? We need to get in the car and start the drive to Dallas before it's too late."

After a moment, the silver-haired woman nodded. "Give me ten minutes. Let me see what I can do."

Rayna thanked her, resisting the urge to ask if she meant ten minutes in hospital time or ten minutes in real time. Instead, she went back inside the room and told Parker and Nicole what the nurse had said.

Nicole nodded, biting her lip.

"I need to take a statement from you," Rayna said softly. "We can talk in private if you like."

Glancing at Parker, Nicole sighed. "He can stay. After what I've been through, it hardly matters who hears about it."

Rayna got out her phone. "Do I have your permission to record?"

"Of course." Nicole took a deep breath and began.

Phillip had pulled up right after she'd taken the photo with the city-limits sign and posted it on Instagram and Facebook. He'd asked her if she was lost and when she'd told him she wasn't, they'd chatted a bit about the weather and the town's history. She'd mentioned Myrna and been stunned when he told her Myrna was his mother.

Starstruck, of course she'd jumped at the chance to meet her idol. She'd agreed to follow Phillip to his place, unaware of what would happen once she did.

Instead of meeting the famous advice columnist, she'd been drugged and imprisoned. There had been one other girl there, sick and weak and seemingly on the verge of succumbing to her illness.

Horrified, Nicole had realized Phillip had not only duped her, but would most likely kill her. Even though she'd tried to run away with her phone recording the chase, after her capture, her phone had disappeared and she had no idea what had happened to her car.

Somehow, Nicole managed to tell them all of her story, only breaking down a few times, but visibly pulling herself together. She was overjoyed to hear that Donella had made it out safely and heartbroken to learn about the bodies in the unmarked graves.

"It's over now," Parker said, patting her shoulder.

"Now all we need to do is get you to Dallas to see John one last time."

A light tap on the door had them all looking up. True to her word, the nurse had reappeared, a white-coated doctor in tow. A few minutes later, discharge papers were signed, a prescription handed over, and the nurse offered to help Nicole get dressed.

Nicole looked stricken. "I don't have any clothes."

"Yes, you do." Rayna pointed to the suitcase she'd placed near the window. "We recovered your things from the house. We knew it was yours because it had Texas Tech stickers all over it."

Eyeing her luggage, Nicole's eyes filled with tears. "Thank you so much."

"No tears." Gently, Rayna hugged her. "Would you like me or your nurse to help you?"

"I can do it myself," Nicole said. "But thank you for offering." Moving slowly, she gingerly got out of the bed and stood, narrowing her eyes for a moment while she regained her equilibrium.

Parker jumped up immediately and went to her side, offering his arm in case she needed his assistance.

"I've got this," she declared. When she reached her suitcase, she wobbled just the tiniest bit before taking the handle and lifting it off the chair.

After that, since it had wheels, Nicole only had to pull it along behind her as she headed toward the bathroom.

"She's a strong person," Rayna commented.

When Parker looked at her, the pain in his eyes made her catch her breath. "So is her brother. Damn, I'm not ready for this."

She went to him then, and wrapped her arms around

him tightly, offering comfort the only way she knew how. He held her back, rigid in his sorrow, though he finally relaxed slightly.

"I'll be back," he told her, his breath warm against her ear. "After this is over…" His voice broke. Pulling away, he visibly steadied himself. "I'll come back to you."

Heart breaking, she nodded. "I'll be waiting," she promised. "No matter how long it takes."

Since all Parker had was his Harley and Nicole wasn't in any condition to ride on the back of the bike, Rayna drove him to Parra's Used Cars on the south side of town. He eyed the car Rayna suggested—a sturdy Volvo with only seventy-two thousand miles on it, and the vehicle he clearly wanted to buy, a late-model black Camaro. Even Nicole's eyes lit up when she saw it.

Parker haggled a little bit and finally struck up an agreement to purchase the Camaro. Rayna walked with him next door to the bank, where he got a cashier's check, and returned to finalize the deal.

"We're going to leave from here," he said, checking his watch. "Hopefully, we can be in Dallas before dark. I don't know what the hospice care center's rules are on visiting, but we'll try our best to get in. I'm not sure he'll even know we're there. He's been in and out of consciousness, but now seems to be completely unresponsive."

Nodding, she gave him a quick hug and then turned and did the same for Nicole. "Y'all drive safely," she said and turned and walked away without a backward look.

She didn't cry until she pulled up in her driveway. Then and only then did she allow her pent-up emotions to spill out.

The biggest case of her career had been solved and, even though the FBI would take custody of Phillip Maple, the arrest had been made by her department, on her watch.

Still, she wept for all that had come before—the murdered girls and for what they'd endured at Phillip's hands. While she couldn't go back in time and save them, she could only hope justice would prevail and Phillip would pay for what he'd done.

By some miracle, Parker had found Nicole alive, which had been the only reason he'd come to Getaway in the first place. Whether or not he'd come back, she didn't know, but either way, she'd found the love of her life and would be forever changed.

When she'd cried herself out, she used a makeup-removal wipe from her purse to clean up her mascara. Then she took a deep breath, straightened her shoulders and got out of the car to head into her house and rejoin her family. As she had in the past, she'd make sure neither Wanda nor Lauren realized anything was amiss. After all, as far as they'd be concerned, she had a lot to celebrate. So she would, keeping a smile on her face even if it killed her.

Chapter 16

One of the most emotional moments of Parker's entire life was watching his best friend's eyes flutter open at the sound of his baby sister's voice. "Nicole?" John had rasped, squinting up at her from his hospital bed. "Are you really here?"

"I am." Nicole smiled softly, though her eyes brimmed with unshed tears. "I got here as quickly as I could."

But John didn't respond. He'd slipped back into his coma.

"At least he knows," Parker told Nicole, patting her shoulder. "He recognized your voice. He knows you're here."

Slowly, she nodded. "I just wish I could talk to him once more. Tell him how much I love him. How much I'm going to miss him."

Parker gestured toward the bed. "Tell him now. There

have been numerous studies that show even people in comas can hear when loved ones talk to them."

She brightened. "I'll do that, then."

Feeling as if she might want privacy, Parker told her he'd be back and went out to his car to call Rayna. But then he realized it was 2:00 a.m., so he texted instead.

Are you awake?

No answer. But then he hadn't really expected one. He smiled sadly, knowing she needed her rest, and decided he'd try again and call her tomorrow.

He went back inside the hospice care center and quietly entered the room.

Though she had to be exhausted, Nicole refused to leave her brother's side. She held one hand while Parker held the other. She talked and sang softly for hours, telling the caregivers that she knew John could hear her and that she wanted her brother to know he wouldn't leave this world alone.

And so he didn't. A few seconds after midnight, the nurse came in to check on them while they dozed at John's side. After checking his pulse, she informed them both that John had gone.

Holding Nicole while she wept, Parker ached with his own sorrow, wanting Rayna, needing Rayna.

The staff took care of the necessary calls, urging them to go get some rest.

By the time he and Nicole stumbled out of the hospice care center and drove to the nearest hotel, he was too numb and exhausted to do anything more than fall into his hotel bed and pray for sleep.

In the morning, Parker got a phone call from the care

center and learned that John had already premade and paid for all his burial and funeral arrangements. John had left sealed envelopes for both Nicole and Parker, private messages he'd wanted them to have after he was gone.

Though Nicole opened hers right away, Parker tucked his into his pocket to read later. His emotions were too raw right now to read it in front of anyone. He carried it with him back to his hotel room and placed it on the small desk. Still, he couldn't bring himself to open it.

Instead, he once again tried to call Rayna, knowing by now she would be at work. But her cell phone went straight to voice mail. Next he called the sheriff's office, but only got a busy signal. It wasn't until he turned on the television and saw Rayna giving a press conference along with the FBI that he understood.

An alleged serial killer had been stopped and captured. Watching as the woman he loved spoke to the press, he knew he had to get to her as soon as possible.

But first, he had to open the letter left to him by his best friend.

Taking a deep breath, he carefully used his fingernail to split the seal.

Don't grieve for me, Parker. Even though this might seem weird to you, I am ready. I fought the good fight and I lost. But I'm okay with that. Really.

I've invested my money wisely and have more than enough saved to pay for the rest of Nicole's education. Since I won't be there, will you become her big brother for me? Watch over her, take care of her, and guide her to make good choices.

*You have been like a brother to me, my friend.
Since I was diagnosed, you dropped your own
life and stepped into mine. You probably already
know how much that means to me, but in case you
don't, I'm going to say it anyway. The gift you've
given me—your time, yourself—has meant the
world to me. Even so, I'm going to ask one last
thing of you now that I'm gone.*

*Live your life. Let go of the past. I've seen
your talent restoring cars, and I know opening
your own shop used to be a dream of yours. Don't
dream anymore. Take a leap, do it. Now. Don't
delay, because none of us are promised a tomorrow.*

*I can see you scowling, my old friend. Don't. I
know of what I speak. I always put everything off
for another day. I didn't understand that another
day might never come.*

*Find a woman you can love and who loves you.
Get married, raise a family, become a respected
member of society. Hah! But seriously, do all the
things I should have done, the things we talked
about while we were stuck in that desert hellhole.
Most of all, be happy.*

I love you, big guy.
John

Parker swallowed, a lump in his throat, his eyes
stinging. John knew him better than anyone, and he'd
often chastised Parker for becoming a drifter. What neither of them had understood was that Parker had never
found anyone who could truly anchor him.

Until Rayna.

* * *

With all her newfound celebrity, the day after Phillip Maple's arrest, Rayna's life became much more hectic than usual. In addition to the ream of paperwork she had to fill out, there were interviews and phone calls and even requests to appear on national daytime talk shows. She'd had to post one of her officers outside Myrna Maple's hospital room to keep reporters from trying to interview her.

Also that same morning, the grateful townspeople of Getaway started bringing food up to the sheriff's office. Baked goods mostly at first. Carrot cake, coconut cake and a three-tiered German chocolate cake that made Rayna's mouth water just looking at it. There were cookies by the dozens, and brownies and Danishes, even two dozen homemade kolacky. Jim and the guys were in sugar heaven. Then one of the ranchers brought up a huge beef brisket he'd smoked overnight, along with a gallon of homemade potato salad and a huge pan of baked beans.

There was so much food that Rayna knew her people could never eat it all, so she asked Mary to look into arranging for the leftovers to go to the nearest church for their next potluck or something.

Somehow that turned into a potluck dinner event that would be held that evening in the church hall honoring the Getaway sheriff's office. Sam, who'd come and paid a visit to his former staff, laughed when he heard about it and told her to enjoy it while she could. It wouldn't, he said, always be so rosy. Rayna had simply shaken her head and retreated to her office.

With Mary fielding so many phone calls, the overloaded and antiquated phone system went down. Rayna authorized a call to their service provider before once again closing her office door. She made a valiant attempt to get at least some of her paperwork done, but kept getting interrupted.

Giving up, she went ahead and held her scheduled news conference, trying to pretend she wasn't going to be broadcast on the national news. Once that was over, she met with the FBI and transferred custody of Phillip, an event that reporters also covered. Then she finally managed to grab a bit of that brisket and potato salad when Mary brought her a plate and ordered her to sit down and eat it. Grateful, Rayna thanked her and headed into the conference room. Maybe there, with the door closed, she could get a little peace and quiet.

Exhausted and hungrier than she'd realized, she dropped into one of the chairs and began to eat. While she did, she grabbed her phone and realized the battery had died. When, she had no idea. She'd been too busy and overwhelmed to notice. Shaking her head at herself, she plugged it in and let it charge while she ate.

Two more interruptions and she managed to finish her meal. She left her phone charging, met with the mayor, who informed her he wanted to have a ceremony and recognize her with some sort of award, and then with Bertha Abernathy and Donella, who both wanted to thank her.

No one asked about Parker, even though he'd played a huge part in all this. Rayna supposed everyone knew he'd taken Nicole to Dallas to see her dying brother. Just thinking about him made her chest ache. Why hadn't he called?

Making a U-turn back into the conference room, she snatched up her phone and saw she had one new text message and two missed calls. All from Parker. The last one had been thirty minutes ago.

She immediately called him back.

"John died this morning," he told her, sounding calm. "He recognized Nicole, and though they never really had a conversation, I believe he knew she was there with him. We both were, right up until the end."

"I'm so sorry," she said. "This must be so hard on you both."

"I'll miss him. But he left me a letter and I'm actually at peace. Nicole got one, too, and said it affected her the same way."

"When's the funeral?" she asked, wondering if she should attend as a show of support.

"John didn't want one. He asked to be cremated and have his ashes spread over a cliff down in the Big Bend. He used to love to hike there." His voice cracked a little at that.

She wanted to ask when he was coming back, *if* he was coming home to Getaway, but bit back the words. Anything he did from this point on had to be his choice. She wouldn't push or prod or beg, no matter how much she might want to.

That night at home, Wanda appeared unusually restless. Constantly in motion, she cleaned and tidied and fussed until even little Lauren asked her what was wrong. Wanda shook her head and rushed from the room, leaving Rayna and her daughter to stare after her in alarm.

"You stay here and play with your puzzle," Rayna said. "Mommy is going to check on Grandma."

Wanda had closed her bedroom door so Rayna knocked. "Can I come in?"

"Sure."

Inside, Rayna found Wanda sitting on the edge of the bed, frantically blotting at her streaming eyes. "What's going on, Mom? Are you sick?"

"Not really." Wanda heaved a sigh. "I've been doing a lot of thinking about what I want for the rest of my life and I feel like I'm trapped between a rock and a hard place. No matter what I choose, I lose too much."

Suddenly, Rayna understood. "Are you talking about Sam?"

"Yes. While he's been here, I've come to realize how much I care about him. I can't bear the thought of him going back to the coast and leaving me here. Yet if I were to go with him, I'd miss you and Lauren terribly."

"Have you considered asking him to stay in Getaway?" Rayna asked. "He has roots here, a lot of good friends. That way you could be with him and still close enough to see me and Lauren as much as you wanted."

"That did occur to me. But honey, Sam hightailed it out of here as soon as he retired. It's always been his dream to live on the coast. What right do I have to ask him to give that up?"

Rayna watched as her mother wiped away tears. "I guess he just has to decide for himself what matters the most to him," she said.

"Exactly." Wanda's mouth trembled. "And honey, I'm so afraid I already know what he'll choose. It will break my heart."

"Like mother, like daughter." Rayna plopped down on the bed next to her mom. "I don't really know if Parker is coming back. He said he would, but..."

Wanda patted Rayna's shoulder. "I saw the way that man looks at you. He'll return. You can count on that."

"Look at us, wallowing in our emotions, when neither of us truly can say what the outcome will be." Rayna stood and held out a hand to her mother. "Come on, let's go have some ice cream. A nice scoop of butter pecan will make us both feel better."

Sam rang the doorbell a little after seven. With her color high, Wanda showed him into the living room and told him she'd be ready in a minute.

"Hi, Sam." Rayna smiled. "How are you?"

"I'm good." Instead of taking a seat, Sam stood, his hands in his pockets. "I talked to Parker. I was so sorry to hear about his friend."

"Me, too. I'm just glad Nicole was able to get there before her brother passed."

Wanda returned, having slipped on a pair of wedge heels with her sundress. "Ready?" she asked, fluttering her eyelashes at Sam.

To Rayna's amusement, Sam froze and simply stared, making her wonder if he'd forgotten to breathe. Finally, Wanda laughed. The throaty sound appeared to snap Sam out of his daze. He held out his arm and Wanda took it. Side by side, they walked to the door.

After they'd gone, Rayna helped Lauren with her bath, read her two stories and put her to bed.

Alone in the living room, Rayna wandered into the kitchen and poured herself a glass of wine. She picked up her phone—something she'd been avoiding—and noted no new text messages from Parker or anyone else. She played around on social media, toyed with the idea of calling him and decided not to yet.

Picking up a novel she'd been trying to find the time to read, she settled in her chair and opened the book. One chapter later, she got up to refill her glass and then checked her phone once more. Again, she debated whether or not to call Parker, even if only to hear his voice. She missed him so much. But then maybe she should try to get used to life without him.

The hell with it. Disappointed in her lack of will-power, she touched the icon for his number. Heart in her throat, she waited for it to ring.

It did. Once. And then so did her doorbell. Since no one visited after nine o'clock at night, she debated simply not answering. Instead, she kept her phone to her ear and hurried to look out the peephole.

Parker stood on her doorstep, his ringing phone in his hand. He answered her call just as she opened her front door. "Hello." He smiled, gazing deep into her eyes. "May I come in?"

Struck speechless, she stepped aside.

As he strode past her, she couldn't keep from staring. Sexy, handsome, strong—he looked like all of those things. As she tried to regain control of her voice, she shook her head. "I was just calling you."

He grinned, holding up his phone. "I know."

Mouth dry, all she could think of was how badly she wanted to jump his bones. Instead, she gestured toward her wineglass. "Can I get you something to drink?"

His grin widened, as if he knew her thoughts. "A beer would be great. But first, come here." He held out his arms.

Heart racing, she stepped right into them, breathing in the familiar masculine scent of him. Tears stung her eyes as he cradled her close to his muscular chest, murmuring words of endearment as he nuzzled the top of her head.

"My beautiful sheriff. Are you happy to see me?"

All she could manage was a nod while she struggled to get herself under control. "I thought you'd still be in Dallas, helping Nicole take care of her brother's estate," she finally said, stepping back from his embrace and letting her eyes drink her fill of him.

He stared right back. "John was very thorough. He took care of everything long before his death. Nicole won't have to do much. He even set up a fund to pay for the remainder of her college. I'll have to go back up there once his ashes are back, but...I missed you. So here I am."

"Here you are," she repeated. "Let me get you that beer and we can catch up."

"Wait." He caught at her arm, tugging her close again. "There are a few other things I want to do first. Like kiss you."

And he did. So deeply and thoroughly she could scarcely stand upright when it was over. Dazed, flushed with happiness, she let him lead her over to the couch. Once seated, she tried to pull him down to her, but he resisted.

"Not yet," he said, his expression serious. "There's something I want to ask you first."

Then, as she gazed up at him, he dropped to one knee and pulled out a ring box. "Rayna Coombs, will you marry me?"

Her eyes filled with tears. "Parker..."

His crooked smile almost did her in. "Don't you dare say no. I love you and I know you love me."

"Of course I'll marry you," she managed to say, crying in earnest now. "I do love you, but there's one thing I need to be sure of."

"Okay." Face full of love, he waited, still on one knee. "What is it?"

"I need to know about Lauren. You'd be her stepfather and I want to make sure she's okay with this."

"I agree." His expression grave, he nodded. "I actually bought a second ring." He pulled a smaller ring box from his pocket. "Once I'd asked you, I planned to ask her if she wants to be my daughter."

She noticed he didn't say stepdaughter. Heart full, she eyed the second box. "That's so sweet."

"How about we wake her up and ask her?" he said, finally getting up off the floor.

"Uh, no. How about we let her sleep and ask her in the morning." She tugged him close, so she could snuggle with him on the couch. "Let me try that ring on and after, I bet we can go to my room. I can think of a lot of ways we can celebrate."

He'd barely slipped the ring onto her finger, when the front door opened and Wanda and Sam came inside. Arms around each other, they both radiated happiness.

"Rayna, look!" Holding out her hand to show off her ring, Wanda rushed over. "Sam proposed and I said yes. We're going to stay here in Getaway. Isn't that perfect?"

"Oh, Mom." Rayna jumped up and hugged her mother fiercely. "I'm so happy for you. Oh, and Parker and I have a bit of news, too."

"Really?" Wanda pulled back, her expression hopeful. "What is it?"

Instead of answering, Rayna held out her own hand, displaying her own engagement ring.

Sam and Parker simultaneously laughed. "I don't know about you," Sam said, elbowing his nephew, "but I sure could use a beer."

"Let's go get one," Parker replied. The two of them disappeared into the kitchen, leaving Rayna and Wanda alone.

"Dreams do come true," Wanda whispered, misty eyed. When Rayna told her about the second ring that Parker had bought for Lauren, Wanda could barely restrain her tears.

"No crying, now." Sam hurried over and pulled his fiancée into his embrace.

"Tears of joy," Wanda promised. "Tears of joy."

For the next hour, the four of them sat around and shared their plans for the future. Parker planned to open up his own auto customization shop, restoring cars either for private collectors or people who wanted to show them. He would come to live with Rayna and Lauren in this same house, if that's what Rayna wanted. Rayna smiled and told him she did.

Sam and Wanda wanted to buy a little house near downtown, close enough to walk to the coffee shop and not too far to visit. "Often," Wanda emphasized. "I'm used to seeing my grandbaby every day."

Finally, Sam stood and told them it was time for him to go back to the motel and get some shut-eye. With a mischievous look, Wanda announced she was going with him. Arm in arm, they practically skipped out the door.

As soon as the two older folks left, Parker held out his hand. Rayna took it and led him into the bedroom. Closing the door, they got into bed, taking it slow. Of course, they'd celebrate their love for each other and their engagement, but tonight they planned to savor every touch, every kiss. After all, they'd have the rest of their lives together.

That is, as long as Lauren approved.

In the morning, Rayna made sure she and Parker were up long before Lauren. Showered and dressed, they sat in the kitchen together drinking coffee when the little girl wandered into the kitchen. "Where's Grandma?" she asked, her eyes going wide at the sight of Parker.

"Hello," he said, smiling at her. "I'm Parker. Do you remember me?"

Shyly, Lauren nodded. "Where's Grandma?" she asked again, going over to Rayna and leaning in to her.

"She had stuff to do," Rayna answered. "She'll be back soon."

Parker shifted nervously in his seat. "I have something I want to ask you, Lauren."

"You do?" Apparently, curiosity trumped shyness. Lauren let go of her mother and walked over to stand near Parker. "What is it?"

Swallowing hard, he pulled the smaller ring box from his pocket. "I've asked your mommy to marry me," he said quietly. "And I wanted to ask you if you'd be willing to be my daughter."

Eyes huge, Lauren studied him. "You want to be my dad?" she asked, incredulous. Turning her gaze to Rayna, she raised both her hands. "Mom? Is that okay?"

"Yes, baby. More than okay. But only if you're all right with it."

Lauren wrinkled up her nose. "I always wanted my own dad," she said. "If you and my mom get married, then that's what you'll be?"

Parker smiled and nodded. "Yes." Finally, he opened the box. "I got you this ring, too. It has three hearts on it. One for each of us."

Solemn now, Lauren eyed it. "For me?"

"Yes."

She squealed and held out her hand, barely able to hold still enough for him to put it on. "Look, Mama." She held out her hand, admiring the sparkly hearts. "It's beautiful."

"Yes, it is." Rayna kissed Lauren's head. "Now let's eat. Then, since it's Saturday and I have the day off, we'll figure out what to do with the rest of this beautiful summer day."

"I've got lots of ideas," Lauren said.

"I bet you do." Getting her little girl seated, Rayna handed over a plate with fruit and a muffin, one of Lauren's favorite breakfasts. She met Parker's eyes over Lauren's head, basking at the love and happiness she saw in them.

"It doesn't matter what we do," Parker added. "As long as we do it together."

"Always," Rayna replied, smiling back.

"Always," Lauren repeated, giggling as Parker blew her a kiss before saying the word a third time.

"Always."

Heart brimming over with joy, Rayna knew she couldn't have asked for anything more perfect.

* * * * *

#2147 COLTON 911: TEMPTATION UNDERCOVER
Colton 911: Chicago • by Jennifer Morey

Ruby Duarte and her daughter are finally free of her ex—but his followers are still a threat. Damon Jones seems like a friendly local bartender, but he's secretly undercover and determined to take down a dangerous ring while keeping Ruby safe. But will his lies ruin any chance they have at a future?

#2148 COLTON K-9 TARGET
The Coltons of Grave Gulch • by Justine Davis

When he came to Grave Gulch PD, K-9 handler Brett Shea never expected to land in the middle of a criminal catfishing case. Annalise Colton may be a part of the family that seems far too entwined in Grave Gulch's police department, but she's also at the center of his current case—and Brett finds himself falling for her even if he's not sure the Colton family can be trusted.

#2149 FIRST RESPONDERS ON DEADLY GROUND
by Colleen Thompson

Determined to expose the powerful family that destroyed his mother's life, paramedic Jude Castleman knows he stands little chance of success. Then widowed flight nurse Callie Fielding comes up with a high-risk plan to find the justice they crave...if their own unstoppable attraction doesn't lead them into danger.

#2150 A FIREFIGHTER'S ULTIMATE DUTY
Heroes of the Pacific Northwest • by Beverly Long

Daisy Rambler's new job in small coastal Knoware, Washington, is a new start for her and her sixteen-year-old daughter, away from an abusive ex. When her daughter goes missing, local hero and paramedic Blade Savick comes to the rescue—but more danger lurks around the corner...

HRSCNM0821

Get 4 FREE REWARDS!

We'll send you 2 FREE Books plus 2 FREE Mystery Gifts.

Harlequin Romantic Suspense books are heart-racing page-turners with unexpected plot twists and irresistible chemistry that will keep you guessing to the very end.

FREE
Value Over
$20

YES! Please send me 2 FREE Harlequin Romantic Suspense novels and my 2 FREE gifts (gifts are worth about $10 retail). After receiving them, if I don't wish to receive any more books, I can return the shipping statement marked "cancel." If I don't cancel, I will receive 4 brand-new novels every month and be billed just $4.99 per book in the U.S. or $5.74 per book in Canada. That's a savings of at least 13% off the cover price! It's quite a bargain! Shipping and handling is just 50¢ per book in the U.S. and $1.25 per book in Canada.* I understand that accepting the 2 free books and gifts places me under no obligation to buy anything. I can always return a shipment and cancel at any time. The free books and gifts are mine to keep no matter what I decide.

240/340 HDN GNMZ

Name (please print)

Address   Apt. #

City   State/Province   Zip/Postal Code

Email: Please check this box ☐ if you would like to receive newsletters and promotional emails from Harlequin Enterprises ULC and its affiliates. You can unsubscribe anytime.

Mail to the **Harlequin Reader Service:**
IN U.S.A.: P.O. Box 1341, Buffalo, NY 14240-8531
IN CANADA: P.O. Box 603, Fort Erie, Ontario L2A 5X3

Want to try 2 free books from another series! Call 1-800-873-8635 or visit www.ReaderService.com.

*Terms and prices subject to change without notice. Prices do not include sales taxes, which will be charged (if applicable) based on your state or country of residence. Canadian residents will be charged applicable taxes. Offer not valid in Quebec. This offer is limited to one order per household. Books received may not be as shown. Not valid for current subscribers to Harlequin Romantic Suspense books. All orders subject to approval. Credit or debit balances in a customer's account(s) may be offset by any other outstanding balance owed by or to the customer. Please allow 4 to 6 weeks for delivery. Offer available while quantities last.

Your Privacy—Your information is being collected by Harlequin Enterprises ULC, operating as Harlequin Reader Service. For a complete summary of the information we collect, how we use this information and to whom it is disclosed, please visit our privacy notice located at corporate.harlequin.com/privacy-notice. From time to time we may also exchange your personal information with reputable third parties. If you wish to opt out of this sharing of your personal information, please visit readerservice.com/consumerschoice or call 1-800-873-8635. **Notice to California Residents**—Under California law, you have specific rights to control and access your data. For more information on these rights and how to exercise them, visit corporate.harlequin.com/california-privacy.

HRS21R

Love Harlequin romance?

DISCOVER.

Be the first to find out about promotions, news and exclusive content!

Facebook.com/HarlequinBooks

Twitter.com/HarlequinBooks

Instagram.com/HarlequinBooks

Pinterest.com/HarlequinBooks

YouTube.com/HarlequinBooks

ReaderService.com

EXPLORE.

Sign up for the Harlequin e-newsletter and download a free book from any series at
TryHarlequin.com

CONNECT.

Join our Harlequin community to share your thoughts and connect with other romance readers!
Facebook.com/groups/HarlequinConnection